READERS SPEAK OUT

"*Immanuel's Veins* **is a heart-wrenching journey of redemption and hope that left me sobbing, laughing and clinging to every word. An elixir of pure love to a thirsty heart.** Like a blanket that covered me, drowning me in the most mind-blowing, cleansing love I ever thought I could feel. **Within five days I had read** *Immanuel's Veins* **three times, and two weeks later I was on reading number seven. You better be ready for a transformation of your very soul.** This book will make you whole again in ways that you can hardly imagine."

— Donna McChristian, 44,
Environmental Chemist

"The moment I closed *Immanuel's Veins* **I wanted to rush the streets**, find my friends, my neighbors—even my enemies—and burst of infallible truth and spectacular love. Yes, *love!* **Inked here in blood is a story so unashamed, so emotionally charged, and so given to its Maker that redemption pulses through the pages**. Ted Dekker indisputably howls at the moon between every chapter in this poignantly penned novel, painting life-altering imagery and even sprinkling thrills of *Circle Series* connections. **For love's sake, uphold this golden chalice and drink it, share it**. *Immanuel's Veins* beckons so."

— Caleb Jennings Breakey, 24,
Journalist

"In the moments after I finished *Immanuel's Veins* **I sat in stunned silence on my couch**. So many times in this book I had to remind myself to breathe. **The intense purity of the love story cut at my heart and tore at my emotions**. Each time I was forced to set it down, I yearned to have it in my hands again. I will read this book again and again, and I have already told everyone I know that they, too, must learn what love truly is by escaping into another world and seeing it with their own eyes. **If I am ever meant to find love, I know it will have to be a love like this-- passionate, enduring**, and mind blowing beyond all logical reason."

— Kelsey Keating, 20, Student

"*Immanuel's Veins* **is a book that grabbed me by the heart and never let go. Even after I finished reading it, I could still feel it tugging at me deep inside.** I couldn't help but immerse myself into this story. It may be considered a fiction novel, but it speaks the truth. **Ted uses his gift of storytelling to once again make us realize that no matter who we are no matter what lies in our past, we can find redemption and love.**"

— Brian Coultrup, 22

"**Once** *Immanuel's Veins* **sinks it's 'teeth' into you, it does not let go. The tension builds like a roller coaster**, then drops you down through twists and turns. When it seems you can't take any more, he throws more at you. Ted confronts you with a question of how far will you go to save someone close to you. The choice should be obvious in a way that only Ted can bring out in Story. **You can't read** *Immanuel's Veins* **and remain untouched.**"

— Rick Balmer, 39

"**In** *Immanuel's Veins*, **Dekker takes his storytelling to a whole new level, engaging the reader and taking them captive in a way that is as breathtaking and marvelous as it is gut wrenching.** Few can explore Truth through fiction as well as Dekker, and among all Dekker's forays toward Truth this just might be his best.

In a tale of love and betrayal, Ted Dekker sets before us a story we have all experienced, but **the height and depth of** *Immanuel's Veins* **takes us to the brink of what our heart can hold. The sheer power of Story drives us to our knees, with eyes to see and weep,** as Dekker peels back the layers and holds up a story as a mirror to our soul. **Should you read this novel, you will not find yourself the same person as when you opened the cover.**"

— Josh Olds, 22, Student

"I read *Immanuel's Veins* in two days, which is unusually fast for me. **I was captivated, longing to find out how this story of love and redemption, and betrayal would end.** Dekker, unlike any other fiction author I have read, can take a theme and magnify it through story and *Immanuel's Veins* only expounds upon this. I highly recommend this to any fiction lover."

— Travis Clarke, 25,
George W. Truett Seminary
Student

"To our world that has forgotten the meaning of selflessness and unconditional love, Dekker spins a tale to remind us not only of what true love really is, but the lengths to which it will go to save a soul.

Completely different than anything else Dekker has written, this book immersed me in a world of long ago and **took me on a journey through one man's anguish, temptation, passion and sacrifice, leaving me with a sense of overwhelming joy.**

Immanuel's Veins **holds the power of transforming minds** by presenting the message of salvation in a fresh way that is rich and honest. It just might shake your world to the core."

— Rebecca Campbell, 30, Mother

"Reading *Immanuel's Veins* **sent me on a personal journey**, examining my own redemptive history. **Never has a story centered around characters from centuries ago been so relevant to my own life.** With such a fantastic plot and epic scope, I saw my own rebellion and restoration vividly retold. The story explored the truths of human nature and the struggle over our souls which stabbed me to the core. By the end, **I found myself longing for more,** but realizing that the way I live my life from this point forward will continue to flesh out this story, my story, our story for eternity.

— Andrew Asdell, 22

"If you are a Dekker fan, this book is the very next Dekker book you must read. If you have never read a Dekker book, this is the very first Dekker book you need to read. **Not since The Great Romance itself has a greater love story ever been told from Dekker's mind**. I simply cannot recommend this book enough. If this is the only book you have time to read this year, this is the book you need to read."

— Gregg Hart, 42, Information Technician

"Even when Dekker writes something that's considered 'inside the box', it seems that he likes to take that box, smash it into bits and then warm his hands by the fire built from the parts. He's a modern day master of the written word. **The story flows so smoothly through your mind that it feels as if the words have flown directly from the Technicolor depths of his mind to the page with little effort.** His style submerges you in the story and even if it feels like you may be drowning in it at times, there's still few other places you'd rather be.

If you have even a passing interest in Dekker's work, don't miss this book. If you've never read Dekker, this is a brilliant place to start. If you ever were a Dekker fan and got lost somewhere along the way, this is the book that will bring you back."

— Lori Twichell, 38, Business Owner

"**Read** *Immanuel's Veins* **and you will quickly become lost in a chronicle so intense that you have to gather yourself together and remind yourself where you are when you put it down** - if you can put it down. I have been gripped by Ted Dekker novels before, but this one had my eyes wide open in constant expectance to the very end. No other storyteller tells tales of such all encompassing love, celebrating the light and all that is good. It is this fearlessness and the purity of purpose that draws me so strongly to Ted's books. **This is a love story and we should all read it, let go of fear and dive deep into beautiful, all encompassing, redemptive love.**"

— Tris Bolstridge, 34, Mother

"**This book moved me in such a personal way, I had a difficult time forming the words of how I feel.** As an avid Ted Dekker fan for the past decade, I look forward to each of his novels with the eagerness of a bride awaiting her wedding day. *Immanuel's Veins* not only doesn't disappoint, it goes beyond my wildest expectations. From the first page, I was held captive by each word. The seductive story grabbed me, pulled me in close, and didn't let go even when I reached the end. I didn't realize **tears of both joy and sorrow had been streaming down my cheeks until several moments after I read the final word.** Ted Dekker's tale of sacrificial love left me gasping for more and longing for redemption. Be prepared to dive deep into the unplumbed depths of immeasurable love in *Immanuel's Veins*."

— Lisa Campbell, 39, Mother

"*Immanuel's Veins* reached down into the depths of my being and tore out my heart in order to lay it bare before me for careful study and examination. **What I experienced was an exhilarating, eye-opening journey of discovery of the constant seen and unseen battle over my heart**. I was washed over and over again by the intense and unending love portrayed in the pages of this book. **The revelation of my love being such a cherished and coveted prize still leaves me with chills and makes my head spin.** I have finished reading this book and put it on a book shelf along with my other treasures, but the message contained in this book will continue to haunt my dreams and thoughts. It has set my heart aflame with a fire that no one can extinguish. I know that for the rest of my life, I will feel the effects of this story as it continues to consume me and wash me from head to toe in its boundless waves of love."

— Amber McCallister, 32,
Computer Technician

"With *Immanuel's Veins* Dekker has clearly outdone himself. This is a story unlike any of his I've ever read. I was surprised, I had no idea the author had something like this inside of him. Nor was I prepared to have my heart ache, pound, and be renewed with a story that runs thicker than blood.** Transporting me to a time where chivalry and romance are at its highest, Dekker again reveals a depth of his skill that utterly amazes. *Veins* is a journey that evokes pure passion and morality from the most wicked and dispirited. The characters and settings entice and entrance making it hard to close the book after the final pages."

— Cory Clubb, 28, Illustrator

"**One of the most unique and powerful stories Dekker has ever penned**. Fantastic characters, gripping storylines, breathtaking imagery. Dekker leaves us with a story that will resonate in our hearts long after reading. *Immanuel's Veins* will spark much discussion amongst readers."

— Jake Chism, 33, Minister

Immanuel's Veins

teddekker.com

DEKKER FANTASY

BOOKS OF HISTORY CHRONICLES

THE LOST BOOKS (YOUNG ADULT)
Chosen
Infidel
Renegade
Chaos
Lunatic (WITH KACI HILL)
Elyon (WITH KACI HILL)
The Lost Books Visual Edition

THE CIRCLE SERIES
Black
Red
White
Green
The Circle Series Visual Edition

THE PARADISE BOOKS
Showdown
Saint
Sinner

Immanuel's Veins
House (WITH FRANK PERETTI)

DEKKER MYSTERY

Kiss (WITH ERIN HEALY)
Burn (WITH ERIN HEALY)

THE HEAVEN TRILOGY
Heaven's Wager
When Heaven Weeps
Thunder of Heaven

The Martyr's Song

THE CALEB BOOKS
Blessed Child
A Man Called Blessed

DEKKER THRILLER

THR3E
Obsessed
Adam
Skin
Blink of an Eye

Immanuel's Veins

TED DEKKER

THOMAS NELSON
Since 1798

NASHVILLE DALLAS MEXICO CITY RIO DE JANEIRO

Published in Nashville, Tennessee, by Thomas Nelson. Thomas Nelson is a registered trademark of Thomas Nelson, Inc.

Published in association with Thomas Nelson and Creative Trust Inc., 5141 Virginia Way, Suite 320, Brentwoood, TN 37027.

Thomas Nelson, Inc., titles may be purchased in bulk for educational, business, fund-raising, or sales promotional use. For information, please e-mail SpecialMarkets@ThomasNelson.com.

Publisher's Note: This novel is a work of fiction. Names, characters, places, and incidents are either products of the author's imagination or used fictitiously. All characters are fictional, and any similarity to people living or dead is purely coincidental.

ISBN 978-1-59554-762-0 (IE)

Library of Congress Cataloging-in-Publication Data

Dekker, Ted, 1962–
    Immanuel's veins / Ted Dekker.
      p. cm.
    ISBN 978-1-59554-009-6 (hardcover : alk. paper)
    1. Soldiers—Russia—Fiction. 2. Kantemir family—Fiction. 3. Dimitrie Cantemir, Voivode of Moldavia, 1673-1723—Family—Fiction. 4. Nobility—Moldavia—Fiction. 5. Triangles (Interpersonal relations)—Fiction. 6. Moldavia—Fiction. I. Title.
PS3554.E43I53 2010
813'.54—dc22   2010016894

Printed in the United States of America

10 11 12 13 14 LBM 5 4 3 2 1

AUG 2010

For king Solomon

To all who have ears to hear:

I am dead. But perhaps you are as well, if you can read this account penned by a dead man.

I, Saint Thomas of Moldavia, make known this report of all that transpired so that any who seek the truth will know what happened.

Some called me a heretic. They said that my dealing with the matters herein could only mean that I was touched by the devil himself. Some said that I was a creature of the night, a dragon, a beast turned into man. Some said that I was mad, and I will attest that I myself once would have believed that this tale could only come from the mind of a raving lunatic.

But I swear by my very own blood that I am neither devil nor beast and that this is not the tale of a lunatic—unless by love I have been driven hopelessly mad, a reasoning that tempts me more often than I dare admit. Judge it for yourself.

I implore you to open your hearts and your minds to this account. Then, when you have turned the last page, if you still do not believe that what you have read is true, you may say that I deserved my death.

Saint Thomas
Lover of his Bride

ONE

My name is Toma Nicolescu and I was a warrior, a servant of Her Majesty, the empress of Russia, Catherine the Great, who by her own hand and tender heart sent me on that mission at the urging of her most trusted adviser, Grigory Potyomkin, in the year of our Lord 1772.

It was a year of war, this one the Russo-Turkish War, one of so many with the Ottoman Empire. I had slain the enemy with more ambition than most in the humble service of the empress, or so it has been said, and having earned Her Majesty's complete trust in my loyalty and skill, I was dispatched by her to the south and east, through Ukraine to the principality of Moldavia, just north of the Black Sea and west of Transylvania, to the country estate of the Cantemir family nestled up against the base of the Carpathian Mountains.

To my understanding, the family descendants of Dimitrie Cantemir, the late prince of Moldavia, were owed a debt for his loyalty to Russia. Indeed, it was said that the path to the heart of Moldavia ran through the Cantemir crest, but that was all politics—none of my business.

On that day my business was to travel to this remote, lush green valley in western Moldavia and give protection to this most important family who retreated to the estate every summer.

Russia had occupied Moldavia. Enemies were about with sharp knives and blunt intentions. The black plague had mercilessly taken the lives of many in the cities. A ruler loyal to Catherine the Great would soon be selected to take the reins of this important principality, and the Cantemir family would play a critical role in that decision as they held such a lofty position of respect among all Moldavians.

My charge was simple: No harm could come to this family. These Cantemirs.

The sun was sinking over the Carpathian peaks to our left as my friend in arms, Alek Cardei, and I sat atop our mounts and stared down at the valley. The great white castle with its twin spires stood on emerald grasses an hour's ride down the twisted path. A tall stone wall ran the length of the southern side where the road ran into the property. Green lawns and gardens surrounded the estate, encompassing ten times the ground as the house itself. The estate had been commissioned by Dimitrie Cantemir in 1711, when he was prince of Moldavia for a brief time before retreating to Turkey.

"I see the twin peaks, but I see no gowns," Alek said, squinting down the valley. His gloved hand was on his gold-busted sword. Leather armor wrapped his chest and thighs, same as mine. A goatee cupped his chin and joined his mustache but he'd shaved the rest of his face in the creek earlier, anticipating his ride into the estate, the arriving hero from abroad.

Alek, the lover.

Toma, the warrior.

I looked down at the golden ring on my finger, which bore the empress's insignia, and I chuckled. Alek's wit and charm were always good friends on a long journey, and he wielded both with the same ease and precision with which I swung my sword.

I nodded at my fair-headed friend as he turned his pale blue eyes toward me. "We're here to protect the sisters and their family, not wed them."

"So then you cannot deny it: the sisters *are* on your mind. Not the mother, not the father, not the family, but the sisters. These two female frolickers who are the talk of Ukraine." Alek turned his mirth-twisted face back to the valley. "Heat has come to the dog at last."

To the contrary, though Alek could not know, I had taken a vow to Her Majesty not to entangle myself while here in Moldavia. She was all too aware of the sisters' reputations, and she suggested I keep my head clear on this long assignment that might too easily give us much idle time.

"One favor, Toma," she said.

"Of course, Your Majesty."

"Stay clear of the sisters, please. At least one of you ought to have a clear mind."

"Of course, Your Majesty."

But Alek was a different matter, and there was hardly any reason to deny him his jesting. It always lifted my spirits.

If I were a woman, I would have loved Alek. If I were a king, I would have hired him to remain in my courts. If I were an enemy, I would have run and hid, because wherever you found Alek you would find Toma, and you would surely die unless you swore allegiance to the empress.

But I was the furthest thing from a woman, I had never aspired to be a king, and I had no mortal enemies save myself.

My vice was honor: chivalry when it was appropriate, but loyalty to my duty first. I was Alek's closest and most trusted friend, and I would have died for him without a care in the world.

He blew out some air in exasperation. "I have gone to the ends of the earth with you, Toma, and I would still. But this mission of ours is a fool's errand. We come here to sit with babies while the armies dine on conquest?"

"So you've made abundantly clear for a week now," I returned. "What happened to your yearning for these sisters? As you've said, they are rumored to be beautiful."

"Rumors! For all we know they are spoiled fat poodles. What can this valley possibly offer that the nights in Moscow can't? I'm doomed, I tell you. I would rather run a sword through myself now than suffer a month in that dungeon below."

I could see through his play already. "From frolicking sisters to suicide so quickly? You're outdoing yourself, Alek."

"I'm utterly serious!" His face flashed, indignant. "When have you known me to sit on my hands for weeks on end with nothing but a single family to occupy me? I'm telling you, this is going to be my death."

He was still playing me, and I him. "So now you expect me to give you leave to exhaust your fun here, then go gallivanting about the countryside seeking out mistresses in the other estates? Or would you rather slip out at night and slit a few evil throats so you can feel like a man?"

He shrugged. "Honestly, the former sounds more appealing." His gloved finger stabbed skyward. "But I know my duty and would die by your side fulfilling it." He lowered his hand. "Still, as God is my witness, I will not tolerate a month of picking my teeth with straw while the rest of the world fights for glory and chases skirts."

"Don't be a fool, man. Boredom could not catch you if it chased you like a wolf. We'll establish a simple protocol to limit all access to the estate, post the sentries, and mind the women—I understand that the father will be gone most of the time. As long as our duties are in no way compromised, I will not stand in the way of your courting. But as you say, they may be fat poodles."

A sound came from behind us. "Who has business with the Cantemirs? Eh?"

I spun to the soft, gravelly voice. An old shriveled man stood there, grasping a tall cane with both hands. His eyes were slits, his face was wrinkled like a dried-out prune, and his long stringy gray hair was so thin that a good wind would surely leave him bald. I wasn't sure he could actually see through those black cracks below his brow.

Alek *humphed* and deferred to me. How had this ancient man walked up on us without a sound? He was gumming his lips, toothless. Silent.

I held my hand up to Alek and drew my pale mount about to face the man. "Who asks?"

A bird flew in from the west, a large black crow. As I watched, somewhat stunned, it alighted on the old man's shoulder, steadied itself with a single flap of its wings, and came to rest. The man didn't react, not even when the crow's thick wing slapped his ear.

"I don't have a name," the old man said. "You may call me an angel if you like."

Alek chuckled, but I was sure it was a nervous reaction without a lick of humor.

"Who inquires of the Cantemir estate?" he asked again.

"Toma Nicolescu, in the service of Her Majesty, the empress of Russia, Catherine the Great, who now rules Moldavia. And if you are an angel, then you may vanish as all angels vanish, into the air of superstition."

"Toma?" the old man croaked.

"What business do you have with this estate?"

"Eh, that is you? Toma Nicolescu?"

His demeanor now bothered me more than I cared to admit. Was this my elder, whom I should honor, or a wandering lunatic?

"Watch your tongue, old man," Alek snapped.

The crow cocked its head and lined up one of its beady eyes for a hard look at Alek; the old man did the same.

"Eh? Is that you too, Toma?"

Alek's brow furrowed. "Stop playing the buffoon. And get rid of that cursed bird."

"State your business, old man," I demanded.

He lifted a bony, scarcely fleshed hand and pointed to the west. "There is evil in the wind. Beware, Toma. Beware the evil."

"Don't be a loon . . ."

I held up my hand to stop Alek, interested in the oddity before us, this ancient blind prune and his all-seeing crow.

"What makes you think there is evil to beware?" I asked.

"Eh? The crow saw it."

"The crow told you that, did he? And does your crow speak as well?" Alek's voice wrung mockery from each word.

Lightning stabbed at the plains in the east. I hadn't noticed the clouds on the horizon until now. A muted peal of thunder growled at us, as if in warning I thought, and I wasn't given to superstition. The devil wasn't my enemy and God wasn't my friend. Nothing I'd experienced in my twenty-eight years had moved me to believe in either.

The old wizard with his crow was staring at me through slits, silent. I wanted to know why the man seemed to sense the threat—it was my job to know. So I dismounted, walked up to him, and dipped my head, an easy thing to do considering his age, for I had always been given to respecting the aged.

The black bird was only three feet from me, jerking its head for a better look, sizing me up, deciding whether he should pluck my eyes out.

I spoke kindly, in a low voice. "Please, if you feel it wise, tell me why your crow would warn us of evil."

He smiled a toothless grin, all gums and lips. "This is Peter the Great. I can't see so well, but they tell me he's a magnificent bird. I think he likes me."

"I would say he looks like a devil. So why would a devil tell an angel that evil is near?"

"I'm not the devil, Toma Nicolescu. He is far more beautiful than I."

I was sure I could hear Alek snickering, and I had half a mind to shut him up with a glare.

"And who is this beautiful devil?"

"A man with a voice like honey who flies through the night." The old man removed his right hand from the staff and used it like a wing. "But God was the one who told me to tell Toma Nicolescu that evil is in contest with you. He said you would come here, to the Brasca Pass. I've been waiting for three days, and I do think one more day might have claimed my life."

"So the crow saw it, and then God told you, his angel, to warn us," Alek scoffed. "How is that possible when we didn't even know which route we would take until yesterday?"

"Perhaps God can read your minds."

"*Our* minds didn't even know!"

"But God did. And here you are. And now I have done my thing and can live a little longer with my crow. I should go now." He started to turn.

"Please, kind sir." I put my hand on his. "Our mission is only to protect the estate. Is there anything else you can tell us? I don't see how a warning of evil given by a crow is much use to us."

The man's gentle face slowly sagged and became a picture of foreboding. "I can hardly advise you, who thinks the devil is only hot air, now can I?"

I was surprised that the old man knew this about me. But it could as easily have been a lucky guess.

"As for your oversexed friend, you may tell him that this valley will certainly exhaust his feral impulses. I suspect that you are both in for a rather stimulating time. Now, I must be going. I have a long way to travel and the night is coming fast."

With that he turned and walked away, a slow shuffle that made me wonder how he expected to reach the path, much less the nearest town, Crysk, a full ten miles south.

TWO

Lucine and Natasha stood on the balcony above the courtyard under a full rising moon, watching the guests who had gathered for this Summer Ball of Delights, as Mother had called it. The name tempted scandal by itself.

"The man in the black coat, there," Natasha said, pointing to a crowd of seven or eight by the fountain that led into the hedge garden.

Lucine saw him now, one of the Russian aristocrats from the Castle Castile. A group of five had come to the ball and shown themselves for the first time since the castle had come under new ownership three months earlier.

"I see him. What of it?"

"What of it?" Natasha cried. "He's magnificent."

Perhaps. Yes, in a way he was, Lucine thought. "A magnificent monster," she said.

Natasha's eyes flashed with mystery. "Then give me a monster." She wore a red silk gown draped over a slight petticoat, white lace whispering around her slippers and wrists. A trim of black satin graced her chest, low enough to provoke curiosity without revealing too much. Her blonde curls flowed over her pale shoulders—positively glowing under the bright moon.

Lucine's twin was a goddess, night or day. The kind of goddess any monster would gladly consume.

"Just watch yourself, Sister. We don't know them."

There was no summer except the summer in Moldavia, Mother said, and Lucine agreed.

It was said that Mother had once been the very vision of proper behavior under the scrutiny of her first husband, Dimitrie Cantemir. He'd ruled her with an iron fist, she said, and she grew to resent her life. But when Dimitrie had died of pneumonia while she was still pregnant with Lucine and Natasha, she had reportedly become a new woman.

Mother had waited six months, then she accepted the full benefits of the Cantemir name and wealth left her, gave birth to twin girls, and, as soon as her body allowed it, set out to find a man who would allow her to live a life full of joy, not servitude.

She and Mikhail Ivanov met a year later and were married in two months, but only on the condition that she be allowed to keep her full name, Kesia Cantemir, and pursue whatever pleasures she wished. For the most part Mikhail lived in a different world, and he rarely accompanied his wife and stepdaughters to Moldavia. At present he was busy conducting his affairs in Kiev.

Mother taught her twin daughters to embrace the full offering of life, and both Lucine and Natasha had, with more passion than most.

Lucine was only seventeen when she'd become pregnant. The father remained nameless, because she'd sworn never to think, much less speak, his name again. The thirty-year-old beast swept her off her feet with all the promises any seventeen-year-old might like to hear.

She'd shoved the memory of what followed to the deepest hiding places in her mind, but it was still there, dulled by time. The way she'd felt a new life grow inside of her belly. The way her passion for this life had found fulfillment in her love for her unborn child.

Kesia and Natasha had joined her in her delight—it was the Cantemir way. But the brute who'd given her his seed did not share any such pleasure. Lucine grew to detest him, and when she refused to be silent about her passion for this child within her, he flew into a rage, tracked her down, and beat her to within a single breath of death. With a stick of firewood he hit her belly until he was certain no life inside survived the beating.

She miscarried that night, while she clung to life. She arose from bed two weeks later, tracked down the beast, and took his life with a knife while he slept.

Then she put the incident behind her and insisted not a word of it be spoken. But she was not the carefree lover of men she had once been.

Four years had passed, and Lucine longed to be romanced by

a true man who would win her for only one kiss if that was all she would give him. A man who would die to protect her.

Her twin sister, on the other hand, still preferred the wild ones with teeth because she was a ravenous wolf herself. And yet, at times Lucine wondered if they, being twins, were really still one and the same, living within themselves and vicariously through each other. Didn't a part of her long for the wolf as much as Natasha did?

". . . more men than I can possibly consider in one evening," Natasha was saying.

"Whatever you say, Sister. I—"

And then Lucine saw the blond man staring up at her.

"What is it?" Natasha twisted her head and followed Lucine's gaze to the courtyard below. "What's wrong?"

He was just a man, a soldier of some kind, dressed in an officer's black suit with short tails, and sporting a black hat. But he was such a fine specimen and he looked at her with such intensity and confidence that she felt immediately ruffled.

The man with the golden mane removed his hat and, keeping his eyes on hers, bowed.

Natasha chuckled. "My, my, does he ever clean up."

"Who is he?"

"One of the two I was telling you about, sent by the empress herself. That one is named Alek."

"Alek?"

"Alek Cardei. They arrived an hour ago and were shown to their quarters. I saw them only from a distance."

The man replaced his hat and stepped back, dipping his head.

"They? Who is the other?"

"The hero, you mean. Toma. Toma Nicolescu. I don't know . . . There he is." She pointed to another man in a similar uniform.

Toma Nicolescu stood twenty feet from his partner, studying the crowd over a drink, which he held delicately in his left hand. His right hand rested on a sword that hung by his side. He was cavalry, she guessed. A horseman.

"Stay if you must, Sister," Natasha said, "but I will not hold myself from this feast for a moment longer. See to Alek and Toma, and leave the Russians to me." And then she was flying down the stairs.

⚜

We had arrived at the Cantemir estate as night fell, and instead of the peaceful home of noble descent that we'd envisioned during our weeklong journey, we found a mansion crawling with lords and counts and dukes and all manner of aristocrats intent on frivolous behavior.

This so-called Summer Ball of Delights. A ball in the country wasn't unheard of, naturally, but considering the urgency with which Her Majesty had dispatched us to secure the estate, I was surprised to find not the slightest concern of danger here.

But then, ordinary people rarely see real danger until the sword has fallen and they lie bloody in the street. They prefer to set their minds on phantom dangers that float through the air unseen. Ghost and devils and ridiculous religious imaginations that cannot be proven.

Still, were they so stupid to allow such an influx of strangers into their home?

Alek and I were shown to our quarters in the west tower, and at first I thought the servant who led us had made a mistake. We were to stay in separate rooms, each lavishly outfitted and beautifully appointed, mine with stuffed silk bedding and lavender drapes that swept across expansive windows framing the towering Carpathian peaks to the west. The velvet curtains sweeping down from an ornate ceiling like sheets of water, the overstuffed golden chair, the writing desk with lit lamp . . . it was all too much.

I was more accustomed to a tent and the ground than this pillow before me. My first instinct was to retreat and ask Alek to exchange rooms, only to find that his was as lavish.

I showered and shaved and dressed in the only uniform I'd packed. We were here for Her Majesty, not on the army's time, so we wouldn't dress in our normal military garb, but Alek insisted on dressing his part if only for this night. Women have always been attracted to the uniform.

Honestly, I felt a bit put off by the levity of the ball.

The old man with the crow's warning whispered in my ear. How had he known we would come through that pass?

Standing in the courtyard an hour later, watching the dancers step with the music, I couldn't shake the impression that we were being watched. But I saw nothing that caused me irregular concern.

There was a group of five Russians who'd only recently purchased the Castle Castile, which lay five miles into the mountains. The mysterious lot dressed differently—the men with long black slacks worn outside of their boots, the women with velvet gowns hiked up in the front to their knees, revealing tall leather boots. But Russia was in a bit of a renaissance now, there was no telling what kind of style or culture might emerge.

"She's stunning," Alek said, looking up at the balcony where the twin Cantemir sisters stood. "God bless the empress. Can you believe our fortune? I would knock a platoon over for her."

On balance, Alek might pose a greater risk to the peace than anyone.

"Which one?"

"Both. But the blonde wants me, I tell you."

"Just remember why we're here," I said.

"We're here for her."

"For her *safety*."

"Can you imagine a safer place than my arms?" He took off his hat and bowed, and I saw the brunette, the sister named Lucine, acknowledge him. He turned and winked at me. "Other than in *your* arms, that is."

But my mind wasn't on love or beauty. Moldavia was a task to conquer, not a pleasure to be plucked.

Five minutes later the blonde sister, Natasha, was down the stairs and crossing the courtyard toward the Russians. Her eyes fell on us and she scanned us flirtatiously, but then she moved on.

"What did I tell you?" Alek growled. "She wants me."

"And she wants the Russian as well."

"Only because she doesn't know me as well as you do, Toma."

One of the Russian women was heading our way. She passed Natasha, eyes set on us, as if this were some kind of exchange. Natasha for the Russian temptress.

"Are you seeing this?" Alek said.

I stepped away to give him some space with her. I had no interest at all.

Lucine, the other twin, was making her way down the stairs.

Her long dark hair reminded me of that crow on the old man's shoulder. But this was no crow. In my view she was unquestionably the more beautiful of the two. For that matter, the most beautiful woman I might have yet laid eyes upon. If Natasha wouldn't warm to his advances, Alek would surely play his games and sweep Lucine off her feet. In all likelihood, he would have them *both* head over heels within the week.

Now, I must say that up to this point, in spite of the old man and his crow, my world was well centered. I was simply a man about his duty.

But that all changed in the next moment.

Looking back now, I can say the series of incredible events that forever changed my understanding of this ordered world began in earnest in that moment. Though I did not recognize or embrace it then, the axis of this planet surely shifted. The stars reversed their course and sent a spell of love and anguish, tears and laughter into the valley, and I was too thickheaded to yet see it.

The scent of the Russian woman reached me before she did— sweet musky flowers—and I turned to see that she'd walked right past Alek and had her eyes on me.

Deep golden eyes that drew me like a warm fire. It's the only way I can describe the feeling I had first looking into those beautiful eyes. I'm not suggesting that I was interested in her, though any man with blood would be, for this woman, not Lucine, was surely the most beautiful woman in the estate.

She moved closer, refusing to shift her eyes. The night seemed to slow.

No, not the night, nor the others in that night, but she. Only she. This vision of beauty seemed to slow right before my eyes while the rest of the courtyard went on. Her arms, the swirl of her black skirt, the bending of her booted legs cutting through the black velvet that hid them so poorly as she walked—it all happened at half pace.

Thoughts of the black plague filled my mind. I was ill, I thought, feverish, hallucinating. Her tongue traced the bottom of her teeth.

I blinked, and the world returned to normal.

"Hello, Toma," she said in low, breathy voice. "You may call me Sofia." And then she winked and was past me. She walked through the archway leading into the main room where half the guests were gathered.

How did she know my name? I glanced at Alek, and to my surprise his eyes weren't even on me, or her. He was fixated on Lucine, who had stepped off the stairs ahead of us.

I must have imagined that woman's voice. Nothing else made sense to me.

Lucine came to us—to Alek—and although I greeted her as any gentleman might, my mind was still clouded and I hardly heard a word.

"Would you mind, dear?" Kesia, the mother, said, stepping up behind Lucine. "Would you show our two guests around? I'm sure they have questions, and I have others to attend to. I can assure you fine gentlemen that no nasty predators will come for us tonight. Eat the lamb, drink the wine, enjoy yourselves."

"But you don't understand, madam," Alek said. He took Lucine's hand and kissed it softly. "When this much beauty presents itself, there is always terrible danger lurking."

Lucine blushed. "Well, now. That's . . . nice."

Kesia smiled knowingly and left them.

And then Alek departed with a slight bow. "If you don't mind,

I must see to other matters." He left us to pursue Natasha, who was already in the arms of another man, one of the Russians.

Lucine turned from the scene and I dutifully followed her into the main house. Slowly my mind was drawn to the gracious movements of the Cantemir sister who led me. As soon as I stepped into the ballroom, thoughts of the Russian who called herself Sofia were gone.

The walnut doors from the courtyard led to a magnificent ballroom with a white marble floor, lit by one of the largest crystal chandeliers I had ever seen. White stairs on either side rose to a second-story balcony that surrounded the entire venue.

Along with the candles in the chandelier, roaring twin fireplaces lit the room. The orange light of oil lamps mounted on walls added shadows. Guests milled about in every corner, tasting pastries that were stacked on four round tables with the drinks.

Lucine led me through the grand space past the curious gazes and into the dining room, where there were no guests. She closed the door, shutting out the party, and I could not mistake her slight sigh of relief.

"It gets to be a bit much, don't you think?" she asked.

Her voice reached into me like a wisp of perfume. I don't know why, but to this day I can't understand why those words affected me so. Perhaps it was the sweet tone with which she expressed precisely what had occupied my mind.

Perhaps it was the sincerity in her eyes, as if she was as relieved as I to be free from the cacophony of meaningless drivel that typified these sorts of balls.

Perhaps it was my being alone with her profound beauty.

I think it was more and less than all of these. I think it was part of what was written in the stars. When Lucine said those simple words, my heart began a most rapid thaw.

"It was a bit much from the moment I entered the house," I said carefully.

She looked at me, hazel eyes brightened by a hundred candles, and then offered me a slight knowing smile. "Was it, now?" She walked past me, along the table, running her fingers on the backs of the carved wooden chairs. Rather small fingers, mind you, but so elegant, like an angel dancing over the backs. Her nails were painted rose as I recall.

"So tell me, Toma Nicolescu, have you seen any criminals among us?" She faced me. "That is what you've come to find, right? Criminals?"

"I don't know what I've come to find, madam. My orders are only to protect you and your family from any danger that presents itself in this time of political anticipation. And that is what I intend to do."

"Then perhaps the first danger you should look to is your stable boy."

"Alek, you mean? He's not a stable boy."

But of course she knew that. She was hurt by Alek. He'd left Lucine to attend to Natasha, and she was jealous.

I suddenly didn't want her to be jealous of Natasha. Alek had enough women running after him.

"You're jealous?"

"What?"

"Of your sister," I said. But I was in no position to stand in judgment of these sorts of things. "Forgive me, that was out of order. I—"

"It's fine. But you misunderstand me if you think I could possibly develop an interest in a man, no matter how beautiful or strong or endearing, at first meeting. Or during the course of a week or a month for that matter."

But this did not cool me. The thaw that had just warmed my heart was spreading, and I felt a little bit of panic. My feelings were confusing to me, and in light of my promise to Her Majesty, offensive. So I forced the interest aside and proceeded with sincerity.

"Then you're not jealous?" I asked.

"Of what?"

"Precisely. I've always tried to understand what women find so appealing about that boy." What was I saying?

"Everywhere we go, they seem to fall all over him. He would never pass up the opportunity to be the life of the party, which he manages like a well-wound clock. Not to mention he's a war hero, skilled beyond belief with that sword of his. I trust him like a brother and would put my life in his judgment any day."

"So then, *you're* jealous," she said. Strands of her dark hair curled around her face like adoring fingers.

"I stand in jealousy of all things better than I, so that I might better myself."

"And do you also look for ways to dismiss one woman for another?"

As you think Alek has dismissed you, I almost said. I was right. She had indeed seen something in Alek that pulled at her heart. I could see it in her eyes and it bothered me.

"I think my sister will like him," she said. "If she can pull herself away from that Stefan fellow."

We spent the next fifteen minutes walking around the mansion, and at every turn I had to remind myself that my awkward attraction to her was only natural, considering her beauty. I had pushed the trivial pursuit of women from my mind so many times for the sake of honor that my thirsty heart was only drinking out of instinct. There was nothing else to it.

She took me to the tower, and from there she pointed out the property boundaries by moonlight. In my need to remain focused, I must have asked her a hundred questions regarding the comings and goings of servants, the proximity of towns and estates, all things pertaining to any potential threat.

None surfaced. But they rarely do before their time.

As I stood by the wall that circled the tower, looking over the grounds, my eyes were secretly and repeatedly drawn back to Lucine. To her dark brown hair cascading over her shoulders. To her neck and her gown, to the curve of her mouth and her small nose. I prayed she did not catch my eyes shifting about.

"I don't really care for horses," she said, resting her hands on the stone wall. Then she caught herself. "Does that bother you?"

"No. Why would it?"

"You're cavalry. Horses are your precious friends. I'm sure I should love them."

"But they don't routinely save your life as they do mine," I said.

"You see?" She turned her light brown eyes to meet mine. "I have no right."

"Nonsense. You can't love something because it saves my life. What does my life matter to you? I don't mean to suggest that you seem like the type who doesn't care if others live or die. People like me. I mean to say I'm sure you value people like me a great deal."

She didn't respond.

"After all, we save the world," I said. "Not that we deserve any special attention for our sacrifice. Or that what we do is really even a sacrifice. I'm just saying."

She responded after a pause, eyes still on mine. "And what are you saying?"

Finally I found some sanity. "That you are free to like or dislike horses as far as I'm concerned. Not that my opinion matters to you."

I think I saw her lips curve into a slight smile. I can't be sure because I was dizzy with my own foolishness. She pointed to the trees and made a remark that I missed about pines.

She could have been the plainest of creatures and I would have felt the same because her spirit was that of an angel's. I was drawn to her values and kindness, her honesty, and the ease with which she led me around, unencumbered by the social pressures waiting beneath us.

She led me down the stairs from the tower, and I could hardly ignore the scent of her perfumed hair. Like gardenias in the summer. If Alek were following her, he would have said something. Perhaps he would have been my savior in this matter. I thought I should send her to him so that I could be free of these ridiculous thoughts.

We returned to the dining room and walked toward the door leading into the ballroom. "You should make a play for Alek," I said.

She paused and tilted her head as if to say, *Is that so?*

"He would like that," I said. "I mean, he likes confident women. And you shouldn't cast judgment before you get to know him."

A roar came from beyond the door.

She stared at me.

Another cry, this time a woman's voice gasping.

I reached the door in two long steps, threw it wide, and stepped into the ballroom. The lights had dimmed by half, candles extinguished. Dozens of guests lined the walls and the balcony. As one their eyes were fixed on the floor beneath the chandelier.

There stood Alek, sword drawn, point pressed against one of the Russian's throats. But the Russian also had a sword stretched out and it lay alongside Alek's throat. They stood two paces apart, glaring at each other.

Natasha lay on the floor six feet from them. There was blood on her face.

"I will kill you for that," Alek said.

THREE

S o obvious?" Stefan asked. His voice was soft but confident enough to send a cold draft down my back.

"Death is always obvious when a woman's honor is at stake," Alek said.

"Her honor? In your jealousy you misunderstand. She *asked* me to kiss her."

I instinctively reached out my left hand and placed it against Lucine's belly, meaning to push her back to safety, then just as quickly withdrew it, thinking the touch inappropriate.

I quickly surveyed the room. The other Russians stood casually in a group, watching with mild interest, except the one who called herself Sofia, who was staring at me with fiery eyes. The other guests had backed up to the walls and wore stark faces.

Kesia Cantemir rushed from the door toward her motionless daughter. "What have you done? What is this?" She dropped to her knees and cradled Natasha's head in her lap. "Darling, wake up! What is this?"

I put a hand out to steady Lucine, who had come to herself and was starting to go for her sister. "Be careful, Alek."

"Stay back, Toma. He's been begging me all night."

Stefan only chuckled. Alek knew as well as I that even if he thrust his blade into the Russian's throat now, the man would have plenty of time to reciprocate before they both collapsed in blood.

"What have you done, you beast?" Kesia cried.

"I kissed your daughter, madam. Clearly she was overwhelmed by the pleasure and fainted. I assure you, she will awake and beg for more."

The room was deathly silent.

"It is your own honor you have put into question," Stefan said to Alek. Now a smile had joined his soft voice and warning bells shook in my head. "But we don't need to kill each other over a woman neither of us really knows. Sister?"

Sofia, who was evidently Stefan's sister, stepped toward the two men locked beneath the chandelier. She left her friends, but I could swear her eyes never left me.

Could the others see this? Was Lucine watching the alluring gaze of this woman piercing my head?

Stefan flipped his wrist and his long blade sailed toward Sofia in a blur. He lifted both hands in a sign of truce and stepped back.

Sofia caught the sword by the handle as if it were an apple

she'd casually tossed to herself. Using only slight movement, she sent it back to one of the others, who snatched it from the air.

"Why don't you try Sofia? She likes big strong warrior types," Stefan said.

I had rarely seen Alek at a loss for words, but he hesitated. His eyes spun to Sofia, who was walking around him as she trailed her fingernails along the back of his shoulders.

"I have no interest in her," Alek said. "The woman you attacked is on the floor. She's under my protection and you will go back to hell before I let you leave this place."

"Hell? Wouldn't that be a rush to the head?" Sofia was coming around Alek again, but her eyes were even now on me, unless I had lost my mind. She kissed Alek's ear.

"I say play his game, Stefan," she said. "I'm much more interested in the other one. The one named Toma."

Sofia left his side and headed toward me.

"Is she alive?" Alek demanded of Kesia.

"She breathes, yes. It's her lip."

"Her lip?"

"Her lip's been bitten."

"You bit her lip and she fainted—you expect us to believe this?" Alek snarled at the Russian.

Stefan shrugged. "She'll tell you the same when she wakes."

"Yet there she lies on the floor. How *dare* you enter this house as a guest and even touch a woman? Go back to your whores in Russia! Your kind aren't welcome in the Cantemir estate."

Sofia had crossed the floor and stood beside me, as if I had claimed her. Lucine on my left, this black-clad seductress on my right. I stood like a trapped deer.

"Be very careful, Toma," Sofia whispered.

She was warning me?

Alek tossed his sword onto the marble floor, where it clattered to a rest. The brows above Stefan's eyes arched.

"He disarms. Impressive. A noble warrior indeed."

"I'll take nobility and shove it down your throat. Leave! This is my last warning."

"Or?"

"Or you will lie dead."

"You'll slice my head off with your fingernails?"

This could not end well. But stepping in would only undermine the group's impression of Alek's judgment, so I held my ground.

"Do not underestimate me."

"My mind exactly. Now you've challenged my honor by accusing me of biting off a woman's lip! I am incensed."

"Leave!" Alek thundered.

You see, I knew that tone in his voice. Alek was not the kind who played games with his sword or knives. Only with his lips and tongue, and only then with women. This dense Russian named Stefan was not hearing his death call. I almost stepped in then, knowing about Alek's throwing blades.

"Then what say we defend our honor in a way that isn't as pathetic or boring as a duel to the death or all that nonsense?"

Alek said nothing

"So you fear me."

"I fear only your ignorance. And I have no desire to make a mess on this floor the very first night of my arrival."

Stefan stepped back a few paces, spread his arms wide, and addressed the ring of observers watching.

"Who is interested in seeing me kill"—Alek was already moving, while the man's eyes were on his audience—"this insolent—"

A blade Alek had dropped from his right sleeve darted across the room like a dagger shot from a cannon. The man was as good as dead.

But as the knife neared his throat, Stefan moved with such speed as I had never seen. His right hand snapped up and clamped around the razor-sharp blade. I could hear the edge slicing through the flesh of his palm.

The room gasped. My hand was on the butt of the pistol strapped to the side of my chest.

Stefan stood still for half a beat, glaring back at Alek with dark eyes, and then in three bounds he was there by Alek's side, the same blade now pressed against my friend's neck.

Slicing already.

I lurched forward.

"Enough, Stefan!"

Alek's attacker froze at the sound of the voice, which had come from the doorway. A warm waft of air swirled around the long black coat of a man standing in the open door. Flames in the fireplace bowed away from the wind that the guest had brought with him. He stood with his arms at his sides, staring at Stefan.

All eyes shifted to this man whom I had not seen before, dressed in black like the others. But he stood taller and carried himself with an air of absolute authority. The tail of his suit fell well below the backs of his knees; his slacks covered black boots rimmed in silver; his sleeves were hemmed with red lace, butting into white gloves; his collar ran high behind his neck, framing a head of black hair.

The door blew shut behind him.

"Step away."

I knew without looking that Stefan would obey. I could judge most leaders' power by their voices.

For an extended moment the room seemed to be held in the embrace of the man's power, as if time had once again slowed. I could hear my heart in my chest, the blood rushing through my veins.

A soft groan broke the moment.

"Natasha?" Kesia cried.

"What's . . ." Natasha sat up and looked around, dazed. She blinked. "What on earth is this?"

"Are you well, my dear?"

Natasha stood, gaining her footing quickly. "Of course I'm well, Mother. What's this about? Where's . . ."

She saw Stefan, who'd backed away from Alek, and her eyes lingered on him. But it was Alek who stepped in and took her arm. The blood was still on her lip and she touched it with her tongue.

"Madam, please." Alek dabbed her lip with a handkerchief. "Are you sure you're fine?"

"*Fine* is not a term we can use to inquire of such a beautiful woman." The late-arrived Russian walked forward and presented himself first to the mother, Kesia. He took her hand and kissed it.

"Forgive the intrusion into your home, madam. These men and women have presented you with a terrible impression of our estate. I am the master of the Castle Castile, a humble guest in your Moldavia. Vlad van Valerik, at your command. Please, call me Vlad, for I am a commoner in your house."

Kesia eyed him, undecided, then faced Natasha, whose eyes were on Valerik. "Natasha—"

"I'm perfectly fine, Mother. Please, we were only having a little fun. Is a woman never allowed to faint with all of this dancing, wine, and heat? It was all perfectly harmless and sweet."

But I could see by the way Stefan was watching Alek that what may have begun sweet had turned bitter.

Kesia turned back to Valerik. "Then I accept your apology. And you are welcome in my home. We aren't averse to a little fun, but please, keep a leash on the pit bulls."

I liked Kesia less for welcoming Valerik into her home but better for the crack of her verbal whip.

Valerik smiled. "Well said."

The room was brighter, and I saw that some of the candles I thought had been extinguished were still lit.

"Would you like me to punish him?" he asked.

Kesia glanced at Stefan, who looked to be struggling between his allegiance to Valerik and his anger at having been humiliated by Alek, though he'd succeeded in laying a small cut along Alek's neck.

So what was driving the dark rage I saw in his eyes?

"What did you have in mind?"

Valerik clearly hadn't expected her response. He stepped over to Natasha, brushed her cut lip with his thumb. "Such a delicate flower. You, my lady, are an exquisite creature who must provoke the dying wish of any man and half the women in this world. We must not judge Stefan too harshly."

"No," she said.

He lowered his arms, clasped his hands behind his back, then walked slowly in a small circle, eyeing the guests. "But some punishment would be appropriate. I wouldn't want my neighbors to think that I am not a fair man. There are a handful of us in the Castle Castile and we are only a few noblemen and women who have escaped Russia for the summer, like you. It's a beautiful land, this Moldavia, and there must be order."

They hung on his words. As, I must admit, did I.

"An eye for an eye, yes?" he said. His eyes came around the room, dark but glistening in the light. They stopped at Lucine. And they seemed to drink her.

When they shifted to me, I felt deep anger, not for the way he looked at me but because he'd looked at Lucine that way.

"Stefan has taken from the one sister. Invited or not, it no longer matters. It would only be fair for the other sister to take from Stefan. You're twins?"

They were not identical twins, but the similarities were plain enough and the twins were well known. But I didn't want this Russian to speak to Lucine. For any reason.

"Yes," Lucine said.

"Would you like to take Stefan for a night and do what you like with him? You could thrash him or force him to bake you a cake or use him for his more natural talents, which go without saying. Assuming your mother likes the idea."

Kesia blushed but smiled.

"You could even make him your mother's slave for the night. If any take from a Cantemir, they will give back, no?"

I was outraged! I hated Stefan for what he might do in this ridiculous punishment. How could Kesia not throw these men out on their tails?

Because snakes are not easily thrown, Toma.

"But you don't understand, kind sir," Lucine said. "I have no interest in a thug like Stefan. His kind are repulsive to me and I would speak for my mother as well. I wouldn't even want him to wash my floors."

The crow's lips slowly twisted with delight. "I'm sure he could change your mind. He's very talented."

"You heard the lady." Alek spoke evenly. "Take your leave, please. Before you yourself become Stefan."

For a beat nothing happened. It wasn't a wise threat, all things considered, but I might have made it myself if Alek hadn't.

Then Stefan was moving with inordinate speed to defend his master's honor. But his knife was on the floor and he had to stoop for it.

I pulled my pistol without thought, and I shot Stefan through his head as he started for Alek.

The man dropped like a stone, dead at Natasha's feet. The detonation shook the chandelier and echoed through the chamber. Blood spread from the wound in Stefan's head.

I cocked my weapon up, so that the muzzle pointed at the ceiling, still smoking.

"Or we could do that," Vlad van Valerik said.

"No man threatens the authority of the empress," I said. "Am I understood?"

"Indeed," said the crow. He faced the lady Kesia, who had gone white, and he dipped his head. "I'm so sorry, madam. But Toma Nicolescu was right. I might have shot him myself if I'd brought a pistol and seen Stefan's foolishness. My only regret is this mess on your floor now."

From behind me I heard Sofia's husky whisper. "Very nice shot, Toma."

Valerik looked past me and nodded at her. She brushed my elbow as she passed me. "I'm impressed," she muttered.

One of the other Russians picked up Stefan's body in his arms and led the others from the room, leaving a red trail on the white marble floor.

"I'm mortified, madam," Valerik said, shifting his look from the thread of blood back to Kesia. "My debt to you is now double. I will do anything to reconcile this unruly fool's indiscretion in your home."

He bowed, arms spread, one foot leading the other.

"Now I must go and teach some lessons."

He walked to the door, then turned back and faced Lucine. "He is a thug. A beautiful thug, perhaps, but a monster through and through."

And then Vlad van Valerik and his clan were gone.

FOUR

Two days had passed since Mother's ball, and it was still the talk of the aristocracy. Having the ball turned on its head with the slaying of a man in defense of honor had immortalized the Summer Ball of Delights.

The name Vlad van Valerik was on the lips of them all. And even more, the name of the one who'd casually drawn a pistol and shot the offender dead in the head, and from a distance of twenty paces no less. Toma Nicolescu. The quiet, tall war hero who had killed a thousand men in battle, a rumor Lucine no longer doubted.

"I can hardly keep my mind off him," Natasha said, balancing on the fountain wall in her wet white slippers. She dipped her left foot into the water, then reached her right foot behind and splashed it too. She stepped along the stone wall with sopping feet, leaving perfect dark stains.

Lucine hopped up behind her, following with both arms stretched out to keep her balance. She wouldn't dip her feet, however.

"You can't keep your mind off which one?"

"The Russian, naturally."

Lucine pulled up short, swaying dangerously before regaining control. "The Russian? The duke?"

"No, silly. Although I can only imagine what he might be like."

"Then who? Surely not that dead one."

Natasha gave her a darting whimsical look as she rounded the far side.

"You can't be serious! He's dead!"

"So he is."

"He attacked you."

"No, Lucine." Natasha spun to face her, nearly falling off. "He bit my lip. That's hardly an attack."

"He was a monster who paraded about as if you had it coming."

"And maybe I did have it coming." Natasha's eyes flashed. She hopped off the wall, jumped up onto a stone bench, and ran along it, watching her feet. "I did ask for it, didn't I?"

"Not to be *bitten*."

She landed back on the ground and sized Lucine up, mouth twisted around the hint of improper secrets. "And what if I did, Lucine? What if he whispered an invitation to me and I said yes?"

"Please, Natasha, this isn't funny. You're not that stupid."

The look of her sister's flushed face surprised Lucine. She

stepped down, confused by this behavior, though she probably had no right to be. Natasha had always been impetuous. But still . . .

"Perhaps a kiss, but an invitation for a man—no matter how appealing—to bite through your lip? It's absurd!"

Natasha hurried forward and grabbed her arm, glancing around as if to be sure no one would overhear. "But you weren't there! Not in his arms, you weren't. I was, Lucine. He asked me if he could bite me and I said yes. I know it was wrong, but I could hardly—"

"He just said that? 'Can I bite your lip?'"

"Not like that, of course."

"Then how?"

Natasha hesitated. "I don't remember exactly. I do believe he just said, 'May I?' and I said yes. But I knew he wanted to bite me because he'd already nibbled my lip."

"You're playing with the devil."

"Then the devil occupies heaven! He bit my lip and I fainted, Sister. I swooned. I have never felt so enraptured."

The puncture had healed already, and it was true, her sister looked anything but wounded.

"I feel positively vibrant!" She drew a deep breath through her nostrils and looped around, head tilted back, arms wide. "The air is filled with flowers, can you smell them? The sun is warm, the sky is as blue as an ocean, my night—"

"Is clearly tortured, judging by the shambles I found this morning. Your pillows were all over the room and the blanket was on the floor. Clearly you're bothered."

"Then bother me again, Sister. If my bedclothes are tossed around, it's because I'm dancing in my sleep. You see what happens when you throw your cares to the wind and embrace love? Even the night calls to you."

"You may not be any worse off, but he's dead," Lucine said, letting the grin go.

Natasha's bright eyes clouded momentarily. "There is that, yes. Because of your hunk of a man."

"Please . . ." She turned away.

"Don't think I haven't seen the way you look at him," Natasha teased. "And I don't blame you. The hero stepped in and saved us from the nasty wolves. He's a beautiful man. I don't blame you at all." Her eyes shot to the garden behind Lucine. "Speak of the devils."

Lucine looked over her shoulder. Toma and Alek were walking abreast past the hedges, deep in discussion. If they'd seen the sisters, there was no sign.

"Let's find out, shall we?" Natasha said. She brushed past Lucine, headed for the pair.

"Find out what?"

"Who loves whom, of course."

"Natasha . . ."

Toma must have heard, because he turned and saw them. Alek stepped around his partner and watched as Natasha glided toward them like a snake.

Toma was dressed in gentlemen's pants and boots to his knees, with a white shirt unbuttoned about his neck. His wavy dark hair fell to his shoulders, framing a strong, smooth jaw.

The cavalryman had remained somewhat busy these last two days, retiring early and staying out of sight except at dinner. Making his arrangements, riding the perimeter, posting several guards—for what purpose, only heaven could know.

His general demeanor did not fit her image of a ruthless warrior. For that matter, neither did Alek's. Out of uniform they were two handsome specimens, clean cut, directly out of Her Majesty's court.

His savagery must hide behind those eyes, she thought.

"If it isn't our two dashing heroes, keeping guard," Natasha said, slowing as she approached.

They both dipped their heads. "Ladies," said Toma.

"Now our day is made," said Alek.

Lucine acknowledged them. "Alek. Toma."

"Lucine was wondering which of you loves which one of us," Natasha said without the slightest pause.

Lucine felt herself begin to blush. Any denial would likely give credence to the question. So she allowed it.

Toma looked at them both, face blank.

Alek, on the other hand, looked delighted. "Well, that's simple enough. I love you both."

"Rubbish," Natasha said. "Well, so be it, fine." She walked behind Alek, picking a piece of lint off his shoulder, then smoothing the jacket. "So you love us both, and who wouldn't want to be loved by two strapping war heroes? Is that how you feel, Toma? You love each of us equally?"

The poor man was caught unaware by the predator in Natasha. But now that she'd so boldly thrown down the gauntlet, Lucine wanted to know his answer.

"How could I disagree with Alek? He's not exactly a slouch in these matters."

"That's why you're blushing? Because you *are* a slouch? In these *matters*, I mean."

If he wasn't blushing before, he was now. "No, that wasn't—"

"Because I was telling Lucine that I had noticed your eye for her, and she called it nonsense."

Lucine wanted to disappear into the ground. She had said no such thing, not really, not while meaning it. Of course she liked Toma, who wouldn't? But that didn't mean she was infatuated with the man. With Natasha it was always all or nothing. Love with abandon, or nonsense.

"Now see, that's what I like," Alek said, beaming. "There's nothing as alluring as a woman who fears nothing."

"Including being chewed on, you mean," Toma said. Lucine immediately wished he hadn't, because nothing good could come from taking on Natasha directly. He would only be humiliated, and the thought of it sickened her.

"Have you tried it, Toma?" Natasha said. "Having your lips nibbled on by a tender woman?"

"Ha!" Alek cried. "You see, Toma? What did I tell you? She's priceless." His eyes remained on Natasha. "I will say, my dear, you may test me anytime."

"If you're so lucky." She winked. "What say you, Toma? Is it nonsense?"

His brow was starting to bead with sweat. He ran nervous fingers through his curls. "Nonsense?"

"Do you have any interest in her?"

Lucine suddenly wanted him silent. There was no good answer. If he said yes, it was as likely provoked as true. If he said no, it would only be to protect her. Either way she might find discomfort in the answer, not knowing why he said what he said.

But two could play Natasha's game.

She stepped toward Toma, wearing a daring smile. "Don't be

silly, Natasha. Of course he has interest in me. Don't you, Toma? I've certainly expressed my own interest clearly enough."

She closed in on him, placed her palm on his chest, then turned away, removing her hand.

"But just because you find someone appealing doesn't mean you throw out restraint. Toma has proven that, and I find it charming."

They all looked at her as if she'd lost her mind. It wasn't her typical behavior. She relished their reaction.

Natasha was the first to burst out laughing. She was delighted and showed it by hugging Lucine, who felt herself blush.

"You think I'm not dead serious?"

Alek couldn't resist the call to join Natasha with laughter.

"Not as dead serious as the man they hauled out of here," Toma said, clearly grateful for an opportunity to change the subject. And all three of them thought that comment hilarious for its brashness. Lucine too, but she was more taken by the laughter itself. Mother would love it.

"Well, there you have it, Natasha," Alek said, still grinning like a boy. "It's all set."

"What is?" Natasha asked.

"This. You and I. He and she. It's practically written in the stars."

"Is that so?"

Lucine sneaked a glance at Toma, knowing already that Alek would later get an earful from him.

"Am I so easy?" Natasha asked with daring in her voice.

Toma's eyes caught Lucine's and he failed to hide a sheepish smile.

"Let's hope not," said Alek. "I detest easy women."

Lucine saw truth in Toma's eyes in that moment. The sparkle, the desperate attempt to hide a secret, the quick shift. He did have feelings for her, didn't he?

"Take a walk with me, dear," Natasha said, reaching a hand out to Alek.

He looked at his superior. "Toma? Are we done here?"

"We are."

Alek took Natasha's hand and they left, high as two birds. The outcome was a foregone conclusion.

Watching them go, Toma looked lost without his partner.

"Would you like to take a walk?" Lucine asked.

⚜

I was a bowl of jelly. My legs were water.

I was a strong man. I could easily lift a man of Alek's size and hurl him across the room into a wall and had done so on several occasions before we agreed to be friends. I had chased down many an enemy on foot, leaped upon them, and slit their throats. I was as comfortable with a sword in the middle of a battlefield, leading a thousand men as they hacked into infidels, as I was drinking tea in the tents with those men.

In Her Majesty's courts I was called the lion.

But there in the garden, standing four feet from Lucine, who had just put her hand on my chest, I was as weak as a lamb.

The turmoil I'd suffered the last few days flashed through my mind. You see, the night after I shot Stefan, I had lain on the plush pillows, unable to sleep, convincing myself that the Russians must have brought a spell with them that infected me. But the only spells I believed in were the ones delivered with a swift blade or a true musket. There was no devil, no God, no power beyond that of man.

What was there in a set of eyes, a mouth, two breasts, thighs, feet, and a head that created any kind of longing? Why did a scent evoke desire and the taste of lips demand obsession? What was in the spoken word that sparked a fire? It was all only flesh that would soon bleed out and rot in the ground.

My uncommon attraction to her couldn't have anything to do with the sum of her parts, I reasoned as I tossed and turned on that obscenely fluffy bedding. Or with her at all. She wasn't falling all over me, offering herself up to me. She wasn't kissing my ears or nibbling my neck. Her hands weren't running up my thighs; her lips weren't whispering undying love; her tongue wasn't . . .

I sat up in bed, terrified at my own weakness. The pain had begun then, when I concluded that the emotions I felt were simply mine, in my heart, my mind. A new weakness had presented itself to me, like a new kind of plague.

But the plague could be controlled. The sick could be isolated and bodies burned until the disease was stamped out.

Still, my own astonishment at the ache in my heart kept my eyes peeled open, gazing at the angels that were intricately carved on the ceiling above me.

I slept little that night and awoke early to drag Alek out of bed. We had to immediately set about the task of securing the estate at every corner, I announced, refusing to hear his protests.

Over the next two days I had done my best to stay clear of Lucine. I stuffed my mind with the challenges at hand, despite the fact that they were the simplest of issues, for there was no real enemy to see and to kill. I ordered Alek to help me extend a rampart at the main entrance.

"Whatever for?"

"Because it needs it."

"I don't see the need. But if you insist, I'll order the servants—"

"You and I should do it."

"What? You've got to be jesting."

"You know me better."

"We already have this barricade. We don't need an extension and certainly not one built by us."

"Look there!" I jabbed my finger in the direction of the forest to our right. "What kind of protection would we have if they came out of the trees with muskets blazing?"

"They? Our enemy is not an army, Toma! If we were in the middle of a war, maybe. Even then, a rock or two would do fine for protection, not all this."

"You're questioning my authority?" I snapped.

"Toma, it's me," Alek cried. "We should be up with our guests, sipping tea and flirting, not muddying our hands to build a rampart we don't need."

"Idleness will not serve us!" I thundered.

I think Alek knew something was going on then, because after a long hard study, he softened and gave me an inquisitive, somewhat knowing look. But it could have been my imagination, because half my mind had taken leave and was hovering around the castle, hoping for a glance, just one peek, at Lucine.

It was horrible, I tell you. With each passing hour, my condition seemed to grow worse. Dinners were the worst, naturally. I kept them short and I managed to be absolutely normal in all regards. I looked into her eyes when I spoke to her and I was nothing but a perfectly courteous guest.

But secretly every word and glance stirred me. I clung to her every laugh and movement of her chin, every bite and drink, all the while wondering how it could be possible.

Slowly the notion of confessing my love became a mandate I could not refuse. Duty was thinner than love, surely.

Now in the garden I felt like that bowl of jelly. I had to tell her. I had to confess my love before it drove me mad, unable to perform any duty whatsoever!

"Yes, we can walk," I said. But I forgot what to do next.

She finally reached out her hand and I quickly crooked my elbow for her to take. I led her down the path toward . . . Honestly, I had no idea where we were going. I was only the puppy on her leash at this point, though I would have rather been damned and dispatched to the flames than let her know even an inkling of my thoughts.

"It's a beautiful garden, don't you think?" she asked. "The red roses are God blushing, Mother says." She motioned to a bed of roses to our right. The garden was terraced with roses and tulips higher, leading around to tall hedges that formed a small maze before spilling out the back to a forest. We were headed the other way, toward the house itself.

"Why would God blush?" I asked, not caring the least why. My mind was on her hand squeezing my elbow.

I could not have felt so reduced by a woman I hardly knew. I wasn't a pubescent upstart, after all. I was Toma Nicolescu, the lion, the one who directed the lives and deaths of thousands.

"God blushes when we thank him, she says. And in Moldavia we are always thanking him because we are surrounded by his very best."

"Oh?"

"Yes, oh." She cast me a sideways glance as we ascended the stone steps toward the fountain. "I hope what I said back there was acceptable."

"Yes."

"I didn't mean it, of course."

"You didn't?" But I knew that she'd said the bit about showing me her affection to rescue me from my pending demise. So what was I asking?

"Should I have meant it?"

"I . . . Well, no. Which part?"

"The part about you having interest in me."

"Heavens, no! What would give you that idea?"

"That's odd. I could have sworn you—"

"No," I insisted. "No, I have no interest in you, madam."

We rounded the fountain and walked toward the main door, which led into what had been the ballroom a few nights earlier, now filled with soft chairs and ornately carved tables and gold candlesticks—a richly furnished living room.

I was mortified, though I should have been ecstatic that she'd given me the opportunity to forever separate myself from her affection.

I dared to look at her face, and unless my imagination was taking over again, she was blushing. "It wouldn't be proper," I said.

"No. But apparently it's acceptable for your man." She was looking past me to a spot in the garden where Alek was whispering something in Natasha's ear. The sister threw her head back and laughed.

"Yes, of course," I said. "That's Alek."

"And Natasha."

"Yes, and Natasha," I said. Her tone struck a new chord in me. One of sorrow. A siren calling out to my own loneliness.

When one lonely person finds another, there is a knowing between them, and in that moment I knew Lucine yearned for love, a deeper kind than what her sister sought. I knew that her heart cried out for the warm embrace of another soul.

I knew that she was asking me to be that soul.

And the instant I knew it, I knew I would confess all. That very night, when under a white moon I would kiss her hand and win her heart.

"But I could as well," I said. Or perhaps I blurted it, I forget now.

"Could what?"

"Well . . . it's not forbidden."

"What isn't?"

"It's . . . You must realize that Alek and I have been fighting side by side for years. I trust him, and he me." I was babbling like a fool. "It was a wonderful ball," I said.

Lucine removed her arms from the crook of my elbow and clasped her hands behind her back. "You enjoyed that, did you? Killing the man?"

"Not at all, that's not what I meant. The whole time was really very nice. Thank you for showing me everything."

"My, I must have had too much to drink. I don't remember showing you anything."

I had to laugh, if only to keep from blushing. So I did, uproariously, holding my breast. Too much I think. I noticed her peculiar stare and coy smile.

We had come to the door leading into the main living room, and I dived for the handle, eager to run back to my room or to the rampart Alek and I had finished building. I pulled the door open.

"Madam."

She stepped through, then turned and stared at me with some fascination. "My, my, Toma. You're full of surprises, aren't you? So strong and willing to shoot a man in the head at the first sign of trouble, and yet so . . ." She stopped.

"He was a threat, madam. If I had not killed him, Alek might be dead."

"I understand."

"And please know I don't like the way this Vlad van Valerik acted. He was eyeing you like a vulture eyes a dead horse."

"A dead one?"

"I must insist that he not be allowed back on the property for any reason. I strictly forbid it."

"Of course. I'll tell Mother."

"Tell me what?" Kesia hurried up, waving at her face with a bamboo fan, fresh from the kitchen I guessed.

"Hello, Mother. I'm to tell you that we are banning vultures because we look like dead horses."

"Really?" She ran her finger down my arm and let her eyes wander over me. "And yet this fine stallion looks very much alive to me."

"Please, Mother."

Kesia sighed. "Fine, no vultures. In the meantime, find Natasha and inform her to cancel any plans for tomorrow night. We have guests coming."

"Guests?" I asked.

"Yes."

I saw two black-clad riders leaving through the main gate before Kesia spoke.

"Vlad van Valerik and two of his clan have asked to bring us dinner. The least they can do, they said. I think it will be wonderful."

I should have put my foot down then, but I was too off center, still too distracted by my own emotions to push my weight around.

Lucine glanced at me. "Toma has forbidden that."

"Nonsense," Kesia said. "I insist. And if they cannot come here, then we will go there. It would be nice to see the Castle Castile again. Would you prefer that, dear guardian?"

I was about to protest in the strongest terms when she suddenly gasped and pulled a sealed envelope from her pocket.

"Oh, a runner brought this for you a short time ago." She handed me the message waxed shut with Her Majesty's seal. "From the empress, it appears," Kesia said. "Most urgent advice on how to stop all the evildoers, no doubt. Come, Lucine, let's leave him to more important matters."

Lucine followed Kesia into the house, leaving me alone with the dispatch. I ripped it open and stepped away from the door. The handwriting inside was from Her Majesty's scribe—I recognized it immediately.

To Toma Nicolescu, servant of Her Majesty,
 I write to you in the most urgent matter concerning the
Cantemir family, whom I have put under your care. Since your

departure it has been determined that Moldavia's allegiance to Russia might best be secured through the union of the Cantemirs with Russian royalty. Interest has been shown.

So then I charge you to protect the life and heart of Lucine Cantemir at all costs. No one less than Russian royalty is to be granted any courtship with her for any reason. Our enemies may have reason to seek her hand. I will soon follow this dispatch with further details for Mikhail Ivanov and Kesia Cantemir, after I secure the necessary commitments.

In the meantime, know that any breach of this understanding would cause a great offense and fracture delicate ties. The result could be devastating in this war of ours.

Catherine

Empress of Russia

FIVE

Lucine hurried through the estate, dressed only in the blue dressing gown she'd thrown on in her rush, hiking the hem so that it didn't drag along the flagstone. It was early, still not yet time for breakfast, and only the kitchen was stirring. Mother was probably awake, being tended to by her chambermaid, and surely Toma was up—she prayed he hadn't left the west tower for a ride or gone out checking on the guards.

Natasha was in trouble! Lucine had to get help, and his was the only name that came to mind for this kind of business.

Dinner service the night before had been an interesting enough affair, as many of Mother's were, with Natasha ogling Alek, and

Kesia doing nothing to temper her. They had all laughed too much between bold statements.

They'd retired to the card room and played quadrille while Toma sat in a chair playing his role as guardian wolf. Evidently he'd given Alek the night off, because the man showed no concern in the world about what assassin might climb through the window to kill them all. Indeed, he had eyes only for Natasha, who was clearly over her loss of the dead Russian.

Toma had excused himself soon after, and with him gone, Lucine's motivation for staying up late was also gone, so she retired early as well.

Toma. She couldn't keep her mind off him, because she couldn't shake the feeling that perhaps Natasha had been right. Perhaps this stallion did have eyes for her and was only keeping them averted to be proper.

If so, she might be flattered, but it wouldn't mean she would fall for him, certainly not the way Natasha fell for her men.

Lucine, whose bedroom was just down the hall from Natasha's, had been awakened by something in the dead of night and had sat up in bed. But all was still, so she had assured herself the noise was only in her dream, and she'd dropped back to her pillow and fallen asleep.

But she'd been wrong.

"Toma!"

She ran down the hall that led to the second guest room, hesitated only a moment with her hand on the door handle, then pushed it wide without knocking.

He was on the balcony, facing the meadow beyond. Hands on hips, dark hair loose and tangled around his neck.

Black pants only. No shirt. No shoes or socks.

Toma was tall, even without boots, but she wouldn't have guessed the strength of the man before her. The muscles on his back wrapped around either side, divided by the channel that was his spine. His shoulders were bunched like a horse's in full gallop; his long arms, though loose now, could surely wrestle that same horse to the ground. She'd seen naked men, but none with such definition.

Nor any with such a pronounced scar as his across their lower backs.

Lucine saw it all in the space of her gasp as Toma twisted back. Their eyes locked. Then he spun around, facing her with concern.

"What is it?"

His chest was as well defined as his back, and his belly rippled like a pond disturbed by a stone.

"What is it?" he asked again, crossing to her.

"It's Natasha." Lucine was breathing hard from her run.

"What about her?"

"I don't know! There's blood and—"

He was moving already, grabbing his pistol, snatching up her hand, pulling her toward the hall.

"Where? Show me!"

"Her bedroom. She's still there."

Toma released her hand, shouting as he rounded his doorway. "Alek, now!" He spun back to her. "Sorry. Can you grab my shirt there?"

"Yes. Yes, of course." She grabbed the white tunic that hung on the bedpost and hurried into the hall with him.

"Now tell me what you saw."

She heard the door to Alek's room open behind them.

"I told you, I don't know."

"You've forgotten? Don't tell me what it *was*, tell me what you *saw*. Is she alive? Is she alone?"

They ran, rounded two corners, then continued down a third hall.

"Lucine!" he snapped. "Is she alive?"

"Yes. I think so. And as far as I could see she was alone."

They were several paces from the white door that led to Natasha's room before Toma pulled up.

"So, no danger that you saw?"

"I don't know."

He took her shoulders in both hands and shook her once. "I need more than that!"

"I don't know, you oaf!"

His eyes widened, then dropped to his hands gripping Lucine's slim shoulders. He withdrew them.

"Forgive me! I . . . I lost myself."

"No. You are not an oaf. I'm just too frantic to think clearly now."

Alek caught them, pulling on his own shirt. "What is it?"

"We're about to find out." Toma plucked his tunic from Lucine's hands and shrugged into it as he strode toward Natasha's door.

He cocked his pistol, pushed the door open, and when nothing happened, he walked in with Lucine on his heels.

The lace drapes floated on a breeze that gusted gently through open balcony doors. A decanter of red wine had been knocked on its side and stained the silk-covered table beside Natasha's bed. Her white comforter sat in a heap on the floor.

Natasha lay in the same position Lucine had found her, sprawled out on her mattress with both arms above her head, hair fanned out on the pillow between them. A soft smile curved her mouth. Her chest rose and fell slowly. Sweet sleep.

The entire right side of her cotton nightgown was soaked in blood.

"I couldn't wake her," Lucine breathed.

"Natasha!" Alek rushed to her. "My dear, my dear, what have you done?"

Toma hurried to the other side of the bed, checking the lock on the balcony doors as he passed them. "What's her condition?"

"Natasha!" Alek looked as though he'd lost his mother. "Dearest Natasha, what has happened to you?"

She moaned softly, smiling from whatever dream had swept her away.

"She's alive! Wake up!" Alek patted her ghostly pale cheek. "Wake up, dear . . ."

But Natasha did not wake. Her smile grew and she began to giggle, then laugh. All the while, Alek watched in stunned silence. She sighed, rolled to her side, hugged her pillow, and settled back into sleep.

Lucine pushed Alek aside and grabbed Natasha's shoulder, shaking her. "Stop this, Natasha! Wake up!"

The twin's eyes snapped wide. She sucked at the air, twisted so that she faced the ceiling, then jerked upright.

"What is it?" Natasha gasped.

Her face was stark white with fright, eyes round like china dishes. The breeze through the open door lifted her blonde hair, showing her smooth neck. There was no blood on her face or her skin, no blemish or cut, no sign of wounding at all. Nothing to account for her blood-soaked gown.

"Are you harmed?" Toma asked.

She faced him. "What are you doing in my bedroom?"

His eyes dropped to her gown and she followed his gaze. "What is going . . ." She saw the glistening red stains and gasped at Alek.

"You spilled wine on me?"

"Wine?"

"You've ruined it!"

But . . . this wasn't wine, was it? Lucine looked at the spilled decanter and considered the possibility. It could be as simple as that. And the bedsheet was also stained on the right side, consistent with such a spill. Sweet relief, if that explained it!

"You're not hurt?" she asked.

A coy smile toyed with Natasha's lips. She lifted her eyes to Alek. "Well, well, what did we do? Hmm? You naughty boy."

"Not this, I swear it."

Toma touched the wet stain. Rubbed his fingers together.

Natasha slapped his hand away. "My dear, don't be so fresh. They're watching!"

"Who's watching?" Alek demanded.

"You are, dear. Some things are meant to be done in private, don't you think?"

She was making no sense. Toma sniffed his fingers. "It's blood, not wine. You have a cut you don't know about. And you left the door unlocked."

"Don't be ridiculous. No one was in this room besides Alek." She slipped her legs off the bed. "Tell them, dear. I can't remember a thing. If there was an intruder after I passed out, it was you."

She looked about sheepishly.

Lucine pressed the point with Alek. "Well?"

"Well, I don't recall everything. I had more than my normal drink. But this is blood." Back to Natasha. "You've been wounded!"

"I have?" Natasha said, standing, looking down at herself. She pressed through the stained clothing, touching her skin beneath. "Then show me where."

"Perhaps someone poured blood on you," Toma suggested.

"Whatever for?" Natasha walked to the balcony door and faced the breeze with her back to them. "It's such a beautiful day!" She hugged herself, tilting her head back, breathing in the air. "The scent of wine and roses, can you smell it all? Love is in the air." She spun around, delighted. "It's positively maddening!"

"What is?" Lucine asked.

Alek was grinning with her, stepping up. He took her hand. "Beauty," he said. "Beauty like this is absolutely maddening."

Then he kissed her on the cheek and spun back, arms wide. "Now let's leave a woman to make herself more beautiful, however impossible that might be here."

"I don't like it," Toma said.

"If it makes you feel any better, I myself will sleep here tonight. To guard against any intruders."

Natasha laughed and threw her arms around him, kissing his face and neck. "You will be my hero. We will dine here . . ." She stopped midsentence. "Dinner! We have dinner tonight! With the Russians!"

In all the fuss, Lucine had forgotten. Her mind raced to an image of Vlad van Valerik and his aristocrats, wondering which two would accompany him.

"I've got to get ready!" Natasha cried, flying to the wardrobe.

Alek's face darkened. "Ready? It's not yet breakfast."

"Oh." She slid to a stop, then turned slowly. "Right. Then there's no rush. Now if you'll permit me. I feel like a bath."

SIX

I endured that day with dread in my belly. Not the kind that precedes outnumbered battle—that sickening realization that today might be your last—but a sense of deep unease, like the feeling of entering a dark unknown space.

It wasn't the fact that the Russians were coming for dinner. I could handle them well enough if they got out of hand. No, my dark unknown was Lucine.

Where I had resolved to confess my love for her, the letter from my empress had cut me off at the knees. Now my duty was clearly drawn, and the consequences of putting my love above that duty would be devastating.

I tell you, I still considered confessing all. Now my turmoil was even greater than before. The letter had made me realize my love all the more.

This was my lot as I begged the hours to pass quickly. I made myself as busy as possible, though there was nothing left to do but stand by and watch Alek's light step as he tracked down any excuse to be with Natasha.

It occurred to me that if I penned my thoughts in my journal, the words might free me from this prison.

I retreated to my bedroom in the early afternoon. I barred the door, took up a position at my desk, and began a new journal entry in the middle of my book, where it would be hidden.

The quill scratched on the paper as I laid down my words.

My dear Lucine—

I stared at the three words, tempted to strike them away. My fingers shook. I dipped the quill in the ink jar and freed my mind so that it wouldn't burst out there, in the public world.

I have exhausted my mind to steer my heart
But it has taken leave of my body and is enslaved by you
I've roamed the night and cried at the moon
But found only an aching that refuses me rest
I am sick with a longing for my heart to return to me
Or to join it there, in your tender embrace
Then I would kiss your lips
Then I would—

I lifted the quill and stared at my words. I could not give in like a child, not even here in my secret hiding.

I slapped the journal closed, tied it tight with the worn thong that secured its leather covers, and slipped it under my mattress. The rest of the afternoon crawled by like a snail navigating the edge of a large pond.

The Russians came at nightfall. My mind wasn't on them until they were framed by the door.

The dining room was perhaps the most spectacular room in the mansion. It was filled with so much crystal that guests had the illusion they were surrounded by diamonds. The long, ornately carved wood table was always set for twenty with nine to a side and one on each end. White china, each embossed with a gold-leaf Cantemir crest, and crystal goblets sparkled under a hundred candles. The walls were lined with cases, some holding old books, some keeping silver plates and more goblets, and some the best silverware.

Kesia Cantemir took her role as hostess very seriously, and there was no better place to entertain guests than around food and drink. This night she had outdone herself, I thought.

A roasted pig from the Castle Castile had arrived three hours ahead of the guests. The head of that boar was now perched on a silver platter as a centerpiece, surrounded by decorative apples and pears. They'd replaced the boar's eyes with pickled cherries.

I didn't see the appeal in the red eyes, but they delighted Kesia and Natasha. And when Lucine said that she found them utterly charming, I liked them immediately.

Lucine was dressed in a long red gown with a slight petticoat that rounded her figure. With dark hair flowing from a blue-feathered hat over white shoulders, Lucine looked the perfect goddess, a standard by which all other creatures should be judged.

I was dressed in a dark blue suit that Kesia insisted her tailor alter for me. At the Cantemir estate all men must have at least six suits for all occasions, she said. It fit well and put me at ease in the company of such stunningly clothed hosts, Kesia in particular. She wore a jeweled emerald gown that spread at her waist like a bell.

There would be eight of us including the three Russians. Four to each side with the end seat left vacant. I was ushered to a chair next to Lucine, across from where our guests would sit, Kesia explained. She was quite particular and she wanted us seated when they arrived to show that we waited for no one.

"A toast before our guests join us," Kesia announced. She held up her crystal goblet, brimming with burgundy wine. "To the Cantemirs. May no one say we did not live."

"To the Cantemirs."

Our glasses were still raised when the doors opened, and Godrik, the butler, stood before us, bowing. "Madam, your guests have arrived."

Two entered, dressed in black as they had been on their last visit. The first was Sofia, wearing a gown that showed her shape without a formed petticoat; it was hiked up to reveal black boots that rose higher than the hem. Another gentleman was with her, hair long and black over a high blue collar. Sofia's eyes were on mine. The man's were on Natasha.

Before our glasses could be lowered or anything said, Vlad van Valerik walked in, dark eyes scanning us all. There was something at once alluring and commanding about his eyes, as if he saw what was desired and could offer it without reservation.

He was dressed in pitch black slacks that ran over tall boots, and the same suit he'd worn to the ball, with its long tails, a red scarf, and red silk cuffs. A white collar cupped the back of his neck.

We stood. "Good evening, kind sir," Kesia said, dipping her head. "Your presence is our pleasure."

"A toast?" Valerik said, crossing to the table, and even as Kesia motioned to the seat opposite her, he lifted the decanter and filled the glass by the plate at the table's head, ignoring her completely. "Then let us join you in your toast. Sofia, Simion."

Sofia stepped up to the seat directly opposite me; Simion opposite Natasha. They lifted filled glasses and stared at us.

"To the Cantemirs," Valerik said. "May no one say you did not live."

He'd been listening at the door? Nevertheless, we toasted.

As one we looked at him, expecting something more from such a bold man. He gave it to us. "Let us drink, eat, laugh, and find the deepest pleasures tonight, before we die tomorrow."

I swear, I should have shot him dead, but honestly, I didn't see the danger then.

He sat at the head of the table, within arm's reach of Kesia. The pork was cut and served, and not a word was said as we all began to eat. If I'd been in another state of mind, I might have found it strange, but I was seated next to Lucine.

Her scent—that of roses, slightly musky yet so flowery. Her hand reaching into my view to pick up her glass—such delicate fingers with red, tidy nails. Her breathing . . . You see, even her breathing distracted me.

". . . just for the summer," our guest was saying. "But perhaps you would like me to stay longer. I can't imagine better company." His voice was smooth, like the purr of a cat.

"And I don't think you would find any," Kesia said. "But perhaps your friends need to learn how to appreciate company without pouncing all at once."

He chuckled. "Discretion is not their strong suit. But they have many others."

Silence settled around us, cut only by the clinking of silver on expensive china. The sound of swallowing drink, the cutting of meat. I chanced a glance at Lucine and saw that her face was flushed and her eyes were angled down. They darted to me, then away nervously.

Then I saw past her to the head of the table, where Vlad van Valerik sat eating, staring at her. At me. And his dark eyes sent a shaft of fear through my heart. There was a line of white around the dark centers of those eyes, and they pulled at me, like a wolf with an undeterred stare.

Sofia was eyeing me as well. Her eyes were dark, rimmed in the same silver. I looked into them and was almost certain she spoke to me.

I find you beautiful, Toma.

My teeth froze around the piece of pork I had just placed in my mouth. Her lips had not moved. Then it had been my imagination. But I could have sworn I heard her.

I lowered my eyes to my plate. The table had gone silent. Only now did I find it strange. It wasn't like the Cantemir table to be so gripped by silence.

Alek broke it. "Well, well, this is quite the scene. Isn't it?"

"It's a beautiful evening," Sofia said. And her eyes were on me still.

"Perhaps we should all appreciate our *own* beauty," Alek said.

"But we are," Simion said, speaking for the first time. His eyes were on Natasha, who had remained oddly quiet. "It's like this, you know," he continued. "The tastes, the scents, the meat, the colors . . . They steal your mind away if you let them. Wouldn't you agree, madam?"

His voice swam with enticement.

Natasha returned his stare. "I would."

"Enough!" Alek slapped his knife down on the table.

"No," Simion said. "It's never enough."

"She's not a piece of meat to consume with your eyes!"

"Alek!" Kesia glared at my friend. "Mind yourself at my table."

Lucine set her hand on mine. The weight of her palm against my hand warmed my blood. I would protect her at any cost!

But I saw no immediate danger, only this flirting. So I remained still.

"Forgive my friends," Valerik said. "Simion. Sofia. Please, a little discretion. I realize they are beautiful." He took a drink of wine and dabbed his lips with the white serviette. "But we are their guests. We're here to honor them."

What region of Russia encouraged these kinds of social graces I didn't know, but this was no way to conduct oneself in public.

Natasha wasn't put off in the least. "You do honor us," she said. "I find it perfectly flattering."

"Then you're flattered by a beast," Alek said.

"Don't be so jealous, Alek," she said. "What lonely man wouldn't find the Cantemir twins attractive?"

It was more than I could bear, this toying with words. "Never-theless, this is too much," I said, setting my fork down. Lucine removed her hand from mine. I tried not to look into Sofia's eyes. "Please, if you can't show restraint, then perhaps you should leave."

"Toma!"

I lifted my hand to the lady Kesia. "No, madam. It is my responsibility to see danger."

"Danger?" Simion interrupted. He laughed softly. "But I see only men and women engaged in fine food and hinting at love. Where is the danger . . . Toma?"

"Second to war, only love kills more men," I said.

"You mean jealousy, which is a form of hate," he returned. Then delicately to Lucine, gazing at her intently, he said, "What about you, madam? Do you have any opposition to love? The kind that you can feel like a waterfall over your head?"

"I have a problem with any emotion that shuts down the mind and encourages stupid behavior," she said calmly.

"Is that what you feel now?"

Natasha looked like she might break apart with delight. "Yes, Sister, what say you to that kind of love?"

"I say it's no love at all."

"Oh, Lucine, don't be a prude," Kesia said. "We all long for love. But there are ways to go about it."

"You're right, my lady," Valerik said, lifting his white-gloved hand. "And I'm afraid we've overstepped those ways." He stood. "We came as your guests and have offended you before the boar has been half eaten. We should go. Sofia, Simion, please."

They made to stand.

"Don't be ridiculous!" Kesia said. "Sit! No one leaves my table without my consent."

Valerik eased back to his seat. "Then we beg your apology."

"Oh, stop it." She took a drink of wine. "And stop doing things that require an apology, for heaven's sake. Let's not waste such a delicious meal and good company. Eat! All of you! Enjoy and talk and be merry."

We did eat. And we made small talk. The weather in Russia. The progress of the war with the Turks. Moldavian politics. The black plague. But none of it seemed to interest our guests much, particularly not Sofia and Simion, who found it difficult not to stare as they were given to.

My mind quickly returned to Lucine and more directly to the fact that she had reached for my hand. I wanted to lean over and ask her if she was well.

I wanted to whisper in her ear and tell her that I loved her.

I wanted to stand and propose a toast to her beauty.

I wanted to do many foolish things that had no root in logic. The very thought that somewhere out there a man with royalty in his blood might take Lucine's hand in a marriage of convenience or for any reason was infuriating. I tried to imagine who the man might be and thought it must be someone who knew Lucine by reputation or not at all, as these things were often arranged. What Russian royalty lived in these parts?

The table had gone silent again. I looked up and saw that Sofia was gazing at me, and that Simion, wearing a tempting smile, was eyeing Natasha. His tongue slowly traced his lower lip.

"Enough!" Alek blurted. He threw his serviette down and stood. "I won't sit here for this!"

"Should I sew my eyes shut for you?" Simion said.

"Or let me gouge them out!"

"Stop this!" Natasha cried. "Alek, your jealousy is unbecoming. Let him look at me, for goodness' sake. It's harmless and I find it charming."

"He's undressing you over there! I won't stand by while he rapes you with his eyes."

"Alek—"

"Stay out of this, Toma!" he snapped.

"You misunderstand," Simion said. "It's true we love beauty, and the Cantemir women have a reputation for—"

"I don't care. Keep your eyes off this one or you answer to me here and now."

"Then it's true?"

"No more words!"

"You are afraid. Does a woman love a man who's afraid?"

I expected Vlad van Valerik to settle his man again, but he didn't. He was leaning back in his chair, glass in hand, eyes on Lucine. I had no idea how long he'd been staring, but the look alarmed me once again.

"Afraid of a man like you? Don't you realize that I've killed a hundred men like you?"

"Like Toma killed Stefan? Without a fair fight?"

"Choose your weapon now and let's be done with it!" Alek thundered.

The dining room rang with the challenge. No one moved. Simion looked completely at ease.

Look at me, Toma. I will show you pleasures that you could never know with her.

Sofia's voice whispered in my head and this time without my looking into her eyes. I was indeed losing my mind.

"That will do, Simion." Valerik's voice rumbled from the head of the table. "I think we have done things backward here. It isn't right for us to impose our own passions on you in your own home. Forgive me, Lady Cantemir."

"Nonsense. I should be the one begging your forgiveness. Please, Alek, sit."

"But now we must leave." Valerik stood and bowed. "It's been a delightful meal."

"But—"

"No, madam. We will go." He glanced at Simion and Sofia, who stood.

Toma . . . beautiful Toma . . .

I felt my pulse quicken.

Kesia stood, as did we all. "Sir, my apologies. I am mortified."

"Nonsense. It was perfectly delightful."

"If there's anything I can do."

"There is," he said.

She blinked. "There is?"

"Tomorrow night we shall have a ball. A private affair, but you are welcome. All of you. At sundown."

"That will be impossible," I said. And then for Kesia's sake, "But thank you for the invitation."

"It's a wonderful idea," Natasha said. "Why not?"

"I am here for your safety, madam," I said. "I do not consider taking leave of this estate to be wise."

"But that's . . ."

"Please don't make a scene, Natasha," Lucine whispered harshly.

Vlad van Valerik took Kesia's hand. Kissed it gently. "I hope you reconsider, my dear. Good evening."

They left, Vlad first. Simion and Sofia both slowed at the dining room door and twisted their heads for one last stare.

Be careful, my darling . . .

Then they were gone.

SEVEN

The dinner with the Russians haunted Lucine's sleep that night. Not the dinner itself, but the eyes.

More specifically, Vlad van Valerik's eyes, watching her, demanding of her, undressing her.

She'd found the man's gaze so unnerving at one point that she'd reached for Toma's hand. A warm hand that felt strong under her fingers. The same hand, in fact, that hadn't hesitated to draw a weapon and shoot one of the Russians dead only three nights earlier.

Touching Toma had washed away her fears. She had no interest in the master of the Castle Castile or any of his comrades. Though

73

she had to admit, they were alluring—those eyes! Dark with gray circles rimming the black moons at the center. Like a lunar eclipse. It frightened her, and if not for Toma's reassuring hand, she might have left the table.

Lucine spent the night tossing. Images she couldn't later remember ran circles around her sleep. She almost got up in the middle of the night to find Toma because she felt unsafe. But the idea of running to him again, finding him in his room without a shirt, bothered her. She didn't want him to get the wrong idea.

She did like the man. Who wouldn't? But she didn't want to send him mixed signals. He was a stallion. A lion among wolves. Still, he was a warrior who killed men for a living, not a lover who could be a father to her children.

Natasha and Mother both said that he was struck by her, and that might be. Though really, Natasha and Mother saw love in the slightest of movements. It was no wonder the Cantemir women had such a reputation throughout Europe.

So then, all the more reason for caution. She didn't want to encourage Toma or hurt him.

Lucine woke late the next morning. Far too late, well past breakfast, she thought. Natasha had locked her door and didn't respond to any amount of pounding.

She went to fetch Toma, but he was already out, for a ride likely. She hurried to find Alek, still groggy, in his room. When they returned to Natasha's room, they found the door unlocked. The bed had been stripped and her sister was in a bath.

A soapy red bath.

"More blood?"

"Please, Lucine! Stop all the fuss with the blood. I feel

positively divine. Would you like to check for cuts? You won't find any."

The soap hardly covered her nakedness, and she bathed with no shame as Alek watched from the door. "Come, dear, give me a kiss and tell me we had a blissful night. Because I don't recall a moment of it."

He came in, leaned over the bath, and kissed her. "It's your loss, then."

"Was it? Blissful, I mean?"

"You'll never know now, will you?"

She flicked bubbles at him and laughed. "Naughty boy."

Alek winked. "Naughty, naughty girl. Did you mean it?"

"Mean what?"

"Your proposal last night?"

"For marriage?" She gasped and covered her mouth with a soapy hand. "No!"

"Well, no." He smiled and winked again. "But that doesn't mean we can't show all the world how to love."

Lucine rolled her eyes and turned to leave. "Please, before I throw up."

Alek and Natasha spent most of the day planning for and then taking a picnic on the property's north side. As long as she remained with Alek, no other protection was needed. They were a sight, those two, walking about with as much grace as they could manage, but in reality they were two lovebirds, chasing each other with twirls of laughter.

Lucine's heart ached to watch. To be loved and to love like that—why couldn't she abandon herself to love like Natasha? It did not matter that Natasha would likely be dead in ten years as a result of her extravagant passions; that she would likely never be the proper mother of many children; that she was likely bound for hell itself.

Natasha wrung pleasure from every cord, every fiber, every man, every moment, and if she died in ten years from a broken heart, she would be buried with eyes etched with crow's-feet from all her laughter.

But even all that was nonsense, Lucine thought, the temptations of wickedness. Still, she longed to be loved so.

Toma was gone to the nearest real town, Crysk, to meet with the church—that Russian Orthodox bishop Julian Petrov. The Russian army had an arrangement with the church to provide intelligence when needed, and introductions were overdue. Perhaps Toma wanted to know more about the residents at the Castle Castile.

"But the bishop will know nothing of them," Lucine explained in the kitchen as Alek and Natasha placed fruits and breads into a small satchel. "The Russians are far too secretive."

Alek's brow arched. "Which Russians? Toma and me? The priests? Or those hyenas in the Castle Castile?"

"The last. They've been here only a short time. No one seems to know much about them."

Natasha gazed out the window, to the west. "If Father Petrov knew, he'd be up to burn the witches already. He turns a blind eye to Mother's doings only under threat of reappointment."

Toma returned and joined them for a lovely dinner, just the five of them, with Mother at the head, Alek and Toma on one side, and the twins on the other. They'd laughed at Natasha's jokes about the boar's head, which Kesia had put on salt and set at the far end.

"There he is, the dead pig who seduces the dead."

Why it was so funny, Lucine wasn't sure, but they could not stop after that.

It felt good to have Toma back. He'd learned nothing at the church, he said. The man he'd met with was a stuffed turkey. This coming from Toma was also hilarious. It was a perfect evening that would have led to a perfect night if Alek hadn't been such a man.

He burst into her room an hour after she'd retired. "Lucine! She's gone! We have to find her!"

Lucine bolted up, fully awake in body but still dead in her mind. "What?"

"Natasha!" He rushed to the side of her bed. "Have you seen her? I've looked everywhere. Her bed is tossed and the doors to her balcony are open."

"What?" Lucine threw her covers off and ran from the room, up the hall, into Natasha's bedroom.

The sheets were on the floor with the bed cover. And the doors leading out to the balcony were open to the wind, which lifted the billowing curtains.

"She's gone!"

"You weren't here?"

"No. I left her two hours ago."

"Then how did you discover that she was gone?"

"I couldn't sleep. What does it matter?" He paced, frantic. "Heaven help us, if she's gone up there . . ."

"What?"

He placed his hand on his forehead. "She said it. She said she would go, but she was drunk and we were laughing and I thought she was only toying."

"Up where?"

"To the Castle Castile. To that cursed ball!"

Lucine was too shocked to reply. By herself? At night?

"We have to tell Toma!"

"No! This isn't his mess. I'll go."

"We don't know for sure that she's gone!"

"I'll find out. The stables, the tracks—I'll know. And I'll take care of this." He brushed past her, now intent on his course. "We'll tell Toma in the morning."

"But—"

"If I'm not back by then, tell him to come for us."

And then he was off, leaving Lucine standing in Natasha's bedroom with a parted mouth and a hammering heart.

She paced and eventually returned to her room, and then, hearing nothing but the wind and her own turning under the sheets, managed to find some sleep.

Lucine woke with the sun in her eyes, late again, for the second day in a row. She pushed herself up and was halfway out of bed before she remembered the night's fear.

"Natasha!" She tore from her room, nightgown flying behind her.

Natasha's room was empty. The bed was as she remembered it, unmade and sheet on the floor. Her sister hadn't returned!

"Natasha!" She flew out into the living room and pulled up sharply.

They were all there, Natasha, Alek, Mother, and Toma. Lucine rushed to Natasha, who sat smiling with pale lips, hair a nest for spiders, and eyes dark for lack of sleep.

"Thank God you've returned!" She hugged her sister. "What happened?"

Natasha offered a short chuckle and shrugged.

Lucine turned to Alek. "Well?"

"She went. All the way up there, if you can believe it."

"And?" Mother asked.

"As I told you," Alek said. "Nothing. It's a large place and I was greeted at the door. They showed her to me and then we left."

"Just like that?"

"Just like that."

"Nothing else?" Toma asked. "She came willingly?"

"I'm here, aren't I?" she said.

"And why did you go, Natasha? When I had prohibited it?"

"I wasn't aware that you governed my life." All this while she maintained a contented smile. But she looked as though she hadn't slept a wink.

"I don't. But I thought we'd agreed."

"Yes. We did. But I changed my mind. Isn't that a woman's choice here? Mother?"

Her mother sighed. "Only if you tell me what kind of delicious experience you had. And it was foolish to go alone. Anything could have happened."

"Please, I can ride as well as most men. And to be honest, I don't really know what happened. I was only there an hour before I was *rescued*." Her voiced dripped with sarcasm.

"You saw no danger, Alek?" Toma pressed.

He thought a moment. "Not that I saw, no."

Natasha stood slowly. "Now if you don't mind, I'm tired. Could you help me, Lucine?"

"Of course."

They left under the others' watchful eyes. The moment Natasha shut her bedroom door, she spun around. "Oh, Lucine! It was won-derful, so wonderful!" She spread her arms wide and whirled, the picture of bliss.

"What on earth do you mean?"

Natasha grabbed her hand and dragged her to the bed, eyes fiery now. Gone were the shadows of exhaustion, the pallor of death. She was beaming and flushed.

"I mean the Castle Castile. The Russians."

Lucine blinked at this. "I thought . . ."

"Because . . ." She eyed the door. "Of course you *thought*, but it's not true. It was the most intoxicating time of my life."

"How is that possible? You were hardly there."

Natasha jumped up and walked around the bed to the open balcony doors and let the breeze flow over her face.

"But I could swear I was there for an eternity, Sister." She twisted back. "And let me tell you, that one, Simion . . . He's a stallion."

"You didn't!"

"I have no idea. No, no, I must not have. But I would, Lucine."

"What about Alek?"

"What about him? He's my lover already. I can have only one?"

Lucine stood, not sure what she should do. "This is . . . Natasha, this isn't right!"

"What isn't right? Hmm, Sister? Why don't you tell me?"

"It's dangerous."

"How so?"

And here Lucine fell flat, because it wasn't really dangerous, not by Cantemir standards anyway. She sat down and let out a long breath.

"Tell me about it."

Natasha did, in halting detail: the grand ballroom, the men and women in black, the wine, the music. But all of it came back to Simion, this man who'd intoxicated her.

All of this was strangely troubling to Lucine. Something didn't sit right, and anything with this kind of alluring power could not be good. Could it?

"Don't tell me he bit your lip," Lucine said.

Natasha laughed. "I don't know, but I will tell you I would let him."

Lucine saw it then, the mark on the inside of her sister's lip when she pulled it out in jest. Lucine grabbed the lip and pulled it lower.

"What are you doing?"

"You've been bitten!"

Natasha jerked away and slapped her sister's hand. "Stop yanking my lip. It's only a sore, silly."

But it looked like a gash to Lucine. And she wondered if it was connected to the bloody sheets.

"Promise me one thing, Natasha."

"And then I have to sleep."

"Promise me you won't return by yourself."

Natasha looked into Lucine's eyes thoughtfully. "But of course, Lucine. I've had my fun. I can't do this all alone."

"That's not what I meant. I'm talking about your safety."

Natasha sighed and dropped onto her bed. "Yes, dear Sister. Yes. Now be a good girl and pull my boots off, will you?"

That was the beginning.

EIGHT

Where is she?" I demanded. But I knew. The flame on the candle in my hand bent with the wind as I moved across Natasha Cantemir's bedroom.

It was midnight.

Kesia and Lucine stood behind me near the door, silent. "Do you have *no* control of your daughter, madam?"

"She's not a child," Kesia said.

"But does she live under no rule? What is it with this family that throws order into the corner?"

Nothing from them.

"If you did not make it clear, then I did," I said, turning back to face her. "Now we have a pattern, and that is the beginning of anarchy."

"What on earth do you mean, setting the order of my house?"

I am here to order you, madam, I wanted to say. *And now you're fighting me and that will make you my enemy!* But I couldn't say that, of course.

I would bow to her authority. The last thing I could afford here was an enemy. Particularly not Lucine's mother.

"Forgive me, then. But I think we should take this seriously."

I gave the room a last look—the strewn bedsheets, the tossed pillows, the empty bottles of wine—and I strode past the women into the hall.

"But what now?" Lucine asked, following me toward the living room.

"Now I'll send Alek after her. Again."

"Alek? But isn't he gone too?"

The thought hadn't occurred to me. I stopped so suddenly that she bumped into me.

"Excuse me, I'm sorry."

"No," I said, spinning. "What are you basing this on?"

"My intuition," she said.

"Wait for me in the main room. Please."

I ran through the house toward the west tower, and with each step I cursed myself for not seeing this earlier. She was right, of course. Alek's affection for Natasha, not any call to duty, was driving him. He'd practically worn his loyalty to her on his sleeve.

He hadn't been forthcoming about his rescue of Natasha, and I'd allowed his reticence, taken with my own distractions. But I should have made things clearer to him. I should have intervened!

"Alek!"

The hall to our rooms wavered under candlelight. I burst into his room.

"Alek!"

His bed was still made. Untouched! What else had I expected?

Lucine was alone in the living room when I entered. No servants, no Kesia. Only Lucine in her white nightgown, flowing against her thighs like angel wings. She was nibbling on her fingernail, nervous as a cat.

I paused, thinking I should excuse myself.

"So?" she said, approaching quickly.

"So, yes. You were right."

"He's gone." She rushed to the door that led out to the garden, threw it open, and stepped out into the back. "Natasha!" She ran out into the courtyard, crying the name of her sister. "Natasha!"

"Lucine!" I ran to stop her. Or to help her, I don't know which. By the time I reached the flagstone, she was already halfway down the steps that descended to the rose gardens and hedge maze. "Lucine!"

"Natasha!" she cried. A quail took flight from the grass on her right, fluttering into the night. She stopped at the bottom, by the second fountain, and gave one last call. But only a far-off owl answered.

"Lucine, please, you should go inside," I said, reaching for her shoulder. I feared that my alarm at her sister's indiscretion in leaving yet again had frightened her. "Please, if she is with Alek she will be safe. I can vouch for that."

"We don't even know they went back to the castle," she cried. "Knowing those two, they're here, hiding out."

"Then they don't want to be discovered. And again, Alek—"

"Your man is no better than she!"

"Please . . ."

"Both of them have that look. It's a mindlessness, the complete falling for a vice. I swear, any man who allows himself such indulgences should be put in a cage!"

The words washed over me like a pail of stream water in the winter. I stood there hovering over her shoulder, and my entire body seemed to freeze.

Was she talking about me? Did she know? She was calling me out! In her frustration with Alek, she was making her will known to me, surely.

Have no emotion for me, Toma. The man with emotion over honor is the crazed man I would punish.

"That's the problem with this crazy Cantemir family," she said, staring at the mountains in the west. "They run on this ridiculous obsession with pleasure and love."

The Carpathians rose black against a full-moon sky, forbidding, gigantic hammers lowered by the gods with enough force to remain immovable for all eternity. The looming obstacle felt like the one in my heart.

"You don't have to worry, madam. I've seen Alek lost in love many times and he never lets it interfere with his better judgment."

"How can you say that? He's gone *with* her."

"Only because he sees no true danger. They are a peculiar lot, these Russians, but they haven't provoked without being provoked. Even if she has gone back, she'll be safe as long as Alek's with her."

She closed her eyes and breathed out, overemotional herself,

I thought. Something besides Natasha was on her mind. Now I faced a rather awkward situation.

I was beside myself for her. My own emotions refused to give me any space. I had put up a brave face and made myself as invisible as possible after much vacillation, but none of it had tempered my feelings.

Now by moonlight she had told me she thought emotions were the bane of mankind. And yet she herself was in need. I was at a complete loss.

Then, to make matters absolutely impossible for me, she took two steps to the stone bench, sat, and lowered her face into her hands.

My heart was breaking! I wanted to rush over and hold her to my breast and assure her that whatever I had done to bring this sorrow would be immediately undone. But I wasn't sure that I had caused her pain. Maybe her sister's disappearance was wholly responsible.

"Lucine . . ." I walked to the bench, then, after a moment's pause with no one watching, I sat. "She'll be safe. I swear it on my life. If I must bring her back myself and chain her to a bed, I shall."

"No." Her voice was tight and she swallowed—I could see her throat move by moonlight. "That's not it. I'm afraid I'm not crying for her. You're right. I'm sure she'll be fine."

"Then whom? Alek?"

She turned her glistening eyes on me and offered a small smile, then faced the mountains again. "I've always lived in her shadow, you see. Natasha has always been the life of society. The crazy one who will take ten men by their tails and throw them onto her bed if she's in the mood."

She stopped there, but she didn't have to say a word more. I could not hold my tongue.

"And I for one would choose you over Natasha without a moment's hesitation."

The night was suddenly warm. Lucine looked at me, perfect in every way: her small nose, her smooth cheeks, her tossed dark hair, and eyes golden by this light. My heart was crashing in my chest and I was terrified she might hear it.

"Not that I'm given to emotion," I said quickly, remembering her comments about indulgence.

"Don't be silly, Toma." She looked away from me and my heart fell to the ground, shattering. "I was only saying that because I am secretly and insanely jealous of her."

"You are?"

"Yes. Which woman would not be? She might be far too loose for my liking, but she is loved. Desperately. By many. Whom do you know who doesn't long to be loved?"

Lucine wanted to be loved.

"Only if that love is genuine. Freely given," I said.

"So they say. So they say. However it is, there's no feeling like love. I should know, I once embraced it with abandon. Now Natasha is washed with this feeling."

She was taking her sister's side, a twin who saw the other side so clearly. Two sides of the same coin, the French said. Lucine and Natasha. Tempered and untamed. Brash and meek. Wise and foolish.

Lucine might see her sister clearly, but I couldn't bear the thought of her changing in any way. "You don't want to be like Natasha, Lucine."

"Why not?" She faced me, chin strong.

"You're perfect the way you are."

"But am I loved?"

"Yes!"

She blinked.

"By you?"

I wanted to vanish into the night.

"In some way, yes. I love many things."

"I don't want to be loved like many things." She stood, pacing now, careless in her nightgown. "I want a beautiful man to leave his life for me the way men throw away their good sense for Natasha. I want love over honor, passion over loyalty!"

She sighed and continued before I could protest any of it.

"But that's all utter nonsense. In truth I'm bound by honor and my loyalty to another code. In truth I can't risk that kind of emotion, so yes, I would put it in a cage."

I rose, rather abruptly. "No."

"No?"

"I mean, yes. Yes, of course, you said that."

Lucine looked up at me, round eyes searching mine curiously. She stepped closer, framing a hint of a smile.

"You're a curious man, Toma," she said in a sweet voice. So close I could smell the flowers in her perfume. "So sweet, and yet inside there somewhere is a ferocious beast who slays men with a sword. And you do like me—Natasha and Mother are right."

I had to cover my awkwardness. "What's not to like?"

She reached up and kissed my bare chin lightly, with soft lips. "A response like that," she said.

And then she turned and hurried up the steps, leaving me flat-footed by the fountain.

The kiss, though only a peck, made my head useless. I think I rounded the fountain twice for no reason before I recalled her last words. *A response like that.* Like what?

If I hadn't been so accustomed to Alek's adventures, I might have gone after them, or at least waited up, worried for their safety. Instead I fell asleep late, with thoughts of Lucine flogging my mind.

Both Alek and Natasha were safe at home, lost to dreams of whatever fantasy had captured them, when I rushed to check on them the next morning. I decided to let Alek sleep. He'd hardly slept these last two days, and there was nothing for him to do now that we'd settled in and secured the estate.

But the moment I saw him when I came in for tea at noon, I became alarmed. His face was white, and dark bruises cupped his eyes. His lower lip looked like it had taken a fist.

On his heels came Natasha, looking like a ghost with the same dark circles, blonde hair down and tangled. She wore a white flounce-trimmed shift under a black leather vest with laces, and a black velvet skirt that fell to her calves. This was a change in fashion for her, and it immediately brought the Russians to mind.

"New look?" Kesia asked, smiling past her cup of tea. "It suits you."

"Thank you, Mother." Natasha curtsied.

"A late night?"

A sheepish grin was answer enough. Natasha walked to the tray of meats, plucked a pickled sardine from a glass bowl, and nibbled on its head. She chuckled once and swayed slightly, like a schoolgirl singing, lost in her fantasy.

All the while we watched, Alek as well, fascinated by her. His eyes caught mine, held steady for a moment, then shifted away as his grin fell flat.

Now, remember, I knew Alek like a brother. I knew his eyes. His heart. His limits. And I knew in that moment that something had happened to push Alek past his limits.

Lucine was looking at me, face ashen. Only she and I seemed to have maintained a grip on common sense and propriety. Kesia was too liberal in all matters, and these two lovebirds had been intoxicated by some elixir of the Russians' making.

I loved Lucine even more in that moment, because we shared the knowledge that only we were the wise ones, the two cut from the same finer cloth. I dipped my head to acknowledge her unspoken request that I step in and make sense of things.

"Alek, a word in private."

He held up a hand. "No. I know, I know, Toma. No need for secrets. Natasha promised not to go back, I promised not to go back. We . . . we, both of us, promised not to go back. Yet we did. But we didn't mean to. We just went out to the garden and found ourselves so delirious with love that we thought we must dance."

"And you can't dance here?" Kesia asked.

"Not like you can dance there, Mother," Natasha said, biting into an olive. "Isn't that right, Alek?"

He started to smile, then grew quickly serious, addressing me. "There is no concern, Toma. I assure you. It's totally innocent."

"How can any emotion that draws you on an hour's journey in the middle of the night for a . . . dance be totally innocent?" Lucine demanded.

"The kind of emotion that eludes you, dear Sister." Natasha sat, slouched somewhat, legs spread rather unladylike.

Lucine faced Kesia. "You see, Mother? This is what your wild philosophy gets you, this disregard for doing things the proper way. This obsession with emotion and pleasure."

"I don't see the problem."

Lucine pointed at Natasha. "She's half dead!"

"Or fully alive," Natasha said, still grinning.

"Enough!" I thundered. "I want to know what is drawing you both up there. Against agreement, I might add."

Alek looked sheepish. "Toma, you know me."

"Which is why I ask. Lucine is right. You've set your common sense aside for . . . whatever this is. Now what is it?"

Alek stood, blurting before he was out of his chair. "Food, wine, women, dance, all of it!" My concern deepened. "What do you think?" he cried. "That we're sleeping with demons up there? Think!" He slapped his head. "We are a man and woman in love and we go to party. Is that forbidden in Moldavia?"

"No. But in my company your tone is!"

He sat. "Forgive me. Sorry."

"And now so are any further escapades to the Castle Castile. Under my direct order, I forbid it. Do you hear me?"

He didn't respond.

"Alek—"

"I hear." He looked at me, eyes grayer than I recalled. "And I obey. Sir."

And with that my concern was even further aggravated.

"Madam." Godrik, the butler, bowed at the door. "You have a visitor."

"Pray tell, who?"

"The duke, madam. Vlad van Valerik."

He might have shot a gun for the shock that followed. Alek and Natasha immediately sat straight up, and I twisted to the door.

"What does he want?"

"To speak with Lady Cantemir," Godrik said, bowing. "He would prefer the garden."

"He would, would he?" Kesia stood and smoothed her bodice.

"And he also inquired if Lucine was in today."

"He wants to see her?"

"He only inquired, madam."

"Well, then . . ."

"Tell him I'm ill," Lucine said.

"As you wish."

"Don't be silly." Kesia walked toward the door.

Natasha bolted to her feet. "Where are you going?"

"Sit, dear. He didn't call for you. Perhaps it's time I find out exactly what this duke's true intentions are."

NINE

The duke Vlad van Valerik remained at the Cantemir estate for no more than ten minutes, walking the garden with the lady Kesia and filling her ear with his lies, surely, before Lucine was called out to meet them both by the fountain.

I watched from a window next to Natasha and Alek, and I was inflamed with jealousy. The orders I'd received by letter now screamed terrible possibilities at me. What if the empress had been referring to this duke, Vlad van Valerik, in her mention of an enemy who might seek Lucine's hand?

"He wants to court her," Natasha said excitedly. "Of all the luck, Vlad wants to court her!"

"Don't be ridiculous," I snapped.

"No, I don't think so," Alek agreed, and I latched onto those words.

But when Lucine came back in only minutes later, she refused to speak of it.

"Tell us, Mother!" Natasha demanded. "What does he want?"

"Nothing. Mind your own business, Natasha."

"He wants to court Lucine!" She was practically jumping, and I swear if Lucine herself hadn't been standing ten feet away I would have slapped Natasha for her delight in such a proposition.

"As I said, mind your own business."

"I knew it! What did I say, Lucine? A big stallion will one day rip your clothes off, and you'll know why you waited. This is delightful!"

Lucine's expression remained flat. She turned on her heels and left the room. I cannot begin to express what kinds of emotions coursed through my veins that afternoon. My whole world caved in on me.

I had once been taken captive by the Turks in Istanbul when my spying on the enemy had earned me a jail cell. They put me in shackles in a dark dungeon, beat me, burned my lips with hot coals. Day and night, I was certain death was only hours away.

But the hours stretched into days and days into weeks and I withstood that certainty, taking strength from my endurance. Three months into my captivity I escaped, having regained enough strength to overtake two guards who'd come into my cell to deliver me to yet another session of torture.

It wasn't the only time I had been taken captive, not the only time I had endured and taken strength from facing my pain. My latest captivity was one of the heart, here at the Cantemir estate in Moldavia, and once again I had withstood my torture.

But now everything changed on me. The moon lost its place in my sky. There was another light edging into my horizon, and jealousy came like a storm to block it out.

The only way to cope, I reasoned, was to physically remove myself from that horizon. And so I took another long ride around the entire property on my dark steed, quickly bringing him to a frothy sweat.

But I could not draw my mind away. The duke Valerik would not court Lucine, naturally. For starters, neither Kesia nor Lucine had admitted that the Russian expressed any such intention. Even so, Lucine would never agree.

Given my instructions from the empress, I had the right to demand that Kesia tell me of Vlad van Valerik's intentions. I was to protect Lucine's heart from any suitor, was I not? Had I been in a clear frame of mind I would have pressed then. But in my eagerness not to show the slightest jealousy, I steered clear.

But if I learned that the duke meant to court Lucine, I would stop him immediately.

It was already dark when I turned my snorting mount over to the stable and headed up to the house. But I couldn't bring myself to go find the others. Dinner was rarely served until well into the night, and I would wait until then to show myself.

Instead I withdrew to my bedroom, where I ordered a bath, washed, and shaved. Then, with the door locked, I read from a book of poetry I carried wherever I went. But everything I read only drew me into darkness. My eyes rested on the first verse of a poem by Thomas Gray, "Ode to Adversity."

Daughter of Jove, relentless power,
Thou tamer of the human breast,
Whose iron scourge and torturing hour,
The bad affright, afflict the best!

Everywhere I looked, relentless power and torture. Who could say that a sword was more powerful than the human heart? I slammed the book closed, unwilling to read any more. I had to write! I had to say what was on my own heart.

So I pulled out my journal and sat down beside the flickering candle at my desk, dipped the quill, and, after a long pause, brought the pen to the page.

Lucine,
    I cannot live but to say that you have taken my heart captive.
Please, I beg you, release me from this cage, for I am bound by
honor to my empress.
    Now you have become my empress, and these words I write
now would be my death warrant.

My hand shook.

But I long to be your captive, Lucine, my love. And any man who so
much as looks at you will be dead by my sword before he can think a
single thought more. I beg you to love me, Lucine.

I stared at these words and they took my strength from me. How pathetic! I was the warrior, not the lover. Let Alek write such words if he could. I was in the sworn duty of the empress, not the toy of a woman hidden away in Moldavia! These words made me a wretched man.

I cursed the page in my frustration. And then I tore it out and burned it in the candle's flame.

A knock came on my door. "Sir, dinner is served. Will you join the lady Kesia?"

I cleared my throat of its stiffness. "Yes."

I quickly cleaned my quill, tied up the journal, and slipped it deep under my mattress. I had burned the page I had just written, but there was my earlier note that I would tear out later.

A splash of water to my face, a dip of perfume. I was wearing a striking black leather vest and a white shirt with closely fitting trousers and boots. A golden cross embedded with a single ruby hung around my neck. Though I wasn't a religious man, I loved the way the piece looked. And I'd fought enough battles in the name of that cross to earn its wearing.

I hurried to the dining room, more eager with each pace. Lucine would be there, and tonight Vlad van Valerik's intentions were surely to be discussed in the natural course of conversation. One could keep open secrets only so well before they became a threat to others.

But the moment I entered the dining room, I knew something had gone wrong. It wasn't only that Kesia and Lucine were the only ones present, but the look on their faces unnerved me.

Lucine spoke before I reached the table. "They're gone."

"Gone."

"Alek and Natasha are gone. To the Castle Castile."

How was that possible? Before leaving on my ride I had been explicit with Alek and received his repeated assurance. Under no circumstances would he visit the castle. Had he truly gone?

This wasn't like Alek. It was so far out of his character that I would have thought it impossible.

"You can't know that," I said.

"Yet I'm right. And tonight they left *before* dinner."

I looked at Kesia. "Madam?"

"Yes, well, according to the stable master they did take two horses for a ride two hours ago. It's possible. Or they might be frolicking about in the woods stark naked, for all I know. I wouldn't put anything past Natasha. She's cut from my cloth, not that I would have it that way, mind you."

I paced behind the chairs, thinking, stroking my chin, aware of Lucine's eyes on me.

"And tell me," I said without looking, "what was the duke's purpose in visiting?"

They exchanged a glance. "He would like to court Lucine, naturally," Kesia said.

"Court?" I said.

"Yes, court."

I had to be delicate, I thought. They did not know of Catherine's arrangement yet, as far as I was aware.

I managed to look at Lucine. "And how do you feel about this?"

She didn't answer at first but held my eyes. "How do *you* think I should feel?"

"I'm not you, madam."

"I think you misunderstand her question," Kesia said, wearing a coy smile.

"Do I?"

"I think she's toying with you. Begging you to tell her that she would be a fool to even consider any other man."

Now I felt flustered. "What on earth could that mean? I look at Vlad van Valerik as a potential threat to this estate and to the empress's wishes."

"Of course," Kesia said, lifting her glass. That she thought my statement a complete farce was obvious from the sparkle in her eyes.

Now I wanted out. And I felt my rage against the duke increase, knowing without question that he had come to secure his position as a suitor for Lucine. I couldn't dare ask if they'd given permission, and that only made my blood boil more.

But rather than upset Lucine here, I would deal directly with Vlad van Valerik and put an end to all of this.

"This has gone far enough," I said, no longer tempering my tone. "I have a man to uncover and a daughter to protect."

Kesia rolled her eyes. "They'll be back by morning."

"Sooner."

"You're going up there?" Lucine asked, sitting up.

"I must. Now, if you'll excuse me . . ."

Lucine stood abruptly, sending her chair toppling back. "I'll go with you."

"No. That would accomplish nothing."

"I will give the duke my mind in person and end all this mystery with Natasha."

I had half a mind to allow her, but the danger would be too much. And her being with me would surely be a terrible distraction.

"No. It's too dangerous."

"Too dangerous? But—"

"No!"

I turned my back and left them alone, determined to do my duty and to recover my conscience and, if fate so permitted me, to teach Vlad van Valerik a lesson or two.

TEN

My pale mount had just recovered from our earlier long ride when I threw my leg over his saddle and nudged him into a trot. We crossed through the estate and past the new rampart by the main entrance. A bright, round moon peered at me around flat, dark clouds. This was the ever-watchful eye of Her Majesty, into whose service I was bound by honor.

But it was also Lucine's face, gazing down on me as if to ask why I would run away from her without confessing my true heart.

I kicked the steed into a gallop and veered onto the road that led west, into the Carpathian Mountains looming black against the moonlit sky. I had taken the road into the mountains to study the lay of the land several times but only a few miles past the property. Now I pushed my mount farther along the thin strip of road that ended at the Castle Castile. Trees rose higher here, clawing for the sky on either side, blocking out the moon's glow. With such little light the way would be difficult for many, but I wasn't so limited by darkness because I had ventured deep into enemy territory under cover of night on numerous occasions. Indeed, darkness could be one's dearest friend.

Even so, the night now bothered me. Or perhaps it was the solitude of my horse's pounding hooves, driving deeper into that night. I pulled up once to listen and heard only a distant wolf's howl. Oddly, no other creatures of the night.

My ride had taken only half of the hour when the road steered to the edge of a cliff that fell several hundred feet to a rocky bottom. The terrain here could be treacherous for any who did not advance with caution, because the path was only wide enough for a single carriage.

As I rounded a corner I saw the Castle Castile in the mountain pass framed by the dark sky. A ravine separated me from it. Four spires stabbed at the moon and were bridged by thick stone walls that looked as formidable as the mountain from which they were carved.

But there was also a wide spread of lawn and garden surrounding the estate, and this, along with the blazing torches at the tall entrance, softened the appearance of the fortress.

Fortress. Indeed it was, I thought. Nothing less. A Moldavian prince had built the castle in the mountain saddle, where it blocked any invasion from Transylvania during the first Russo-Turkish war. Exactly how it had fallen into the hands of the duke, I had no clue, but gazing up at that mountain, I wanted to know.

It alarmed me to think that Natasha Cantemir had come this way alone before Alek joined her. What kind of madness had pulled at her?

A single flap of wings brushed the air over my head, and I jerked my neck back to see a large black bird wing directly over me. It soared across the ravine and was quickly absorbed by the dark foliage.

I could have sworn it was a crow. And the only crow that came to mind was the one that had settled on the shoulder of the old man who had warned us. But that was impossible, I thought, and I guided my steed back down the road, toward the Castle Castile.

It took me another bit to make my way up to the pass—surely they saw me coming. But I took solace in my conclusion that in everything I'd seen of these Russians, they did not seem to be aggressive in matters beyond love. Valerik had stepped in to stop aggression on the part of his man Stefan before I'd killed him. And he insisted on leaving the Cantemirs when Simion and Sofia were unable to show restraint at the dinner party.

Indeed, the true threat here was Natasha and Alek, their abandonment of common sense for the sake of whatever revelry called to them from beyond those tall, dark walls. But they had come and gone of their free will and had not been harmed, not that I had seen.

I was not concerned for my life.

I tied my horse to the post at the bottom of stone steps that rose to twin banded doors, lit by torches on both sides. Though I left my sword in the scabbard, I felt more comfortable with my pistol at my breast, loaded and ready to fire quickly.

I pounded on the door, then stepped back.

No one came. Strange, because I was sure they would have seen me.

I pounded again and waited. Still no answer. Now I was concerned. What could they mean by not responding?

The door suddenly swung open an arm's length, and a pale-
faced man stuck his head out. "Yes?"

Something wasn't right about the way he looked at me. His
eyes were odd.

"Toma Nicolescu calls. I have come to see to my man, Alek
Cardei, and the woman under my charge, Natasha Cantemir."

This fellow looked at me without blinking for some time, as if
he wasn't sure what to make of the creature on his doorstep.

"Is that so?"

"It is. Are they here?"

"That depends. Are you going to see to them or make them
leave? Assuming they are even here."

"Please, sir, I don't have time to play with words. They are
under my charge and will do what I ask. Are you going to invite me
in or leave me out here in the cold?"

"Is it cold out there?"

An unusual fellow, to be sure. If not for my frame of mind, I
might have chuckled at his way.

"What do you think? It's the middle of the night," I said.

"But it isn't. The night's only just begun! If you swear not to be
too bossy and march about trying to give orders, I will let you in."

Bossy? "Stand aside, man!"

But he just stared at me, so I thought it best to work with him.

"Fine, I promise not to be too 'bossy.' I've just come to do my
duty."

"And are you capable of having any fun whilst doing your
duty?" he asked. "Because we do not favor party poopers in here."

What was this manner of his speaking to me?

"What do you mean, 'party poo . . .'" I dropped it. "Listen to me, young man—"

"I am not young. But I am beautiful and so are you. So I will let you in. Just try not to put a damper on things, will you, please?"

"Of course."

He swung the door open and swept his arm wide to usher me in. I stepped into the Castle Castile for the first time. The door shut behind me with a dull thud that echoed throughout a small vacant atrium. To my right, several coatracks were heavy with clothing. To my left, seven white wax candles burned in sconces. And ahead, another arched door.

My host was standing still, watching me from the side, and I saw what was wrong with his eyes. His pupils were so dilated they nearly blotted out his irises.

"My, you are beautiful, Toma Nicolescu." He reached for my shoulder and brushed his fingers against me as if to test whether I was real or a ghost. "My name is Johannes. From Rome." He pulled his hand back and rubbed his fingers together delicately. "Italy."

"Yes, Italy."

"Then let's let the others get a look at you, shall we?"

You have it backward, I wanted to say. *I'm here to take a look at them, then extract my charge.* My experience thus far was nothing like I could have imagined, and it put me at considerable unease.

"Yes."

He pulled a string beside the door, likely ringing a bell inside, then opened it.

"Welcome to the festivities, Toma Nicolescu. Don't worry, no one will bite."

I offered a courteous smile and walked into the inner chamber. There I stopped, facing an expansive ballroom that was dimly lit by thick candles. These blazed in elegant brass sconces along the walls and in a single chandelier that hung on a massive chain at the room's center.

The ceiling's dome was engraved with a horrific creature that might be a devil made to look like a wolf with wings and red eyes. The walls were made of stone and wood, all darkened with age and draped extensively with long black and red velvet curtains. Wide sweeping stairs rose to a balcony on either side of the room.

The floor was made of marble, a rich golden brown, at the center of which was inlaid a large black circle perhaps fifteen feet across. Tables and chairs were set about the room, some filled with bowls of exotic-looking fruits and meat and wine.

But it was the people who arrested me. Not just a few, mind you, or a dozen, but thirty, perhaps as many as forty guests had positions around the room. Some lounged at tables in small groups, some draped over the balcony, arms limp, watching. Some sprawled out on couches and stuffed chairs, goblets held as if permanently affixed to their fingers. Men and women, no children.

Most were scantily dressed in black and reds, and their attention was directed toward the center of the room, where a group of about ten gathered around a slight man. He had long blond hair and was dressed in tight-fitting black leather trousers and a red satin shirt with a black jacket. Both of his arms were spread wide and his head was bowed so that his hair hid his face.

The whole room was fixated; not a breath seemed to break the stillness. I stood rooted by the intensity.

"Now," someone whispered. Just that one syllable.

And the man in leather threw himself up and back as if to do a backward somersault through the air. But this was no trick I had ever seen. He blurred, graceful and very high, with an arched back and fully extended legs that didn't tuck but treaded the air above him as if he were on an inverted walkway. His jacket flapped behind him as he smoothly completed the rotation and landed on both feet, knees bent, light as a feather.

Whistles cut the silence, a cheer from the group around the flier.

I scanned the others loitering about the room. Most had turned their eyes on me without showing any reaction to what had happened. Indeed, even their gaze on me showed only partial interest. Brooding looks set in dark wells.

"They like you," Johannes said softly at my shoulder. "But I knew they would."

Their eyes lingered, emotionless, like cats' eyes with wide black pupils. I wanted to ask what was happening here, but the answer seemed obvious. They were in revelry. Then why did it all seem so strange to me?

In the shadows across the room, a shirtless young man with dark hair arched backward over the arm of a chair. The eyes in his inverted head stared at me. A woman dressed in a burgundy shirt sat on the floor, holding his head in her lap. She idly ran fingers through the man's long hair as she watched me.

Caught staring, I turned. But everywhere I looked, I was surely staring. Though there was no overt sexuality on display here, the room was drenched in sensuality, in tracing fingers and weaving arms and smoldering looks that drew out the wildest imaginations.

The women were dressed like men, with trousers and shirts worn loosely, as if an afterthought. I saw only a few gowns, and these were cut high on the leg. All dark colors—blacks, purples, greens. The guests were exotic, they were beautiful, and they were affecting my breathing.

"I must . . ." A frog was in my throat, and I cleared it. "I must find my man Alek immediately."

"Nothing is immediate here, my man. And reminding, you promised not to throw a sack over the fun." A woman no more than eighteen or nineteen approached Johannes from behind.

"Who is this delicious man you've brought us, Jo?"

"A warrior named Toma," my host said. "He's agreed to play."

"I've come to collect my man," I said.

"Play with me first," the young woman said. Her eyes were rimmed in gray, swallowing me as she glided up to me and touched my chest. She toyed with the strings that tied my vest. "I am very good with men."

Half of my mind was on the fact that Natasha and Alek had been so easily bewitched by these Russians. I now understood why.

"I'm not here to play," I said.

"Then I might show you out," my host said, wrapping his arms around the woman's shoulders from behind. He gazed at me, his cheek against her flowing mane. "It's cold outside, remember. No party pooping."

I gently removed the woman's hand from my chest. Her fingers raked my palm as I released her.

"Johannes, please, I beg you help me. I won't be a problem, I only want to take my man aside with a message. Then I will leave you. No 'party pooping,' as you say." I couldn't believe I was

engaging this man with these words. A shrill laugh from the circle
behind me. "But I'm your guest so I . . ."

Then I recognized the laughter and I spun back.

The slight man dressed in the shiny leather pants had his arms
spread wide and his chin tilted to the ceiling, screeching with
laughter as the party around him lifted chalices in a salute.

I knew that laughter, surely.

"She lives with us!" the leader cried.

"She lives with us!" they all repeated.

And then the man, whom I now saw to be a woman, lowered
her head and drank deeply from a brass chalice given to her by the
man who'd called the salute.

This was Natasha.

Her eyes caught mine and she froze. Immediately the others
noted the sudden change in her and turned. The man who'd fed
her from the chalice swiveled to see what she'd seen.

Me.

Now every eye in the room was surely fixed on Toma Nicolescu,
warrior sworn to the duty of the Russian empress, Catherine the
Great.

"Toma!" Natasha dropped her chalice, ignoring the splash
of ruby wine at her feet. Her eyes sparkled with excitement.
"You've come!"

But my eyes were now on the man beside her. This was either
Stefan, the man I had shot dead three days earlier, or his identical
twin.

Natasha was rushing forward. She flew at me, threw her arms
around my neck, and kissed me on my lips. Then she grabbed my
hand and dragged me toward the group.

"Everybody, this is him! Toma, the one who shot Stefan. A brute of a man, as quick and sharp as a whip. The one who loves my twin sister."

I was too stunned to speak.

"Dance with us, Toma!" She released my hand, having maneuvered us among the others, and twirled. "Dance, dance, dance!"

Stefan, risen from the dead, watched me with a steady, haunting stare. No, his twin, I decided. A fiddle played by a musician who walked out of the shadows drew one long, mournful note.

"Alek will be so excited," Natasha cried. "Did you bring Lucine? Please say you did. Not even she is prude enough to resist magnificence."

The long violin note lingered, then spilled into a string of notes from very high to nearly a growl. Natasha spun in rapture to the sound while I stood at a loss. The others watched, waiting for something, perhaps Stefan, who now wore a mischievous smile.

He stepped up to me, leaned forward, and kissed me on the cheek. "All is forgiven," he whispered in my ear. "Call me by his name."

Then he lifted his arms over his head, clapped twice, and started to dance with Natasha. The others laughed and twirled, and the fiddler's fingers flew over the strings at a dizzying pace.

The dance resembled no movement I had ever seen—a twisting, twirling affair that might be better suited for dervishes than ladies and gentlemen. It was at once beautiful, even breathtaking, and terribly sensuous, in part because of the way the women were dressed in their tight-fitting leathers and boots.

"Natasha," I managed to croak, now flushed with uneasiness.

She cast me a coy smile and rotated her hips. "Dance, Toma." Her face was pale like her hair; dark circles swept under her eyes.

Stefan stepped up to her, took her into his arms, and kissed her lower lip. He took it into his mouth. She closed her eyes in rapture.

He was biting her? Biting her! The blood on her bedsheets . . . Surely it hadn't been from her mouth.

All of this took only moments as I stood like a tree, rooted in stone.

Stefan pulled away, leaving her laughing with her head thrown back. Blood glistened on her lip.

The sight pushed me to the edge of panic. "Stop!" I cried. And when they did not, with my full chest, I thundered in the hall.

"Stop this!"

Now they did. The fiddler ceased midstroke; the Russians froze in dance; the entire room came to perfect stillness.

"What did I tell you?" a voice murmured behind me. Johannes, reminding me of my promise.

"What's the meaning of this?" I demanded, glaring at Natasha. "Where is Alek?"

From behind again. "You promised—"

"Quiet!" I shouted, twisting back.

Johannes still stood with the young woman, his chin on her shoulder. Neither looked affected by my rebuke.

"It's for your sake, not mine," he said.

Another spoke. "Leave us." I could hardly forget Vlad van Valerik's voice, now reaching to me from somewhere in the room.

When I spun back to find the source of that voice, the space was empty. I saw the blur of one moving through a doorway to my far right. Between the time Valerik had issued his command and my own turning, the Russians had all vanished.

All but the tall master himself, who now stood in the middle of the room, dressed in his long coat perfectly cut to form. And Natasha, who looked forlorn on the dance floor.

The duke started to walk toward me, boots clacking on the marble floor. Then another sound came from my left: lighter feet, clipping on the same floor. I turned to the sound and saw the Russian seductress who had stared me down at the Cantemir estate.

Sofia. And her eyes were no less alluring.

Vlad van Valerik stopped five paces from me. Sofia crossed to Natasha, kissed her on the cheek, and spoke in a soft, kind voice.

"Leave us, dear. Go see to Stefan."

Natasha smiled and hurried out the back like a girl running to share a secret with her playmates.

"I have come for her," I said.

"And you will have her," Valerik said.

Sofia walked up to me, placed one ruby-nailed finger on my cheek, and drew it to my chin.

"Hello, Toma."

ELEVEN

Lucine Cantemir paced by the fireplace, torn by her thoughts. She was at once confused and certain, adamant and reticent, found and completely lost.

"You worry too much about your sister, Lucine," Mother said. "She's not a child."

"And yet she acts like one. I can't bear this."

"So you'll what? March up there and redeem her? Toma's sword isn't enough for you?"

Lucine lifted her fingers to her cheek and brushed it lightly, feeling the slight tremble in them. "He's as lost as Natasha."

"Toma? Please, you know nothing about him."

"I think he cares for me."

"Nonsense."

"You said it yourself."

"That was confusion. Either way, I can assure you he isn't a man you want."

"And you would know?"

"Your mother would know. Yes. Be mindful of that." Kesia looked past her, out the window at the black night. "You'll need a man of standing and wealth, one who can command a country, not a battle in the field."

She was talking about the duke, naturally. But Lucine found the suggestion offensive, not because she had no interest in a man of the duke's standing, but because Mother held such double standards for her and Natasha.

"Natasha can run off with a man like Alek, but for me—"

"You are not Natasha! You are Lucine, my daughter, and I know my daughters. Both of them. Natasha was born for a warrior. You were born for an emperor!"

Lucine had never heard her speak like this before. Mother might mean well, but such a broad proclamation only increased Lucine's offense. In her own way, Mother had steered Lucine and Natasha in these directions for years now without saying as much. Lucine recoiled.

"You know your daughters, but I know myself. And I'm not indifferent when a man looks at me. How can I mistake the way Toma looks at me? If I did allow myself to be taken by someone like him, it would be my decision, not yours. You've always encouraged us to think for ourselves."

Her mother's face fell flat, and fire lit her eyes. "You can't be serious, he's a warrior!"

"He's a war hero."

"He's a ruffian."

"He's wild, and tamed when he needs to be."

"He's not even in the same league as the duke!"

That was it, of course. Mother was infatuated with Vlad van Valerik. Until he had come along with his courting call, she had winked at Toma's apparent interest in Lucine. Now she saw it as a threat.

This attitude only inflamed Lucine's interest. She held her mother's stare.

Kesia stood and walked to the window, clasping her hands behind her back. This was the precursor to the most earnest talk. With her chin firm and the last hint of smile and tenderness gone from her face, she spoke evenly.

"You must consider the duke, Lucine. I demand it."

"What on earth has gotten into you, Mother? A single Russian blows into the country with a single credential and you demand your daughter lift her skirts for him? This isn't like you!"

Mother faced her. "He's not any single Russian who's blown into the country. He's the son of Peter Baklanov, cousin to the empress. He has royal blood. And some would say that he's the rightful heir to the throne of all this land, if he chose to pursue it."

Lucine stood, disbelieving.

"Wealthy beyond measure. In any case, it is in his power to run Russia if he wishes. Toma would serve in the duke's army, hero or not."

"I've never heard such a thing. How do you know this?"

"He told me. And he showed me a letter confirming it."

"Then why wasn't I told?"

"Because he insisted he win you without any advantage."

"But I don't want to be won by him!"

"And I'm telling you, Daughter, you need to find a new senti-ment. His path is entirely noble. He could rip this land from us. And I can tell you by looking into his eyes that few can woo like him."

"Then let him woo you. I'm not interested."

"Why?" Mother cried.

Why? Because of the way he looks at me, Mother. The way he undresses me with his eyes. The way he thirsts for me. But she could not say this.

Kesia said it for her. "You're afraid of raw desire?"

"Please."

"He's royalty! Does that mean nothing to you?"

"Am I a slave?"

Her mother blew out some air in frustration. "You can be so stubborn at times."

"Like my mother."

"I swear on my grave, if you let this pass, I will never for-give you. And if you think Toma cares for you like Alek cares for Natasha, you're sadly mistaken. You're no longer the kind who can draw any man the way your sister does. You've been scarred by your history."

Lucine felt the words more than heard them, each cutting. She was speaking of the miscarriage.

"How dare you speak of that."

"I'm being truthful."

Lucine forced her bitterness down and took a deep, calming breath.

"You are wrong, Mother. It's not that I can't devastate any man I choose at any time I choose. It's that I choose not to. And I'm telling you now that I choose *not* to have the duke. I don't care who he is, because as I see he's the devil. And in my eyes, Toma could put him on his back and slit his throat before that devil could draw his weapon."

"Well, isn't that a wonderful trait? Then the two of you could run off and live in the hills like paupers while all of Russia hunts you."

Lucine felt her resentment for the Russian deepen. In that moment Toma Nicolescu and poverty looked the better choice by far.

Mother must have seen the look of resolve on her face, because she spoke quickly, with urgency. "Don't be a fool. Toma loves you no differently than he loves Alek. He cares for those he serves, that is all. He's loyal to the bone, and that loyalty is for the empress."

"This isn't about Toma. And it's certainly not about royalty. It's about your daughter, Natasha, who has lost her mind."

Lucine turned on her heels and walked from the room, mind resolute.

"Where are you going?"

"To bed, Mother. Good night."

But she had no such intention.

It took her only a quarter hour to change into riding clothes—pants and a long jacket—and slip out the balcony door. Her reasoning was simple and she rehearsed it with a fixed jaw.

She wasn't willing to be shoved aside while Natasha trampled their reputation and cavorted with danger.

She trusted Toma's ability with a sword, but even he had shown some weakness in dealing with his emotions. Hadn't the Russian woman Sofia flustered him? Whatever had seduced Natasha and Alek could just as easily seduce Toma. This business had gone too far.

She would drag them all back if she had to, and while she was there she would give Vlad van Valerik a reason to leave her alone forever. And while she was at it, she would see for herself what all the fuss was about. Natasha wasn't the only one with a heart.

Lucine saddled her own mare, hoisted herself on the horse's back, and set out under a bright moon for the Castle Castile.

TWELVE

I stood facing Sofia at a momentary loss. The whole business seemed to have unraveled me somewhat. This realization rang warning bells I could not ignore.

"Please, madam, step aside."

She smiled. "Such a gentleman. Yet with so much blood on your hands I can smell it. I find the combination irresistible." She stepped to my side and faced the duke.

"I hope Sofia's attraction doesn't confuse you, Toma Nicolescu," he said, wearing only a faint grin.

"I'm here to see you, not her. You have my man Alek and my

charge Natasha Cantemir. All I ask is that you allow me to return them to their rightful place."

The duke raised his arm slightly and held his palm out. Sofia moved to him, like a dark angel, gliding more than walking. I could not ignore her beauty, but she held no appeal to me because I had given my heart to another, however I might have denied it. Surely Sofia saw in me no return of her own affection.

She took his hand and he lifted it to his lips. Kissed it. Then released her and she stepped to one side.

"As I said, we will find your Alek and you may do what you like with him."

"Find him? Bring him, if you don't mind. And Natasha."

"Find him. As you can see, the castle has many rooms. Even more beneath us. He could be anywhere. Yes, Sofia?"

"Anywhere," she purred.

"Any man who can speak a word and make his subjects vanish can surely speak another and bring them out. I have no desire to make a search for—"

"But I'm telling you, good sir, that this is the way it is here. I command only those loyal to me. Your man isn't in my charge. You'll have to find him. I would think that you, being a man who understands the value of knowledge, would appreciate the opportunity to know more about our"—he indicated the walls with one hand without removing his eyes from mine—"home."

He made a good point. Only my uneasiness with the Russian's peculiar personality gave me pause, I reasoned. My anxiety wasn't born of any physical threat but of my own reaction to their demeanor. By *not* examining the castle I was indeed weakening my position to understand any true threat.

"Then I will accept your invitation."

"Splendid. You will find that we are only a few men and women who love living and teaching others who are inclined to embrace life as we do. A lot of fun and many very late nights, but harmless to body or soul."

"Forgive me if I reserve my judgment until I've recovered my man."

"Of course. Sofia will be happy to show you whatever you want. My castle is yours."

"Why her?"

"You would prefer my company to hers?"

To say yes would have been rather pathetic. Either way, he spared me the choice.

"I assure you she knows every nook and cranny of this place. I'm afraid I have business I must attend to. You could wait for me, an hour at the most—"

"She will do fine."

"Splendid." He hesitated. "Take your time."

Then he left us, just Sofia and me, alone in the large hall that had only minutes ago been ripe with revelry.

Sofia glided up to me, took my hand without showing the slightest indication she'd been hurt by my comments, and led me toward the back of the hall. I wanted my hand back but would have felt foolish if I'd yanked it away. I had never been in such a discomforting position as I was in that castle that night.

"Madam, I find it difficult to think with my hand in yours," I said as we reached the door.

Sofia stopped and turned into me as if she'd expected this. We were in the shadows. "Now listen to me, Toma Nicolescu," she whispered, looking up at my face. "All of a thousand men peering at us now would beg to be in your position, my dear. Please, if you can pry it out of yourself, enjoy it."

It was then that I felt my first shifting toward her. Not that I wanted to, mind you, but I could not deny the way she pulled at me. I didn't know what to say, because honestly, I did not want to hurt her feelings. She'd done nothing but show me affection.

"I love someone," I said, then felt like a fool for saying it.

Sofia watched me for a moment, then reached up and kissed me lightly on the lips. "Yes, I know. Lucine. And she doesn't know it. Such a terrible pity, to be loved by such a beautiful man as you."

"You know?"

"One look in your eyes the other night and I knew. So does Vlad."

"So he intends to court her, then."

"Vlad will do what Vlad does. He will win the world."

I had already said far too much, enough to earn my head on a platter if this Russian ever reported my confession to Her Majesty. So I did not press the matter. But with Lucine brought back into my mind, I wanted to run from the Castle Castile, take Lucine in my arms, and vow my eternal love for her. Let Alek and Natasha find their own condemnation here.

For a moment I thought I might do just that. Maybe I should have. I have relived that moment a thousand times and wondered why I couldn't throw honor and duty and loyalty to the wind just once and rush to the woman I loved with all of my heart.

Sofia released my hand. "I like you, Toma. You would make a worthy adversary." Then she walked through the door, and I followed.

The hall beyond was only seven paces in breadth, but the arched ceiling was so high I could barely see it in the shadows. All wood here, with a long line of candles burning along both walls, illuminating a treasure trove of appointments. Large oil paintings, brass candlesticks, chests filled with bolts of cloth and unusual artifacts and instruments meant for medicine and navigation, but much of it very old looking. Books. Many ancient volumes, stacked or opened on the tables.

Arching doors appeared halfway down on either side and one at the end. Sofia led me down the hall, past the two doors that remained closed.

"What is this place?"

"The way into the main chamber," she said. "Or do you mean the paintings?"

"All of it. Did you bring it from Russia?"

"Impressed, yes? You should see Vlad's collection. Perhaps he'll show you. Truly impressive."

"And the doors we just passed?"

She stopped, walked back to one of them, and swung it open. A dark storage room was filled with wood barrels.

"Oh, Alek," she called lightly. "Come out, come out, wherever you are."

I had to smile. And she returned it. Then she checked the other door, another storeroom, in the same manner. This time I allowed myself half a laugh. We headed back down the hall.

"May I ask you a question?" I asked, feeling far more at ease.

She spun around, cocked her head, and eyed me mischievously. "Don't tell me: you want to know why you're so drawn to me."

"Well . . ."

"You do, don't you, Toma?"

What could I say?

"But you're the one asking the questions, not me. So I will answer that question and tell you why you find me so attractive." She came back to me. "It's because I am, in some small way, you, Toma. I am what you long others to find in you."

I was unprepared for this.

"No, don't feel uneasy with that," she said softly. "I'm only saying that you want the power I have over you. And who wouldn't want to be able to draw others to themselves the way I draw you to me? I can give you that power, Toma. Vlad can. We all can."

I could not answer. Perhaps she overestimated her effect on me, but I could hardly deny that I was in part drawn to her for this reason: where she showed boldness with me, I had shown only cowardice toward Lucine.

"Now ask me what you really wanted to ask," she said, turning back down the hall. "I owe you any answer."

"Natasha's bedsheets were bloody. Do you know why?"

She hesitated. "Stefan bit her lip. The cut must have opened. When humans are bitten, they bleed."

"But was she bitten again?"

"My brother is a consuming lover. You'll have to ask him. Does it bother you?"

"Naturally. The sheets were wet with her blood! More than that, she was pale. And now she manages this stunning feat—this astounding tumble in the air—that not even I could do."

"Ah, the aerial maneuvering. But even I could show you that, Toma. It's not that difficult with a little practice and rivers of motivation."

"I'm not sure I follow."

She turned, slid up to my ear, and whispered, "Love, my dear. Rivers of love." Then she pulled back, winked, and threw open the door at the end of the hall.

I was going to ask if she meant Natasha's love for Stefan, when my eyes caught sight of the room beyond. Another great hall, like the one inside the entrance, only slightly smaller.

At least twenty of the Russians sat or stood about in silence, eyes fixed upon us. The sight of so many dark eyes looking at me made me stop in my tracks. Sofia slipped her arm around my back.

"Vlad has given him to me to love," she said, and nearly as one they seemed to lose interest in me. "Don't worry, they are harmless lovers, not fighters." She steered me to our right, taking my hand again. A cool hand now.

"How many live here?" I asked.

"Seventy-three."

"So many? How is that possible? How can you even feed such a number?"

"With money you can do anything. We have our means, and thanks to Vlad, more money than anyone could spend in a lifetime."

We crossed through the room, moved down a short hall, and came to a door made of wood that looked older than any of the others.

"Your man was with my sister the last time I saw him. Dasha. They've taken a bit of an interest in each other." She pushed the door wide and we faced a flight of stairs chiseled from stone. It curved down and out of sight, lit by flickering orange light from below. "Watch your step."

We descended into a round atrium brightly lit by two large torches. Between them was a single arched door, burned black. More tables, more books, more artifacts. The space was dry and smelled like cedarwood, a pleasing scent.

"Through here." She opened the door.

I couldn't get over the quantity of relics I'd laid my eyes on in the last ten minutes alone. To say that the duke was wealthy would understate his value. But how had he managed to place all these treasures here since purchasing the castle only a few months earlier?

Inside the door, yet another round atrium, this one with six doors.

"This is a dungeon?" I asked.

"Heavens, no. We're in the subterranean levels. A system of tunnels that once provided harbor and escape for those who lived in the fortress. But it's been largely changed. The sixth tunnel"— she turned to the door on our right—"is a work of wonder."

Sofia put one hand on the door's handle and paused. Then turned back.

"I should tell you, Toma. This is a place of temptation. Your man, Alek, isn't weak willed, as you know. But Dasha is even more alluring than I."

My curiosity had grown with each step through the castle, and I knew that I had to see what Alek had gotten himself into, because she was right. Alek, however impetuous, knew his limits. For him to come up here at all was a surprise. For him to be up here without Natasha for whom he'd come—an even greater one.

"Then take me to Dasha," I said.

She hesitated. "I fell in love with you the first time I set eyes on you, Toma. So I will tell you, do not let my sister get inside your head. She and I have that ability, you must know. She can call to people when they look into her eyes, like I can."

I didn't know what to say.

"Stay close to me, Toma. Don't let her seduce you. That's for me."

She kissed me on the cheek, opened the door, and stepped past it before I could object to her renewed assumption that I was interested or inclined to be seduced. Her direct manner and courage were hard to ignore.

We entered a tunnel of sorts, hewn from rock, the kind you might expect to find moss and worms living in, but it was bone dry and lined with cedarwood. The floor was polished marble, the same I'd seen in the great ballroom. All was brightly illuminated with thick orange candles that ran along each side. How they lit the many candles I'd seen since entering the castle was beyond me. They must have had an army of servants, though I had not seen a single one.

Light laughter reached us from farther in.

There was excitement in Sofia's voice as she grabbed my hand and urged me forward. "Let me show you. Remember, stay by me, yes? You are mine, not Dasha's. Don't let her get into your mind."

"Sofia, you must not get the impression that I—"

She spun and placed a finger against my lips. "Later. They will hear."

"Who—"

"Later." Then she pulled me along.

We passed several doors and I thought I could hear murmuring voices behind some. But Sofia went farther until we came to twin doors on the right side. With only a pause at the doorway, she pushed her way in and stood at the entrance.

I peered over her shoulder at an expansive library. Thousands of volumes were neatly arranged on ancient cases that hugged the walls. A large crystal chandelier, brimming with white candles, lit the room, and below the lights, a grouping of stuffed sofas surrounded a low leather-covered table.

There was no one in the room that I could see, unless they hid in the shadows behind the bookcases.

Sofia walked in and immediately headed toward a door at the back of the library. But I stopped at the center and gazed about the room. It was most unusual to see such a place carved out of the rock below a fortress.

As in the halls upstairs, great paintings with ornately carved and gilded frames hung on all the walls not hidden by bookcases. Portraits, of both men and women, and by their dress I guessed those rendered had lived long ago. Most were handsome enough, but a few looked oddly disfigured to me.

The wall to my right was clear of bookcases, featuring instead one large writing desk with books stacked and open on its surface. Two lamps stood to either side of a single large painting directly above the desk. It too was a portrait, but not of any human.

This was an image of the same creature I'd seen carved in the dome of the ballroom, a large batlike being with the snout of a wolf and large wings folded around itself. What kind of strange religion or worship invoked such a being, I did not know, but it recalled stories I'd heard about deities in the Far East and in ancient times.

Thoughts of the church and monasteries flooded my mind. But surely, Vlad van Valerik was no monk.

"What is this?" I asked.

Sofia came up behind me. "Later," she whispered. "Hurry. It's just a painting." She guided me by my arm and pushed open the door at the back of the library.

Inside, a heavily draped room filled with smoke and incense. Orange flames lapped at the oily air and cast shifting light over a round table at the center.

There lounged four Russians, three on armed chairs around the table, and the forth on a green couch that faced a fireplace. I could see only her shoulders and head. I recognized only one man, Simion, from the dinner party at the Cantemir estate. No sign of Alek. They talked in low tones, chuckling, fingers toying with brass goblets.

Their dark eyes turned lazily to us. I would ask about those dark eyes. Why did they all have the same here, and why did their eyes look golden in different light, as I'd seen at the Cantemir estate?

"Hello, Dasha," Sofia said. "I've brought my lover."

It wasn't my place to object here.

Conversation stalled. The woman on the couch faced us. I was staring at Sofia's sister, and I could see the resemblance. Older, I guessed. Her eyes bored into mine, and a smile tugged at the corner of her mouth.

Hello, beautiful Toma.

This from her, clearly in my mind. How it was possible I could neither guess nor dwell upon.

You are mine, Toma.

This from Sofia. Or perhaps all of it was only in my mind, bent as I was by this strange castle. I had heard Lucine calling to me a hundred times these last few days. But not like this, not so vividly like a voice in my head. Evidently only these sisters and others like them had that ability.

Let us see you, beautiful man. Take your shirt off for us. This from Dasha.

Her eyes went to Sofia. "So nice of you to join us, Sister," she said. "You've come to play?"

"No," I said. "I'm here for my man Alek."

A man, until now hidden by the stuffed green back of the sofa, pushed himself up. Alek. His hair was tangled and his eyes were wide, still blue by the light. He wore a white shirt half undone and slacks. No jacket.

"Toma?"

He tried to get to his feet, but the woman had to move first. He clambered up and faced me, smiling like a delighted child.

"You've come!"

Alek leaped over the couch and hurried up to me. He gave me a tight hug—something he'd only done once, while weeping at the loss of our friend Johan on a battlefield in Turkey—then stepped back. "You've come, my friend."

"What is the meaning here?"

"Love, my friend. Decadence. And revelry!" His face suddenly flattened and he placed a hand on my shoulder. "Is there a problem at the estate?"

"Yes, Alek. There is. The estate is missing you."

He broke into a grin. "Of course! I am needed." He turned to the others. "I am loved and dearly missed. What did I tell you? Everywhere I go they desperately need Alek!"

"As do I, lover," Dasha cooed, standing now. She wore a short red dress that clung to her form and covered only her upper thighs. No stockings or shoes. Rounding the couch she walked up to Alek, snaked her arms around his waist, and gazed up at him. "As do I."

They both looked at me wearing dumb grins.

"You want to take him from me?" Dasha asked.

I hesitated. Truthfully, they looked so contented that I didn't feel as compelled as I had only minutes ago. This was surely because of my own state of mind, having for so many days now been in a state of love itself.

I envied Alek for the lover who craved him.

"Alek, this is not why we are here," I said.

He blinked, then loosed himself from her arms and led me into the corner. He spoke in a low voice, turned away from the others.

"No, you're wrong, Toma. All is well at the estate, yes?"

"Yes. But—"

"And half of our charge is here, not there."

Natasha.

"We will take Natasha with us," I said.

"No, my friend, you will not. She has a mind of her own. She follows her own heart, and that heart is here. She will return in the morning as she wishes."

"And your heart, Alek? I see it's here as well."

He looked over his shoulder and smiled at his lover. "Yes, well, there is that. But I am fully aware of how critical my charge is, and I insist on fulfilling my duty to keep a watchful eye on Natasha."

However twisted his motivations, he made perfect sense. And he was right. Forcing Natasha back to the estate would be unacceptable protocol.

"Quite convenient," I said.

"Quite," he agreed.

And there it was.

"So you do see a danger here, then?" I asked.

"No, not at all. At first I thought so, but then I realized that however different this coven is, they are only lovers, not fighters, and they will consume only what is given. What better virtue in love can there be? I can assure you, there is no danger here, not even a drop."

"Why do they have dark eyes? Why can I hear their voices? How can Natasha move like a tumbler at a circus? None of this bothers you?"

"They have dark eyes because of their diet. You can't hear their voices; you only interpret what you want to hear because they call to your heart. And I haven't seen Natasha move like a performer, so that is new to me."

He gripped both of my shoulders and spoke in an earnest whisper, eyes bright. "The power of love in these halls is fantastic, Toma. These Russians have found an elixir of sensuality and passion that cannot be found in all the world, I tell you. You must stay for a while. If you stay and are bothered, then leave."

I was now drawn, I cannot lie. And Alek took my hesitation as answer enough.

He put his arm around my shoulders and turned me back to the group. "My friends, I give you Toma Nicolescu, slayer of wicked infidels, hero of Russia, servant of Her Majesty, Catherine the Great, friend to us all!"

THIRTEEN

The moon was high and bright when Lucine rounded the bend that first offered her sight of the Castle Castile, and she pulled the mare up, stunned by the sheer scope of the behemoth across the valley. What was she thinking, coming up here alone?

But she wasn't alone. Natasha was up there. And Alek. And Toma, the ferocious warrior who would throw himself over a hole in the road if it would save her life, surely. Mother had made her claims of Toma's lack of interest in her, but if nothing else, he was indeed loyal to the bone and sworn to protect her. Staring up at the monolithic structure illuminated by moonlight, she felt drawn to that loyalty.

To Toma.

This is what she told herself as she headed on. Now that Mother had thrown down the gauntlet, casting Toma in such a negative light next to the duke, her mind had more deeply explored her own opinion of the warrior.

She'd toyed with him in her own way, even that first night when she mistook his loyalty for attraction. Why? Why had she flirted with him at all? She had, hadn't she, if only a little? Then why?

The answer was simple: she longed to be loved. Was that so careless? Who did not long to be loved?

As she rushed up the mountain, her mind searched back through each time they'd been together. The looks, the words, the kiss she'd given him on his chin. The kinds of things Natasha did by rote as a way to test or maintain opportunity.

Did this mean she was taken by him? No, because he had made it clear that he would not be interested in her beyond his charge. But what if he *did* love her?

The thought made her heart quicken, which surprised her. And it made her even more eager to dismiss Vlad van Valerik, regardless of Mother's demands.

She recognized Toma's stallion and she tied her mare off next to it. How long had he been here? What if harm had come to him?

What if they had fallen on him and her sister and killed both of them?

She went up the stone stairs with a tremble in her legs, thinking she would be wiser by far to flee back to her horse and fly down the mountain. But Natasha was here, and not for the first time . . .

The door opening when she was only halfway up the stairs interrupted her thoughts. A young man dressed in a frock stepped out and looked down at her.

"Are you a party pooper as well, then?"

She opened her mouth but didn't know what to say.

"Well, get out of the cold if you must. He's waiting for you."

"Who is? I'm sorry, I . . ." Words were flowing like tar.

"You are Lucine Cantemir?" the man asked.

"Yes."

"I am called Johannes. Then get yourself up here quickly. You're expected. But I must insist on one thing. Yes?"

She climbed the stairs, still at a loss. She was expected? They'd seen her as she approached, of course.

"Yes?" the man asked again.

"Yes."

"You must not spoil any fun like the last one. You must play with us and play our games."

She climbed the last step. "Is Toma Nicolescu here?"

"My, he didn't tell me how beautiful you are." Johannes reached out and touched her dark hair. "An exquisite creature. So many will like you."

"Please, sir. I'm not your toy to play with. I demand to be taken to Toma, the warrior who rides that black stallion down there."

"Demands. Always demands. If he hadn't sent me to collect you, I might leave you out here in the cold, because I can tell you're not going to play nice."

"Then take me to the duke. Immediately."

His right brow arched over a dark eye. "So very demanding. As you insist, then. Follow me."

The Russian led her into the castle through a set of inner doors that opened to a grand hall with a large domed ceiling. The room was lit by a hundred candles, at least, but it was vacant.

"This way. Come, come. And there's no need to waste the journey to the tower, it will take us a few minutes and we could at least have some fun with words."

The initial threat she'd felt by the oddity of this man was fading, replaced by the realization that he was indeed only wanting to play, as he called it. As if he were a puppy sent to fetch her to the master.

"No?"

"I don't think so," she said. "No."

"Party pooper, then." She had no idea what that meant and didn't care to ask.

The Russian led her through a dining room, then up stairs that circled a full rotation before landing at a richly appointed atrium.

The duke's wealth was apparent everywhere, from the original oil paintings to what were surely antiquities on shelves along the walls. The large brass chandelier alone might fetch a year's wage or more. Perhaps much more.

Royalty. Wealth beyond comprehension. The power to buy and sell countries and women. She found it all vaguely revolting.

Her host made a great show of presenting her to the door, bowing deeply and sweeping his arm out in dramatic fashion. "The duke awaits, madam."

Despite the circumstance, she felt no threat from the man, only good nature. She could resist her revulsion.

"Thank you." With a slight curtsey. Then she immediately

chastised herself and stepped up to the door. Before she could reach the handle, her host bounded up.

"Allow me." He gave the door a little shove.

Lucine walked into a small, lavishly appointed library, built in the round. No sign of the duke Vlad van Valerik. The door shut behind her and she spun, startled.

Nothing. The tower, as Johannes had called it, was lined with finely crafted wood. The smell suggested it was cedar. More paintings here, each illuminated with its own pair of candles, old portraits gleaming by the flickering light.

"Welcome."

She started and whirled. The duke was seated at a desk that had only moments earlier been unoccupied. He leaned back and eyed her for a long moment, then spread his arms wide.

"Welcome to my home, Lucine Cantemir. I am so delighted you chose to accept my invitation."

"I didn't," she said.

"But you are here." He stood. She'd forgotten how tall he was, a lean form perfectly fitted in black.

"I came to find my sister."

"Then you shall."

The duke stepped around the desk and walked to the center of the room. "My home is your home."

"I have my own home."

Valerik smiled. "And a beautiful home it is." He scanned the walls of his library, then walked to a bookshelf filled with leather-bound volumes. He ran his fingers along a row of spines, brushing them delicately.

"Did your mother tell you who I am?"

"She did. And I must tell you that it's of no concern to me. I appreciate your interest, but I'm not of a mind to be courted by anyone not of my choosing, regardless of their status. I would like you to dismiss me and never consider me again."

"*Appreciate* is such a weak word, Lucine. Does my attention flatter you?"

She thought about the difference between the words. "No, I don't think it does."

Valerik faced her and his eyes showed not a hint of discouragement. She wasn't doing this well enough.

"The realization that I can give you whatever you desire, be it wealth or servants or property or power to rule, doesn't interest you?"

"No, not really."

"Then only a little. And that's what I find irresistible about you. You aren't a woman who rules her world. You are not easily beguiled by the first serpent who comes along. You are the daughter of Eve, pure and lovely, searching for that perfect Adam."

An interesting choice of metaphor, she thought.

"Then you will understand why I have no interest in this serpent."

"Yes. But you are too naive. Your lack of knowledge is your only weakness. I'm the Adam, not the serpent, in your life."

"Don't be so presumptuous. I know what I need to know, and I know that you're a bewitcher of women. Where are Toma and Alek? I demand to see my sister immediately."

"She is being fetched already." He walked closer and stood over her. She could smell the scent of lilacs on him. His chin was strong and his dark eyes haunting. "I would never presume to have your love, Lucine. If you leave my castle without any interest in me, then I will never call on you again."

Lucine wasn't quite prepared for this approach of his. "Yes."

His hand reached for her hair. Long, strong fingers touched it gently as if he were coaxing silk from a cocoon.

"But for a moment let me tell you about myself." His voice was far too gentle for her image of him. *He's a witch, Lucine.*

She stepped away and ran her hand over the hair he'd touched. "Are you always so forward with women?"

"I have not been with a woman in many years."

A lie, naturally. "But you fall for me the moment you lay eyes on me, is that it?"

"No. However romantic, no."

"Natasha's my twin. Surely she fancies you."

"But I have no interest in Natasha. The world is full of women who seek the first catch that comes their way. But not you, Lucine."

"So you desire me because I am your challenge. Like a trophy kill?"

He smiled sheepishly, an odd look for him. She'd made royalty blush?

"If that is what you think of me, I would rather take my leave and live in regret. You have misjudged me, my dear."

They stood facing each other until Lucine felt she must remove her eyes for fear that she might change her mind about him. It was how that terrible form of seduction worked, and she wanted none of it.

But he would not give up.

"Let me just tell you one thing, Lucine, before you go."

His eyes looked sad now, genuinely regretful.

"If you will allow me, I will show you why I must love you and you alone. But if you do not allow me, then you must at least know that I will never again touch a woman without feeling vile regret for not being loved by you. My heart has been waiting for a thousand years. With my love you will never die. It is eternal."

There was such conviction in these words that each was a hammer upon her breast. Lucine could not move, could not breathe.

"You are Lucine, and I am your Adam. We were made for each other. This castle is yours to do with as you please."

A knock sounded on the door.

He waited for an extended moment, eyes on hers. "Come."

The door opened, and Lucine intended to see who it was, but her eyes lingered on his gaze another breath.

"Lucine!"

She turned to see Natasha rushing in, a flight of ghastly white flesh reddened with blood about her mouth. Her sister threw her arms around Lucine's neck and hugged her close.

"Dear Lucine, you came!" She held on like a slave freed from torture, body shaking as she wept with gratitude.

Hot alarm crashed through Lucine. What beast had done this to her, the poor girl! Rage boiled. Vlad van Valerik was manipulative beyond measure!

"I'm so sorry, Natasha! Forgive me, I should have come sooner— I wanted to but it wasn't my place. Forgive me!"

Natasha spun away and danced with arms spread wide. "It's no matter, you are here now! I thought you would never join us."

Join us?

Lucine blinked. She'd misread the situation. Her sister wasn't tormented, she was in rapture!

Lucine twisted back. The duke was gone.

"Toma has come as well, Lucine," Natasha cried. "Isn't it wonderful? Did Vlad show you the castle? It's magical, Lucine! Magical!"

Lucine faced her sister, furious. "How can you say that? You look like death warmed over!"

Natasha wore men's clothing, shiny leather pants and a red shirt without stays or a shift to make herself modest.

"No, Lucine. I've never felt so alive." Natasha rushed up to her and took her hand, kissing it. Then she rushed over to a door on the far side. "Is he gone?"

It was rhetorical. They were obviously alone.

Natasha faced her, calmer now. "I'm told that he loves you, Lucine. Is that true?"

"Don't be ridiculous. He doesn't have a clue what love is."

"Then you're a fool, Sister. I didn't know true love until I came to the castle. There's not a woman here who would not sell her body to the devil himself to be truly loved by the duke." Natasha's eyes were wide. "Don't tell me, he approached you?"

"Yes."

"I knew it! And you . . . you didn't . . . ?"

Lucine's silence was her answer.

Natasha threw her hand to her mouth in horror. "No, you didn't dare turn him away!"

"Of course I did." But there was no conviction in her voice. "Look at you!"

Natasha rushed up and took Lucine's hand in both of hers. "You don't understand! Do you know who he is?"

"Some sort of royalty."

"Yes, but that's not it. Do you know what that man is capable of?"

Lucine wasn't sure what she meant.

Natasha stepped away, pacing, hands to her head. "Such a fool!" You'd think she just learned that the sky had fallen. "Think of Toma," she said, twisting with urgency. "Hero of all Russia. No one compares as a warrior. Now think of Vlad, heir to the throne, a lover of the heart. Gentle and kind and raw and the father of a thousand children. If Toma is a god to his soldiers, Vlad is a god among all lovers. And you have just snubbed him?"

"You're overstating everything."

"I've said only the truth. You have it all wrong, like a country girl who's offended by streets because the horses make too much noise on them. You are utterly naive."

"This from the girl with blood dried on her mouth. You've lost your mind."

"Blood? No, Sister, wine. The thickest, richest kind of wine from the duke's own vineyard." She wiped at her mouth and looked at her fingers. "It can make the lips swell if you're unaccustomed, but even that is delightful."

"Then . . . ?"

"You have it all wrong. All of it! You've made the single greatest miscalculation of your life. Ask Alek. Ask Toma."

"I can't for a moment believe that Toma would be a party to this. He came here to rescue you!"

"And instead I rescued him. He's still here, isn't he? And no worse off for the wear. Likely with that seductress, Sofia, last I saw anyway."

Lucine's pulse spiked. "That whore?"

Natasha laughed. "Nothing of the kind. If you only knew.

While you run around trying to save the world, your Natasha and Toma are dancing with the angels."

Natasha looked at the books along the wall, then, suddenly distracted by them, turned and walked to the shelves. Like a child first discovering books, she ran her hand along them. "Isn't it beautiful, Lucine? There is magic in this world after all."

But the thought of Toma with the Russian woman who'd visited their dinner table contradicted any notion of magic for Lucine.

Natasha gasped and spun around. "If the one sister rejects him, perhaps he'll find love in the arms of the twin." She stroked the ends of her hair with thin white fingers. "I'll dye myself a brunette and win him."

Was it possible Lucine had been so wrong about it all?

"So you won't go back with me?"

"Never."

The blood was only wine. Valerik, a god among lovers. But surely Toma was not with the Russian seductress; Lucine could not accept that. It would only prove that Mother had been right about him.

"And you really are well?" she asked.

"Better than."

"But Toma is not here with that whore."

"Sofia isn't a whore. I don't know where he is."

Lucine paced, mind lost.

"Tell me more, Natasha."

FOURTEEN

I didn't forget my honor in that den of smoldering seduction, but with each passing laugh my ease grew. Alek and I had traveled the world together, crossed seas, marched over countries, descended into the deepest dungeons, and climbed the highest peaks, but we had never experienced anything remotely similar to this. I began to understand the delight in his eyes.

To say that I was of two minds would be wrong, because my core duty was not shaken. But happiness and pleasure are not always at odds with duty.

Alek introduced me to the other two women—Marcel and Serena—who both came to me and kissed my hand before Sofia quickly reclaimed me with an arm wrapped around my neck. I didn't have the heart to push her away because I saw that she felt threatened by the others. Perhaps Dasha was the stronger sister and was used to having her way, which might explain Sofia's boldness.

Alek bounded over to the shelf and poured wine into two brass goblets, which he rushed over to Sofia and me. "To Toma!" Alek cried, snatching his own from a side table.

They lifted their drinks and tipped their heads to me, then drank. The wine was red and dry, an excellent variety.

When I lowered my glass they were looking at me, smiling.

I knew I had to engage them if only to lead and not be led, to regain direction myself. "So this is what you've found, Alek," I said, looking about the room, which to me seemed to have no purpose but this lounging. "Revelry in the mountains with women, wine, song, and dance."

"Is that what you've reduced us to?" Dasha asked. "Objects of desire?"

"Aren't we all?" I peeled away from Sofia, set my cup on the table, and slid into a chair. She was immediately behind me, hands on my shoulders, kneading gently.

"Alek," Dasha said, lips twisted playfully, "help your friend understand who we are."

"They are the model of love. The pounding of the heart, the touch of lips. They are God's gift to the world, to love as you would be loved, with intense affection."

"And so we are," Dasha said. "God's gift to the world."

I could see it, in a strange way. My mind drifted to Lucine and I wanted her to be with me now, here in this room. Only to hold her and tell her that I loved her and that I would die if she did not learn to love me. Only to woo her into letting me serve her and kiss her and waste my life for her.

". . . don't you, Toma?" I had missed Sofia's question. I wondered if the heavy scent of spiced incense was clouding my mind.

"Hmm?"

"Of course he does!" Alek leaped over the back of the couch and landed on the cushions. "Who in their right mind would not? Sit here, Toma."

Dasha joined him and Sofia tugged at my shirt, so I stood, rounded the couch, and reclined there. Three sofas formed a box that faced the fireplace. The others slid over the sofa backs with the ease of cats and tucked their legs under themselves or sprawled out, heels on the table between us.

Sofia curled up against me, and Dasha with Alek, one arm around his neck, lightly stroking his cheek. The other two women pressed close to Simion, one on each side.

"I really should be going," I said.

"Nonsense," Alek said.

"Please stay awhile," Sofia purred. "If not for our pleasure, then for the sake of Russian royalty."

"Royalty?"

They looked at each other and Alek made the point. "You don't know? The duke is part of the royal family. Where would you suppose all of this came from? He's a potential heir to the throne, Toma! Valerik is a very important man here."

Alek was delighted. I was horrified.

Royalty? Surely this was not who Catherine had in mind! My head reeled with revelation. It took the wind out of my voyage to save Lucine from a suitor who might be at odds with the empress.

If Vlad van Valerik was indeed a royal . . .

But the empress had not specified any suitor. Until she did, I was right to ward off any suitor who might upset Catherine's choice. Just because Vlad was a royal didn't mean he was the one the empress was dealing with.

Still, the man I considered a potential enemy was more closely linked to the empress whom I served than I myself. In fact, it could one day be *him* that I served. Perhaps I'd been too hasty in my judgment.

On the other hand, I loved Lucine, and I could no longer contain that love.

I thought then that I really needed to learn more about these Russians. So I began asking questions, simple ones, only to hear them talk about themselves.

They came from Russia, but from the world over before that, drawn together by Vlad, an ensemble of like-minded creatures who valued love and liberty and the pursuit of happiness above duty and honor.

Vlad's wealth provided all. Most of their supplies came from the west, Wallachia and Transylvania, on large weekly shipments drawn by horse over the pass.

The conversation rolled on in muted tones, entirely different from the ringing that had egged Natasha on in the ballroom upstairs. I could see where Alek and Natasha had found different groups, one reveling in song, the other infused with an opiate that slowed their movement and kept them satiated.

They lived in the wells of each other's eyes.

By rote they played with each other's hair and ran their fingers over skin, as if they could only think if in contact with at least one other human. Without any prompting they would lean over and kiss their lovers' lips or ears.

I had the distinct perception that Dasha and her friends were so burning with desire that had they not been relaxed with wine, they would try to devour me. Sofia had warned me about them.

Yet I felt no threat from them. Everything they did began to look and feel natural to me. After all, they were simply men and women in need of love and loving. I might not agree with the arrangements between them, but I neither knew nor cared to judge the nature of those arrangements.

Alek had given himself to Dasha, heart and soul, and he looked delighted to demonstrate that fact for me. Rather than feel concern for him, I was glad for his joy.

I couldn't have kept Sofia's hands off me if I wanted to. It just wasn't their way. Pushing her away would be like rebuking a puppy for licking my fingers. But she did not overstep herself, content to keep her fingers on my hair and arms and shoulders and chest.

Naturally there was danger; only a fool would not see that. But the threat was that I might be ensnared by vice, not by any harm they intended.

We talked of Moldavia and the occupation, of the church and of the Russo-Turkish war. They demanded I tell them of some conquest, which I reluctantly did. Then they wanted another story, and another, and they were all quite impressed by my abilities on the battlefield.

Alek and I had just finished a tale about our time in Lithuania, when we'd taken refuge in a harem to escape an army of infidels, when Dasha rose amid the laughter and crossed to the cellar that stored the wine. She returned carrying a dark bottle with a red cord around its neck.

The glass was stamped with the same crest I'd seen throughout the castle, the image of that strange batlike creature.

"My friends, what can you tell Toma about duty and honor?" she asked, approaching.

Simion twisted his neck and kissed his lover's forehead, smiling. "That duty and honor are the slaves of true affection, not the other way around."

The words hit me like knuckles tapping on my forehead. "Is that so?"

"It is God's way," Dasha said. "We aren't machines meant to perform, but creatures of love, of emotion. Ultimately we all give our loyalty only to that for which we have true affection. Our dreams, hopes, and desires lead us, not our duty to a master. Unless we have true affection for that master, yes?"

In that moment, perhaps for the first time in my life, I understood the certainty of what they meant. I, like they, was led by my heart, not by duty.

I looked at Alek, who was grinning. "It's true," he said. "Only a fool would deny it."

"And when your affection opposes duty?" I asked.

"Following any duty for more than a few days or years requires a desire to do so," Simion said. "That is its own kind of affection, the desire to follow a system. But in the end our hearts rule our lives."

I had never thought of my duty in those terms. For me, this was a moment of epiphany that made me think of Lucine.

"You know, Toma," Dasha said, "we tend to live in the extreme here."

"Is that what you call it?"

"We make blood oaths. For us, we must live, really live. But only blood can give any of us life. Cut your wrist, bleed out on the ground, and you die. Without blood there is nothing for the heart to pump, and it goes limp."

Blood.

"Blood. Lifeblood. Yet so many living, breathing souls on this earth have shriveled hearts and shrunken veins. They are neither hot-blooded nor cold-blooded. They are only bloodless."

She said the truth, though I was uncertain about her figure of speech.

"Yes?" she prompted.

"Yes," I said.

"Without the shedding of blood, there is no remission, isn't that what the priests say?"

"Something of that kind."

Dasha pulled the cork from the bottle with a soft pop.

"Have you ever wondered why?" She stood holding the bottle, waiting for my response.

"I'm not very religious," I said.

"Why did blood have to be drawn from the veins to cleanse the guilty stains of even the most righteous? Hmm? Why did Christ drink from that cup called death and bleed out for the world? You never think of any of these things?"

"On occasion, but as I said, I am not so religious."

"Blood," she said. She lifted my chalice and tipped the bottle as she spoke. "Not a substance, but life itself. One life for another. The wages of sin." A thick fountain of blood poured into my brass goblet, but she quickly lifted the bottle, leaving only a taste at the bottom.

"Stealing life from one soul to feed the lust of another is eternal death to the thief, I can assure you of that." She swirled the wine. "And the blood is life."

"And yet I sense no shortage of lust here," I said.

"No shortage, no. We do lust. But we don't steal others' souls to feed that lust. We take only what is freely given. There is not a shred of infidelity here among our clan."

I could only take her word for it.

"This is why wine is so important to us. It represents blood. Take and drink in remembrance." She sat next to me, drew her legs up to one side, and leaned close, sniffing the goblet.

"This wine is our own blend, thicker than most, almost like the blood it symbolizes. It's easy to confuse sometimes."

Natasha's bedsheets.

"It's strong enough to burn your mouth if you drink too much and aren't accustomed to it." The room had grown deathly silent. She brought her mouth to my ear and spoke very softly. "We share it only with our closest lovers."

Then she handed me the goblet, like a treasured offering.

It smelled odd, not fruity or acidic like most wines. Musty.

"Drink it," she said.

I looked up at Alek and saw his eagerness for my tasting. He nodded once. So I lifted the chalice to my lips and I drank their wine.

It was lukewarm. And I could swear that it did indeed taste like blood, with only a hint of grape juice to cut the flavor. But it did not revolt me.

I took only a sip, then wiped my mouth with the back of my hand. It came away bloody red. Dasha took the goblet from my hand, pushed me back against the couch, and brought her lips to mine.

A soft tongue licked at my lower lip to taste what I had left behind. Her mouth hovered over mine, her breath warmer than the wine. I started to lift my hand to push her away.

"He is mine, Dasha," Sofia said.

And it was enough. Dasha withdrew before I could remove her. Her eyes were fired and her mouth parted. She pushed off me and collapsed back on the couch beside Simion.

Alek leaned forward. "Well?"

But my eyes went to Dasha first. "I don't mean to be rude, but I am not your private chalice to drink from." Then back to Alek. "It tasted a bit rotten."

He laughed and slapped his knee. "Of course!"

"Of course, what?"

"The finest wines always do."

They do?

And then they were all laughing. Even Dasha, who'd been rebuked. Even I, who'd done that rebuking, chuckling.

Dasha's face suddenly fell flat and she bored into me with fierce eyes that cut to my bone. "I will drink from whomever I wish," she said.

Only a beat of silence.

Then she laughed again and the rest with her, as if this was a ridiculously funny statement.

It was then that I first felt my head start to spin.

The room began to bend.

FIFTEEN

Lucine stared out the only window in Vlad van Valerik's round tower library, lost in thought about all that Natasha had told her—in part because much of it made no sense, in part because it all made perfect sense.

Hearing of Natasha's nights up here had filled her with a sense of regret. Once again she'd missed out, even though on nothing that would normally draw her. What was revelry but an invitation to debauchery?

But there was more to Natasha's descriptions of the Russians' tireless pursuit of pleasure, a kind of wonder and mystery that was born out of true love, not the typical abuse of one party for the gain of another.

One might be convinced Natasha had stumbled upon the truest vein of nobility, not a den of vain conceit.

Could such pleasure be a good thing? They were Cantemirs, of course, known for extravagant balls and unabashed celebration. But next to these Russians, they would all be called prudes.

Lucine had spent half an hour watching Natasha twirling about the library as she spoke of Simion and magic and love, such a ridiculous obsession with love. Natasha was curious as a cat, bounding about, daring to touch the paintings, sniffing the candles, sitting in Valerik's chair, and running her fingers over the desk. After all, this was where Vlad sat. This painting might actually have been painted by Vlad himself—he was a painter, did Lucine know? And these books surely contained Vlad's secrets, whatever they might be.

The room had grown quiet behind her. She turned and saw that she was alone.

"Natasha?"

Alarm flashed down her neck.

"Natasha!"

"Shh!"

Lucine spun to her right and saw that the door at the back of the library was open.

"Natasha?" She hurried up to the door and peered through.

Natasha stood at the foot of a large canopied bed, gazing around at the furnishings in a richly appointed bedroom.

"This is his bedroom!" she whispered. "He sleeps here."

The hide of a large bear lay on the wood floor beneath Natasha's boots. She ran her fingers over a silk bedspread the color of red wine.

More portraits on the circular walls, spaced out in perfect order. Swags of red velvet that draped from ceiling to floor framed each painting. Tall golden candlesticks holding a dozen flaming candles stood on either side of the bed.

Lucine was sure she'd stepped into a king's bedchamber. It was utterly magnificent.

"Have you been in here?"

"Never," Natasha said, turning. "Wouldn't it be wonderful, though?"

"I can't say."

"Then hear it from me, Lucine. There would be no greater honor, no finer pleasure, nothing so intoxicating as spending one night alone with this king."

"Now he's a king?" She said it as much to distance herself from the idea as to ask a serious question.

"Haven't you been listening to me? A king, an emperor, what's the difference? This place calls to me like the blood itself."

"Blood?"

"Life. It's our way of talking about life."

"Wine. Blood. Life. And now it's *our* way, not their way. However innocent it may all be, you've gone too far, Natasha. Surely you can see that."

Her sister ignored the challenge. "Stefan and I are to be wed," she said.

Lucine wasn't sure she'd heard it right. "What do you mean?"

"I mean we will have our wedding. I am going to stay with him."

"But . . ." She was appalled by the idea. Mother would be furious.

Natasha closed the distance between them in two long steps. "It's a bond to royalty, Lucine. Mother will be delighted!"

"You were just talking of throwing yourself at Vlad, but you plan on marrying this—" She stopped cold. "Stefan, did you say? He was killed."

Natasha caught herself. "Well, no. He wasn't as dead as we all thought after all."

"How is that possible?"

"You'll see. Don't worry about it, Lucine. You must join me! We could join them together. You with Vlad, me with Stefan. Mother would be ecstatic; you know how much she loves Moldavia. It would be a match made in heaven!"

"Please, no, you are moving too fast! I haven't even agreed to allow the man to court me. I know so little about"—she flung her arms at the walls—"all of this."

The idea of it was dizzying.

"I have to speak to Toma!"

"Toma? What does he have to do with this?"

"He's the voice of reason in my head now. You and Alek are crazed and half bewitched for all I know. Mother is hardly better. Please, we have to find him and sort all of this out."

"There is nothing to sort out. You either desire Vlad or you don't. And Toma is no match for Vlad, not in any kind of way. I can't believe you even think of him."

"He's sworn to protect us!"

"He's a servant!"

"He's the reasonable one."

"He's at the mercy of another."

That whore again. And the reminder of it stung Lucine more than she cared.

"Then show me. Show me that Toma agrees and I will reconsider it all."

Natasha looked at her for a long spell, then gazed at the room one last time and sighed.

"Fine. Follow me, dear Sister."

⚜

I knew that something was wrong with my senses, but the nature of that wine's intoxication was such that I was hard-pressed not to enjoy it.

No . . . no, it was more than that.

I was quite sure that something other than wine was in that goblet from which I had sipped. The feeling of rapture that engulfed me came as a delightful surprise despite my knowledge that my state of dissociation could not be entirely healthy.

But as my world began to bend, I longed for it to bend even more.

I managed to push myself to my feet. "I think I should be going now, Alek," I said.

"So soon?"

"I think I'm seeing things."

To this they said nothing.

Sofia was up and I could feel her whisper in my ear. "Don't push it back, dear Toma. It will help you accept love."

Other than bending my world, the drink freed my heart and loosened my tongue. Restraint fell from me like severed chains.

"I am in love with another woman, Sofia," I said. Tears sprang to my eyes.

"Yes, but we aren't made for just one."

"You don't understand," I cried. "I haven't told her! I am bound by an oath to my empress, Catherine, so I haven't allowed myself to love the way my heart longs to love. But I love her! And the world is gone from me now, bending and twisting away because I've lied!"

"No, Toma," I heard Dasha say. "Your world is bending under the power of the blood."

"I drank your blood?"

"Not mine."

I walked to the fireplace and faced them, overwhelmed with emotion, tears wetting my cheeks. "But I love Lucine, Alek! And I haven't told her."

He sprang to his feet, then rushed to me and wrapped his arms around me. "Don't worry, Toma!" My man was weeping with me. "All's well. She knows."

"I have not told her!" I cried.

"She's seen it in your eyes!"

"I denied it."

"She knows, Toma!"

"My heart breaks when I see her because I am bound by duty and I cannot tell her."

I stood bellowing like a bull, forcefully convinced that I must return to her. That I had to confess my unabashed devotion to her.

"I love her, Alek!" Clever words failed me entirely. "I will die . . ."

Then I was moving, pushing him off me, striding for the door, through the library, into the tunnel and left, toward the entrance. Tears were streaming down my cheeks as I strode in long steps. The hall was bent before me.

The others made no attempt to stop me, but they were beside me, behind me, like a pack of wolves. I could feel their breath and their eyes on me.

"Let it take you, Toma," Sofia said. "Let his blood take you."

I began to run, a stumbling gait that threatened to propel me to the floor or throw me against the wall. But I kept my legs and I ran, down that hall, into the atrium outside, through the outer door, up the curved stone stairs.

When I reached the main floor, this blood they talked about had reduced me to my most fundamental instincts.

"Where is the way out?" I cried, lost and directionless.

"Ahead, Toma. Through the doors."

So I lunged forward, through those doors, into another room, the one that had been filled with others an hour earlier, now vacant.

But I only made it halfway through the room before my mind started to shut down and I forgot where I was going. I stopped by a couch and I wept.

Arms were around me. Whispers in my ear. "I love you, Toma." I heard only Lucine, though I can tell you I knew it was not her. I knew it was Sofia.

I sat heavily, embraced by a warmth of love like I had never known. I felt fingers pulling at the ties on my shirt. Lips on my neck and face.

"I am here now, Toma."

Then my sight faded and I let myself go.

The room went dark.

"Where are we going?" Lucine asked.

"To find your precious Toma," Natasha said.

"You know where he is?"

"No. But he's here somewhere, that I can promise you."

They walked through the grand ballroom, emptied of any human. The scope and beauty of this castle were enough to draw the interest of any architect, raise the eyebrow of any ruler, knowing that another ruler lived here.

"What if he's left?" Lucine asked.

"No one leaves so quickly. You fail to grasp how powerful Vlad is, Sister. How irresistible love can be."

And you fail to grasp how strong Toma is, Sister.

But she didn't say it. Instead she wondered what about Toma had convinced her of his strength. Perhaps because she was no fool and knew even by his side glances, by his running off to tend to frivolous tasks, by his silence in her presence, that he loved her. Which could only mean that his refusal to demonstrate that love was caused by his loyalty to duty.

But she could be mistaken.

"For all I know, he's in the tunnels with Sofia and Dasha," Natasha said, leaning into a door that led out the back of the ballroom. She pushed it. "But he's here somewhere. I can promise . . ."

She stopped.

Lucine stepped up to her sister. "What is it?" And then she saw. Toma.

She knew immediately it was him sprawled out there on the couch with his shirt half undone and his head in the lap of that whore, Sofia. She saw the truth, but she rejected it out of hand. The sight did not align with her understanding of him.

They were alone on the couch, washed by a low orange glow from the candles. Sofia looked up and stared at her as she ran delicate fingers through Toma's hair.

"He is mine," she whispered.

Rage blazed through Lucine with those words. Insane jealousy. And utter shame.

She'd been wrong about him.

She'd held out a standard for Toma that now shattered like a crystal chandelier loosed from its chain. A thousand shards sliced through her.

She had been wrong! All of it, wrong.

Lucine spun from the doorway and ran, panicked by the confusion and pain swatting at her.

"Lucine!" Natasha cried.

Lucine veered toward the main entrance. Natasha had been right.

"Lucine! Where are you going?"

She couldn't find her voice. The door flew open beneath her hand. She staggered through the outer atrium and jerked the outer door wide.

"I tried to tell you, Sister!" Natasha cried.

Then Lucine fled into the night.

SIXTEEN

Heat lay against my face. The hot tongue of a beast. Her breath on my neck, in my ear.

I love you, Toma.

Fingers traced my chin, my mouth. Teeth delicately held my lips. Then a sting, just the smallest one that left me longing for a deeper cut.

The teeth clamped down. Pain stabbed.

My eyes snapped open.

There was no beast. No woman. And during that first heartbeat against my breast I felt a profound disappointment. Then it was gone and I jerked up.

I was in my bedchamber in the Cantemir estate. Hot sun rays stabbed the room. I was wet with sweat. That breath I had imagined was a warm breeze that drifted through an open door to the balcony.

My dream was feral and terrifying but I had already lost the details. And I had slept so late? A warm breeze meant the sun had already heated the air.

I threw my legs over the side of the bed only to discover that I was still dressed. My vest was gone and my shirt torn. Trousers and boots still on. I could not remember then how I had gotten into bed.

The last thing I remembered was . . .

Details of my night at the Castle Castile flooded my mind. The ballroom, Natasha's aerial leap, my descent into the dungeon. Dasha and Alek, smiling.

That sip of blood burning my mouth and throat. Or had it been some elixir distilled with wine?

Dasha's soft voice whispered through my mind. *"Do you know why blood had to be drawn from the veins to cleanse the guilty stains of even the most righteous, Toma?"*

None of it made sense. But there was more. I had blurted my love for Lucine.

Lucine.

Heart now pounding, I rushed about the room, pulling on a clean shirt and a vest. The trousers would have to do. It could all have been a dream, I thought. I might well have conjured up the whole business in my sleep, driven by my shame for loving Lucine and not confessing it to the world.

But if it was all real, then I had to make a change to my thinking.

Royalty or not, surely Vlad was a beast who would harm Lucine. My love for her had found a new path—I would confess all to her and make sure she did not fall into the claws of that monster. The empress would have to either understand my actions or punish me for them, but I could no longer stand by without following my heart.

The sun outside was already past the noon hour!

I flew down to Alek's room, still tucking in my shirt. His door was cracked open so I barged in without a knock. "Alek!"

His bed was made. The chambermaid may have cleaned up already. Or he may not have slept here.

I spun and ran through the estate in long strides. They had to be in the main room, Lucine, Natasha, Alek, and Kesia. But they weren't. Only a maid was there, dusting the paintings.

The dining room then.

"Where are they?" I thundered. My voice was strong enough to shock the maid, so I ran into the dining room to see for myself.

Kesia was pouring herself a cup of tea at the table, humming. Sweet relief! Her eyes lifted and she smiled.

"Well, well. Look who's dragged himself from sleep. I was just going to check to make sure you hadn't run off to Russia with your man."

"Where are they?"

She poured a second cup. "Sit, Toma. Relax."

I crossed to the table. "Where are the others?"

"Tea?"

"Madam, please, I must know. Where is Lucine?"

"Ah. Lucine." By her condescending smile I knew all could not be well. "Always Lucine. Please, sit, my strapping warrior."

I did not like her tone. But she was still my duty and I couldn't dismiss her. So I forced myself to sit and tried to take a sip from the cup she'd poured me. My fingers weren't entirely steady. I withdrew my hand.

"I should find Alek," I said.

"You should. But I doubt you'll find him here. I'm told that both he and Natasha spent the night at the Castle Castile."

So then, at least that part of my memory wasn't a dream. I had to return there immediately and fetch my man. He had been bewitched by the blood wine that I had tasted, surely.

"This doesn't bother you, that your daughter spends the night in a stranger's home against our strongest urgings? Please, madam, you must allow me to do my job. Tell me how you know this?"

"Vlad told me."

"Vlad."

"Yes. That royal who just left an hour ago."

"He was here?" I was shocked.

"All morning. He and Lucine left for a picnic in the carriage."

I stood abruptly. "Lucine went with him?"

She eyed me with a raised brow. "Am I stuttering, Toma?"

"She . . . Lucine is a *party* to this?"

"Of course she is. The duke seems to be set on her. And it appears that Lucine has had a change of heart. She granted him the right to court her." She sipped from her cup. "So now she will be in his charge, not yours. I think the empress would approve, don't you?"

"But he's a dangerous man!" I paced, torn by this terrible news. "Have you all lost your minds here?"

"He's a perfectly respectable gentleman, sir. Clearly far out of your league. And Lucine is not yours. She belongs to her mother and herself. Please remember that before you berate us."

She could not know what I knew, and I didn't have the patience to persuade her of the danger. I turned and marched from the dining room.

"Where are you going, Toma?" Kesia asked entirely too casually.

"To see to my duty," I said.

It took me only minutes to learn from the guards which direction the carriage had gone, and I took after it on my stallion. I realized I had left my pistol behind—indeed, I wasn't sure where it was—but I didn't have the patience to go back for a weapon. I didn't think violence was the worry here.

The true concern was rightness of mind. When one lost his mind, he lost his way, as I myself had almost done, if only for a night. So long as Lucine was in my charge, I could not allow her to be put in harm's way.

On the other hand, the duke presented no direct threat to Lucine. And there was the letter from the empress, which might be read for or against him. Perhaps the only danger was a threat to her virtue.

Or to my own love for her.

I pushed the thought from my head and rode hard because I didn't care any longer. In confessing my love for Lucine to the Russians last night, I had learned how much I needed to admit the same to Lucine herself.

Now she was with this royal! Without knowing of my love for her! How I hated myself.

I found the carriage under a grove beside the road soon enough, and I pulled back on my animal's reins. There was no sign of Lucine or Valerik, only the driver. They must have brought horses.

I veered off the road and circled around to the south, keeping my eyes to the trees, where he had surely taken Lucine to be alone with her. The thought of it . . .

They've gone to the clearing, I thought. I'd seen it during my wanderings through this wood as I scoped out possible approaches for an invisible enemy, never imagining that the enemy had already been in the house on the night we first arrived.

I rode straight there, far too noisily for my own good, but I wasn't determined to go in like a ghost. I had been a ghost in her world for too many days already.

But then I heard that low rolling laughter and I changed my mind. They were indeed ahead in that clearing. And at least Valerik was enjoying himself.

What if I was wrong about her? I couldn't storm in and pronounce my love if she was laughing with him. I had to first determine her disposition, then step in when Valerik showed his true nature.

I tied my horse to a stump and crept up from tree to tree. My vantage of the clearing opened up when I rounded a particularly large trunk, and I pulled back into the shadow of that tree then slowly peered around.

The horses grazed in the grass nearby. Valerik, in black, walked by her side with his hands behind his back, the perfect illusion of a gentleman.

Lucine was dressed in a baby-blue dress cut from the sky itself. A white hat shaded her head. It was a mere stroll without a hint of any danger.

The duke suddenly laughed again, took her hand, and kissed it.

I could not remove my eyes. He was kissing her hand . . . That monster was placing his lips on her hand and she wasn't jerking it away like she wanted to. I very nearly ran out then to stop this obvious infraction. But as I watched, my outrage turned to horror.

Vlad van Valerik drew her closer, leaned over, and whispered something in her ear. She chuckled.

She did not slap him, she chuckled.

Then he kissed her cheek and walked on.

She did not slap him, she walked.

I pulled back, barely able to breathe. My head pounded. New thoughts crashed into my head, insane ones that might get me locked up if voiced. I wanted to kill him, or find a way to banish him from Moldavia. I wanted to challenge him to a duel, to break his legs, to drop a tree on his head.

But I kept my senses, turned from the large tree, and hastily retreated to my horse. The only way to approach this was to expose Vlad for his less than honorable intentions, whatever they might be, and expose Lucine to my own love. But not here like a fool while she skipped along by his side!

I had already made my own grave here by putting duty above love for too long; I would not lie down in that grave so quickly.

I let the better part of an hour pass as I made my way back to the estate, keeping to the high ground so I would see that black carriage rolling back. But they seemed to be in no hurry, and each passing minute gave birth to new imaginations of what he might be doing to her. Questions crowded my mind.

Why had they gone by carriage, why not just by horse?

Why leave the carriage, once in the wood?

Why leave the estate at all when so many rooms had tables for tea?

Why had Lucine granted him the right to court?

And these were just the most obvious. There were many more that had little bearing in common sense, subjects that I had rarely dwelled upon, like what kind of perfume that beast was wearing.

More than once I nearly turned back to check on her again, but I chided myself and pressed on.

The sun was already heading behind the towering Carpathian peaks when I entered the house, and still they had not returned. No longer able to contain myself, I went straight to find the lady Kesia in her sitting parlor.

She was humming.

"Toma! You've returned. Did you find them and shatter their dreams?"

I paced, torn.

"Yes?" she pushed. "Is she in mortal danger?"

"More than you could possibly know."

"He's attacked her, then? Ravaged her there in the wood?"

She was playing me and I had no patience for it.

"I must tell you something, but I must swear you to secrecy," I said. I had to tell someone.

"We keep no secrets here."

"There are too many secrets here! I beg you, don't breathe a word of what I say."

"How delicious! The strong man makes his confession. I swear."

For a moment I considered fleeing before I opened my mouth and ruined myself. But the urge to unburden myself was too much.

"I am in love with Lucine," I said. My voice was unsteady.

"Yes? But what is your secret?"

"I am smitten!"

She just looked at me, and now I had done it, so I said it all.

"From the first night, I was taken. She is my everlasting love. I can't remove her from my mind. I can't sleep or eat. I can't do my duty. I am a slave to her."

I believed I might weep with those words, so I said no more.

"Is that so?"

I had said too much.

"Then you are a fool, Toma."

"A complete idiot," I said.

"What kind of man doesn't tell the woman he loves that he has deep affection for her?"

"A man bound by duty and order."

"The man who puts duty above love is the fool."

"Then I am a fool."

I stood there looking at Kesia, who was seated, staring back at me. For a moment I thought I had found a friend who could help me.

"What do you intend on doing with these feelings?" she asked.

"If I can't vow my love for her, then I will die. So I will forsake my duty."

She sighed, stood, then crossed to a bottle of wine. "It's too late for that."

"I saw her there in the wood with him. And I couldn't bear the sight. This isn't something that we can take lightly any longer. I am beside myself with it!"

"If you had won her earlier, then she wouldn't have considered the duke."

"I was bound by duty!" I thundered.

She faced me, glass in hand. "Then bind yourself again, Toma. Because she has decided for the duke, and you are now outmatched."

"She will decide that." I pressed closer, aiming my fingers to the west to make my point now. "I was there last night and I found it to be a very dangerous place."

"Do tell."

"There's bewitching up there! The drinking of blood. Obscene intoxications!"

"Sounds fun. I thought you didn't believe in God or the devil."

"This is worse. I fear your daughters are in mortal danger there."

"Oh, please, Toma! This from the man who is raging with jealousy. Of course the duke is a devil in your eyes. He's just stolen your bride!"

She was driving me mad with her calculated rhetoric. Her logic was too persuasive for my liking.

"Say what you will, I know only one thing now," I said. "I will confess my heart to her and then let the stars fall if they must. I cannot live with myself otherwise."

"I told you, Toma, you are too late."

"And I told you that she will decide when I tell her."

"But I doubt you will be telling her of your love."

"What do you mean?"

"I mean that Lucine may be gone."

"Gone where?"

"The duke has invited her for dinner tonight. She told me that if she does not return by eight, then it is because she has decided to go with him to the Castle Castile."

I felt the blood drain from my face.

Kesia smiled. "I think she will go. So you see, my friend, you will tell her nothing, at least not tonight."

SEVENTEEN

It had all happened so quickly, Lucine found it hard to believe that she was here, at the Castle Castile, being wooed.

The night before had been the kind she once imagined nightmares were made of. But having walked through this valley of death, she had only found a new life.

"A toast, my friends," Vlad said, standing with his glass.

They were seated at a long, dark wood table bordered in gold leaf, Vlad at the head, she on his right hand, and Alek, Simion, and Stefan across the spread of food. Pork, veal, carrots, red potatoes, and caramelized onions with all the trimmings were piled on gold platters between tall white candles. Beside Lucine, Natasha and the sisters, Dasha and Sofia.

They all rose, but when Lucine lifted her glass to stand, Vlad's hand rested on her shoulder. "No, my queen. We honor you."

She felt awkward with all the attention, and reticence warmed her face. But she couldn't deny her appreciation for their honor. She'd never been held in such a lofty regard.

"To the woman whose mere consideration of my devotion sets my world upon a new axis," Vlad said.

"To the woman," they said. And they all drank.

"To the blood," Vlad said.

"To the blood." They drank again and then sat.

Blood, which was wine, held a central part in all Vlad talked about. She'd never heard such poetic words as those that came from him. He was a romantic to the bone, as Natasha had said.

Last night she'd rushed from the castle, cursing her own shame for clinging to an ideal that had failed her. She'd collapsed into bed and cried herself to sleep.

And when she awoke, she resolved to embrace a new kind of love, freed from the restraints of convention that had bound her for so long. She would no longer be the prude twin, reserved and proper, while the rest of the world found satisfaction in abandon.

But she hadn't immediately associated that new kind of love with Vlad van Valerik. His presence had haunted her dreams, and she couldn't deny that her impression of him had been reshaped by the night's events.

Mother was the one who'd sent for the duke, Lucine learned later. When he appeared midmorning and bowed before them, she knew that she must entertain his offer to court her. Not that it would go anywhere, but she could not keep sending opportunity into a dark corner while she awaited the perfect suitor.

If Natasha swore by this man's love, then she must reconsider.

So she'd gone with Vlad to the wood, and there he'd spoken like a true gentleman, always considerate, full of wit. And beautiful. As beautiful as Toma, who slept off his revelry in his room.

When Vlad asked if she had decided whether to join him for dinner that night, she had surprised herself by answering straightaway.

"Yes." Then even more: "I would like that."

He'd kissed her hand and her cheek. The sensation of those hot lips on her skin lingered still.

When Natasha had been summoned, she threw her arms around her sister. "Oh, Lucine! I heard." She immediately checked her exuberance and dipped her head at the duke, took his hand, and kissed it. "Thank you, sir. Thank you."

Then she'd bounced around and clung to Stefan and generally showed her delight that Lucine had returned. "What did I tell you, Lucine? What did I tell you?"

Lucine had been ushered into the main hall, where sixty or seventy of the coven waited. They stood as Vlad walked in with Lucine on his arm, and to a person they'd bowed.

"Now you see her, as I said you would," Vlad said, and his voice held them in a trance. "She is mine. And the castle is hers."

They stared at her with dark eyes rimmed in gray, a stunning sight caused by the variety of wine, Vlad said. In the sun his own eyes had looked golden brown, but here in the dim light, they too were dark.

His companions bowed when she left the room again, followed by Natasha and the others who now sat at the banquet table—Vlad's lieutenants. She didn't bother to ask why they used rankings if they were simply aristocrats. These Russians referred to everything in poetic terms. Queen, blood, coven . . . it was all said with a flair for the unconventional.

Even the way they dressed was sensuous and made a bold statement of exclusivity. *We stand above it all and are proud to do so. We are royalty.*

She felt conspicuous in her own blue dress, like a nun at a ball.

The banquet was presented in silence by two servants. They kept staring at Lucine, but not a single word was spoken. The unnerving stares from their first dinner with these Russians now struck her as hauntingly beautiful. She had a hard time keeping her eyes off of them as well.

She might have expected Alek and Natasha to be more talkative, but both seemed content to play the role given to them by their host. Something about their state still bothered Lucine—the look in their eyes and their pale faces—but with as much wine and as little sleep as they took here, it wasn't hard to understand. They had thrown themselves at these Russians. Too much. Lucine would have to take them aside and talk . . .

But no. No, that was past now. She would not play the spoiler here.

"Then eat!" Vlad said, snapping his serviette. "Drink! And above all, love."

He said it with his eyes on Lucine, and she felt herself blush.

"To love!" Stefan said. And again they toasted. Lucine watched Simion drink, eyes on her. When she turned back to Vlad, his chair was empty. He was behind her, warm hand on her shoulder. He traced her neck with his finger and whispered into her ear.

"Tonight belongs to you, Lucine. Whatever you desire. I am your servant." And he lifted her glass from behind and fed her a sip of wine.

She was at once embarrassed by his extraordinary attention and thrilled by it. His finger trailed off her cheek and he walked to a great window draped in purple velvet. He grasped the curtains with both hands and flung them wide to show the night.

Vlad stood there with his back to them, arms wide on the drapes. His black suit was cut long, hanging down to his knees, gathered in the middle of his back with a brass buckle. He released the drapes, took his collar and dropped the coat off his back, then threw it across a chair.

Such a magnificent specimen, Lucine thought. She could see the strength of his shoulders through his shirt.

Vlad spoke, facing the night. "Some kinds of love are worth the wait of a thousand years." He spun, eyes sparkling with mischievousness. "I'm afraid that I have lost my appetite for this mortal food." He was positively beaming. And in a moment he was seated again. "But I will eat with you anyway—I'm told the veal is delectable."

It was all so very strange, yet so fascinating. No wonder Natasha had returned again and again. Had she been treated like this? Lucine doubted it, but seeing the Russians with unmasked eyes now, she suspected any interaction with them would be intoxicating. They were like honey drawing bees.

Knives and forks chimed on the plates. The scent of freshly cooked meat was heavy. A fiddler's mournful tune drifted in from another room.

Together they ate and drank. And they watched each other,

feeding as much on each other's gazes as on the veal and pork. Lucine felt like she was on the cliff, ready to fall. But even that apprehension drew her, if only to know what awaited in the black chasm beneath.

Natasha had been there and was grinning like a child.

Alek had descended and come back with dumb happiness.

Toma had let himself go . . .

Lucine hardly had an appetite and the wine was getting to her head.

"May I ask a question?" she asked.

"You must," Vlad said. "You must have so many."

She smiled. "Naturally. Is this normal?"

Vlad looked at the others, then back. "You mean the food? We eat very well here."

"No . . ."

"The wine then? We drink even better."

"I'm sure you do. But I was thinking about the . . . well, this general atmosphere. Is everyone so taken with everything all the time? It's a wonder, don't get me wrong, but isn't it just . . ."

"Unnatural?"

"Yes. Unnatural."

"Well, we do have our fights, if that's what you mean. Passion is something we demand of each, but not everyone embraces love and beauty the way we do, and at times they put up a fuss."

"Why would anyone come against you?"

"For the same reasons you wanted to," he said.

There was that.

"Love isn't easily understood by the wicked." He leaned back and toyed with his goblet. "Ask any martyr."

"You believe in God here?"

"Only a fool would not."

"All except Toma," Alek said.

They looked at him strangely.

"Just pointing that out."

"He's still here?" she asked.

"If not, we should invite him," Vlad said.

She wasn't sure why, but the idea sounded premature to her. Unbecoming even.

"And you, Stefan, you heal so quickly?" she asked.

He touched his hair. "Yes, well, it was a nasty blow to be sure. They tell me I almost bled out. I'm sure when the wound heals it will leave a ghastly scar. Three cheers for hair to keep me beautiful."

They chuckled, Natasha laughed in her high pitch, and that was the end of it.

"Which reminds me," Vlad said. "I recall the time Simion fell from the balcony of that dreadful castle near Venice. Trying to save a woman perched on the railing, yes? Instead you fell and bled on my floor."

"How could I forget?" Simion pointed to his head. "My skull is still lopsided. But I do believe that is my secret. Women love to hold my head, thinking it's still hurt. It has proven to be the perfect lure."

"To women," Alek said, lifting his cup. And again they obliged his toast.

Conversation began in earnest then, having been broken open by Lucine, who mostly listened. It was as if they had respectfully waited for her to break the ice before beginning table talk. They told stories about more countries and wars and women than she could believe anyone could possibly have crossed, fought, or loved in a single lifetime.

The more she heard, the more she felt at ease with them. And the more Vlad doted on her, the more she wanted him to.

He was clearly on the prowl to find the slightest way to serve her, rushing to the kitchen for a fresh bottle of wine and pouring it himself, or fetching her a clean silver fork because the gravy had soiled hers. Each time he rose he found an excuse to pass behind her, to touch her hair, or to lean over and ask if she needed anything.

Anywhere else, his attention would appear obsequious, but not in this banquet room. Not with these candles and these paintings and drapes and wine, and certainly not with these Russians, who didn't seem to know any other way to behave.

In so many ways they were perfect gentlemen, sharpened with just enough of an edge to keep her guessing how deeply they might cut if provoked.

Like Toma in that way. Yet so different.

Dasha and her sister, Sofia, on the other hand, were hardly the image of perfect ladies. Far from it. They lusted openly, objects of great desire who knew how valuable they were and had no interest in pretending otherwise. Completely comfortable in their own skin, surely with or without clothing. In that way they were both queens.

Royalty.

They took their time—two hours at the table, at least, in no hurry to rush the taste of each morsel, unwilling to release each gaze too quickly, wringing satisfaction from each word spoken.

But mostly they all seemed delighted to take pleasure in her, as if Vlad was sharing his queen with his court and he didn't want to rush their experience.

True to his word, Vlad hardly ate. Or drank for that matter. But his eyes were drinking her already, and the thought of it made her head spin.

"Now I must ask you one question, Lucine," he said when they had finished as much food as they could eat. "You've eaten with me twice, once there with that other man—what was his name? Sorry, yes, Toma. And your mother, of course. And once here in our company. Which has pleased you the most?"

"I wasn't aware that it was a contest," she said, laughing. The wine had certainly softened her good graces, but here good graces were not so highly valued.

They all laughed with her. And toasted.

"No, of course not," he said. "It only gives me context. You might love red, but only when you put red next to purple do you know which color you prefer on the walls. So it is with people."

"And I can only hope you find my red more alluring than that purple."

She said it quickly and was feeling too loose to moderate herself. He stared at her, as if trying to know if she'd said what he'd heard.

"Then," he said, smiling, "I would choose red over purple even if the red was soiled beyond repair."

She wasn't sure what that said about her, but the rest obviously thought it a great compliment, because they lifted their glasses for the twentieth or thirtieth time.

"So be it."

"So be it."

And they drank.

"Now leave us," Vlad said, dismissing them all with a slight movement of his hand.

As one they rose, dipped their heads, and, with one last look at Lucine, left without another word. One moment they were seated, drinking, and the next they were gone, leaving Lucine and Vlad van Valerik alone in the dining room.

He reached out his large hand for her small one. She gave it to him. He kissed it lightly.

"I worship you," he said.

Deep inside she knew this was too much, but too much of what? Love? And what was too much love but too much of what she did not have? Were torrential rains in the dried ravine of her heart too much to coax forth life?

She let a timid giggle leak from her mouth and felt easy with her response when he smiled. "Thank you," she said.

"Then I will worship you even more."

He stood, still holding her hand, and brought her slowly to her feet. Then he drew her to the large window. For a while he seemed content to stare out at the night.

Clouds had gathered, she saw. Not a star to be seen. Fingers of lightning cracked the horizon in silence. A storm was coming.

She felt at such ease with him and yet so unnerved at the same moment, like that serene sky, split by flashes of hot light. If this was what had driven Natasha to her unabashed pursuit of men all these years, then Lucine pitied herself for not experiencing it sooner. It sounded scandalous, but in that moment, so pleased to stand next to such a powerful, romantic suitor who vowed his love for her, Lucine thought she might be falling in love with the duke.

"You are a mysterious man, Vlad van Valerik," she said.

He leaned over and kissed her forehead. "Then can I unwrap part of this mystery for you?"

"Please."

His eyes drifted back to the stormy sky. "It begins with another man, who is my mortal enemy."

"Really? You seem to have enough power to crush any mortal enemy."

He chuckled. "Perhaps. You know that I stand to inherit more than this world? That in reality, I possess it? That I have the power to pull its strings and own the hearts of all men?"

A rather poetic, if odd, way to put his position. "I've heard that you are very powerful."

"More than most would care to know. But I don't wear that power like a red cape to show the world. I may have the teeth of a wolf, but I prefer to walk among them in sheep's clothing."

"Then you should be praised. There is too much struggle for power, too many wars and too much bloodletting in this world."

"Well, I didn't say I wouldn't drink their blood. I just won't let them know I'm doing it." He smiled and she laughed.

"So who is this mortal enemy of yours?"

"Someone who doesn't know that I am who I am. That I will rule, that in so many ways I already do rule from the shadows. If he did, he might one day kill me."

"Then you should make sure he never finds out. Or you should deal with him now."

"Yes, well, I am."

Lucine felt the effects of the wine weighing on her mind. "So how does this unravel the mystery that surrounds you, Vlad van Valerik?"

"It came to my attention that this man has an eye for the Cantemir twins," he said. "And when I met you, I immediately understood why."

"Truly? Why?"

"Because you, my dear, are exquisite. I'd heard of your reputation, of course, but I never expected to be so crushed with jealousy for your love."

She laughed with less reservation. He certainly had a way with words, and as long as they poured such affection into her, she would welcome them.

"I knew immediately that you were the one I have waited for. I must have your love. Nothing else will ever matter to me more."

"Because of jealousy?"

"If winning you from our mortal enemy is jealousy, then let it fill my bones and rage for you."

He was too gracious to be real.

Vlad turned to her and took both hands, holding her as if she were made of delicate tissue. "Before I take you back tonight, I would like to show you one thing."

Outside, lightning stabbed the earth; thunder rolled. She glanced at the window. Rain was falling.

"The road will be treacherous," she said.

"Nothing will harm you; I'll get you home safely."

She wasn't sure she wanted to go. Natasha and Alek had spent the night here, hadn't they?

"So show me," she said.

"It's in the tower."

"Then take me to your tower."

His eyes searched her face, moving from one eye to the other, then to her lips and back to her eyes.

He bent and touched his lips to the bridge of her nose.

"No wonder he loves you."

EIGHTEEN

I waited. Wrapped in a tight fist of raw nerves, I waited for Lucine to return to me. Not to her mother, not to the Cantemir estate, not even to safety, but to *me*. Because now I knew that if I could just persuade her of my deep affection for her, she would surely reconsider.

Such was the state of my mind as I paced the lawn and rode out to the gate and finally retreated to my room for release in my journal. This page I would never burn.

My dear Lucine—

Forget who I was yesterday when I was an unwitting child.
Today I am your savior. I am your Solomon and you are my song.
And that wolf who stalks you—I can't bear to think of it!

You must know, it was religious duty to Her Majesty, not
any lack of devotion to you, that muzzled me. But now . . . now
I would scream my love for you from the mountaintops. Now I
would slay a thousand beasts to bring you from the valley.

You, my Lucine, my cherished one, have stolen my heart. One
look from you and I would be ravished. I beg you, Lucine, come to
me and let me wash your feet with my tears.

My shame knows no bounds; my regret has no bottom. This
breast can no longer contain my love. I beg you to return to me. If
you do not, then I will die there on that cross of shame.

My words are like rocks here, blunt and worthless for their
refusal to express my love . . .

My quill hovered over the page. But I could not write another
word. She might be approaching already. I thrust the journal back
under the mattress and ran outside to find an empty road.

A hundred times I considered rushing up the mountain, but
I remained at the estate for fear that I would miss her return by
another route. I nearly ran back out to the meadow where that wolf
had taken her, but if she was still there . . . I couldn't mortify her
like that, exposing how he'd damaged her.

My thoughts replayed the events of the previous evening
over and over, and I could not make my suspicions a certainty.
Had I ingested some bad drug or wine that had softened my will?
Had anyone threatened me or Natasha or Alek? Had anyone

spoken a disparaging comment about Lucine or the Cantemirs in my charge?

No. No, and it enraged me because, I tell you, there was something hidden up there, and I wanted to go up with an army and break the castle to pieces until I found it.

Valerik was a wolf in sheep's clothing come to kill, steal, and destroy. He was that snake in the garden, beguiling with a smooth tongue and wicked eyes. He was that monster under the bed who waited until all slept before feeding on his prey.

He was none of these things, of course, and he might not present any physical threat to my charges, but that was now beside the point.

Vlad van Valerik was surely robbing any fondness Lucine might have for me. He was stealing her heart away from me. He was destroying any chance I had to win her, and that was now all that mattered.

So then, Vlad was my mortal enemy.

I swore to wait until the eighth hour, but when I saw that first stab of lightning on the horizon, I could not wait. He must have taken her to the fortress! The thought of him up there wrapping his slender fingers around her hand had driven me to the bitter end of myself.

I rushed to the stable, sword at my side, pistols in my bag, and I whipped that horse until it galloped for his life.

The rain began to fall when I was only halfway up the mountainside, and my fear began to mount. Thunder hammered the earth, lightning split the sky, and I pushed my stallion faster. He lunged through the trees, splashing through mud, scattering rocks.

What if Lucine had returned to her mother after all? I was on a different road. I would have missed her entirely. But I was now committed, so I threw the thought aside and pressed on.

When I rounded the bend that first allowed full sight of the Castle Castile, the falling rain was so heavy that I could not see it across the ravine. I let my horse have his head and prayed I was not too late. Too late for what, I wasn't sure. But my warrior's instincts were raw with alarm.

There were no horses tied out front when mine slid to a stop at the post, but Valerik would have put them in the stable in this storm.

Rivers of water ran from my head and shoulders as I climbed those steps to the sealed doors. The wind whipped my coat about my legs. If the doors were locked, I would find another way inside—those stone walls could not keep me out.

Sword trailing at my side, I pounded on the door. Stealth would not be my friend here, because I had not come to take on an army, only confront Lucine with my love. But if anyone got in my way, I was sworn to put them to the side.

The door did not open, so I pushed the lever and shoved. It swung wide. I stepped into the atrium and let the door blow shut behind me.

Now I was here, in the silence, and for a moment I just stood. Then I shrugged out of my coat and let it fall to the stone. I gripped my sword's handle and let the blade trail behind me. My determination would be clear, but I wasn't foolish enough to go in swinging.

I hesitated for one deep breath at the door that led into the great hall where I'd first found Natasha. Then I pushed it open and stepped into the Castle Castile.

The floor was empty. I stood dripping on their marble and let my blade rest on the ground.

And then I saw them, lined along the balcony shoulder to shoulder, a dozen of the Russians, staring at me.

This was their welcome. They'd been waiting. And they wore knives on their thighs. A rage settled over me.

"I demand an audience with Lucine Cantemir!" The water on my lips sprayed with the force of my words. "Bring her to me! Now!"

NINETEEN

Rain poured from the sky. Lucine could hear it pelting the roof above, but here in Vlad's tower it was only a distant, comforting murmur. Even the crashes of thunder were shut out by this magnificent fortress.

"It is beautiful, isn't it?"

"What is?" she asked.

"The sound of the rain."

"Hmm."

Look into my eyes and see my love for you, Lucine.

She looked at Vlad, who was staring at her from the bookcase. Had he spoken to her? In his hand he held a brown leather book that was worn from years of handling. His eyes invited her to live in them. "I want you to know who I really am, Lucine. No secrets between you and me."

"You've been keeping secrets?"

"Never from you. But it takes time to unveil all. It's the only way to embrace true love."

She smiled, toying with him and pleased to find herself in the position to do so. "And what is true love? As much as I appreciate all of this more than I ever would have guessed, is it really the stuff of true love?"

"No." He approached her, holding his book in one hand. "It's only one page of the whole. Still, you do find"—he glanced at the portraits—"all of this beautiful, yes?"

"Yes. Yes I do."

"But it's only a taste, I agree. The rest of the story is found in the rest of the pages. In the full truth of the matter."

He turned from her and opened the book's leather cover gingerly. "The problem with most people is that they're afraid to look at the whole story. They live in fear of what they might find, because they cling to such a thin thread of hope that any disappointment might snap it in two."

He was speaking about her, she thought, her own reluctance to embrace a hope for true love, her fear it might not exist. She felt her smile fade.

"And their greatest fear is of the wolf. The priests have done a good job of that, don't you think? 'Look here, the wolf has eaten your chicken. Look there, the wolf has killed that man,' they say. But no one ever sees that wolf."

"Perhaps."

He paced slowly, fingering through his book. "Meanwhile the wolf prowls freely, dressed in a cloak made of sheep's clothing."

The soothing waves of his voice calmed her. "Yes," she said.

Vlad looked at her sideways. "The Pharisees put up their fences: 'Don't touch, don't eat, don't drink, don't cross the road on this day or that.' And all the sheep bleat their agreement. 'Yes, yes, yes, don't, don't, don't.'"

He was so bold, this royal named Vlad.

"While religion is busy putting up fences to protect their young, the wolves walk through the front doors. And no one wants to strip them bare for fear of what they might find. It makes the wolf's hunt so much easier."

"I suppose it would."

"Do wolves scare you, Lucine?"

Considering the wine and company, she felt somewhat fearless. "No, not really."

"Perhaps if you spent more time looking at them, they would," he said. "Because the real wolf comes to kill. To steal. To destroy."

"Then I'd prefer not to look at them," she said.

He smiled and closed the book with a thump. "No. No, I suppose you wouldn't. Which is good for us both." He lowered his eyes to the cover, rubbed his thumb over the embossing. "You wonder what makes me and my coven so unique." Eyes up, drilling her, he walked to her. "So magical."

"Yes." In a whisper.

He reached for her chin and lightly brushed it with his forefinger. "Mine is a world in which the stakes for true love are higher than you can imagine."

She felt her breathing thicken as he spoke.

"The beauty you see here is only a fraction of all I possess. If you would step with me beyond the pages of this story you see about you, I could show you a new kind of love."

She didn't know what to say.

Vlad grinned, then turned, crossed to his desk, set the book down, and splashed some wine into a tall brass goblet.

Lucine cleared her throat so that she could speak. "That's what you wished to show me, this magical book of yours?" she asked.

"No." He lifted the glass and stepped across the room to her.

She took the glass.

"Don't drink it yet, my love. It is a very special wine." He winked at her. "The kind that opens the eyes of mortals to true wolves and true love and to God himself."

She laughed. "Then it's what Natasha has been drinking, no doubt."

"No doubt."

"She's never had a problem running after love."

"But you, my dear Lucine, are the more beautiful by far." He drew her hair off her cheek with his fingers. "You are exquisite, and if I were so humbled to have you as my queen, together we would rule the world and show them all love."

"And put all the wolves into cages," she said.

"May I kiss you?"

She felt her heart stop for a beat, then resume with more force.

Vlad slid one arm around her waist and gently pulled her against him. Then he brought his lips to hers and he kissed her. Like a dove. And it made her head spin.

He lifted his lips and spoke in a whisper, only inches from her mouth. "Will you remember me forever, Lucine?"

Her heart pounded and she let her restraint slip.

"Yes."

"Then drink this wine in remembrance of me." And he pushed the goblet up to her lips.

She took only a drop of the musky-smelling liquid, barely enough to slide down her throat, and then the goblet was gone from her lips. He kissed her again, and this time she returned the kiss, softly at first, but then with hunger.

"You will be my bride soon, Lucine. Forever my only bride."

TWENTY

They were twelve and I was one, and we faced each other across the hall, I the lone lion with my teeth bared, they the wolf pack with dead eyes.

They did not answer my demand. They gave no indication they had even heard it.

They did not circle nor reach for their weapons. They only stood on that balcony and stared down at me like generals watching a battle in the valley below. Nine males and three females.

I staggered forward three steps and stopped, sword still low on the stones. They were all dressed in black trousers, some with shirts open in a V to their bellies, some of the men bare-chested. All were lean and well muscled, pale as the moon.

I recognized only two, Stefan and Dasha.

"Where is she?" My voice echoed through the hall.

Stefan spoke quietly. "You are no longer welcome, dark twin. Leave us."

It was true, *Toma* means "twin," and a thousand dead infidels might have called me "dark," but in the Castle Castile I was surely the beacon of light.

"Let Lucine tell me that I'm not welcome," I said.

"She loves another."

My hand began to shake. "Then take me to your master!"

I swear I could see a grin on that Russian's face, though his lips were flat. "He's in her embrace. Your love is wasted here, dark suitor."

Until that moment I did not know how far I would go, indeed if I would use my sword at all, but when I heard those words my mind lost all thought of sparing even one of those infidels. I became that man who could step onto any battlefield without fear for my life.

Cold calculation, not blind rage, determines the warrior's fate, and I became ice.

My mind skipped through the weapons at my disposal. Two throwing knives, one pistol, one sword. The hall was open for maneuvering. I could take twelve men if tremendous fortune was on my side; I'd done it before. But my first purpose was to find Lucine, not slay these fools.

I was confident that their master resided in the western tower, because he'd taken that direction when he left Sofia and me the last time I was here. The door he took rested shut across the hall to my left. It would be my goal.

Slowly I walked out to the center, eyes on them all for the slightest movement. "Then give me my man Alek," I said, hoping to engage their minds. "Give him to me and I will go."

In answer, the twin of Stefan, the man I had shot at the Summer Ball of Delights, threw his legs up and to one side, vaulting over the railing as if hopping over a small tree in the forest. His shirtsleeves fluttered as he fell ten feet, and I swear he did not remove his eyes from me as he dropped, not once.

He absorbed his landing with a light spring in his knees.

"But Alek is no longer your man, Toma." Stefan stepped toward me, unconcerned, knife still fastened to his thigh with buckled black straps. "He's Dasha's man."

Dasha dropped over the railing and landed with the same ease Stefan had. So they were accomplished gymnasts, but such tumbling could not stop a blade.

Stefan halted ten paces from me, lips twisted in a whimsical grin. "And you should know that Natasha is mine. She became mine when I kissed her at your ball."

The thought distracted me for a moment. Then this was the man I had shot?

"We heal rather quickly," he said.

My sword was still touching the ground and I remained as ice, despite that bell of alarm ringing in my head.

Dasha stopped beside Stefan. "Did you like our wine, Toma?"

"You have bewitched my man with this drug."

"No, not a drug. Blood, lover boy."

"Then this is your way of loving? To drug your victims with blood so they become pliable in your arms?"

"We force no one to drink. And no one may drink from us unless they beg. Would you like me to drink your blood? Then you would be my lover."

Natasha. And Alek.

I didn't know what kind of coven I had fallen into, what kind of witchcraft or evil proceeding. I was ignorant of religion, as I have said. But my lack of faith was wearing thin. Surely what they suggested could not be entirely true. Only the raving mad might drink blood!

Drink this blood in remembrance of me. Holy communion. I had never understood how the civilized could talk so openly about drinking blood. Christianity was obsessed with blood—the blood of Christ, the blood of the lamb, the blood of the saints, always blood. It was one reason I considered priests to be the better part of mad and churches their asylums.

I was one who spilled blood on the battlefield, not on an altar.

And now Lucine was in the monster's arms, drinking his blood? The thought of it made my bones tremble.

"Let me pass."

Stefan stepped forward. "You shot me," he said. "It's only a memory now, but I can't say it did not hurt. Would you like to try again?"

The door was to my left, a good twenty paces. At a full spring I might make it before they got to me.

"I'm not here to kill you. I am only here for Lucine."

"And yet Lucine is my master's property. None of us take kindly to thieving."

"Then you have twisted her mind and taken what is not yours to take!"

"You were not listening to me," Dasha said.

I had listened, but I could not embrace her talk of blood. It did not seem feasible to me. They clearly had some powerful drugs, but they were not devils. I wasn't so naive.

"Fight me," Stefan said. "Kill me again, and they will let you see Lucine, whom you have lost to our master."

I had only three options. I could retreat and return later with more men. I could make a break for the door on my left and trust my speed to carry me past these two. Or I could engage Stefan. Kill him.

I was never a man to delay unless it was to my distinct advantage. And it no longer was.

I took a deep breath. "Then I must insist . . ."

My arm flashed.

It was my practice to house a single, perfectly balanced throwing knife as part of the hilt in my sword, released with a single clasp by my forefinger. I had released the clasp as I took that deep breath.

And now with the snap of my arm that steel blade rushed toward Stefan.

It sliced into his chest and thudded to the handle. He made no attempt to deflect or duck. I don't think he moved so much as a hair, not even after it drilled him.

No one moved. I expected him to fall, earning me an

undisputed victory. Instead he calmly reached up, grasped the handle, and pulled the knife out of his chest.

Blood ran down his belly. He held the blade for a moment, then let it fall noisily to the floor.

"Very nice throw," he said. And then he moved.

Not a sprint, not a leap, not a swerve. He was a blur shifting from his position five paces away to my side, knee drawn back, and then smashing against my ribs as he reached me.

I had time only to brace for the blow and fall with it. I landed on my shoulder and rolled, grasping for the blade at my side.

I saw the room in one glance as I came to my feet. Six of them were dropping from the balcony like crows settling for a landing; the other four streaked to my left to cut off the approach to the western tower. They covered twenty paces in the space of one breath.

But I saw more. Dasha's face looked bleached, and it had narrowed. Her eyes were bright red. And her fingers were longer, like claws with extended nails.

I knew then that I was outmatched. Swords and knives and bullets were no use against twelve of them. Nevertheless, I threw my second knife.

It took the nearest in his forehead. The force of the blade kicked his head back so that he faced the ceiling. Blood drenched his hair and he crashed to his back like a felled tree.

If I had more blades . . .

I had my pistol in my hand and discharged the load into the shoulder of Stefan. The bullet spun him once and dropped him to one knee. But he waited only a moment before pushing himself back up.

I was trapped. Out of blades. The pistol was too slow. There was only one unguarded door, and I had no idea where it led.

My heart was broken for Lucine. I had failed! I would have rather died than lived with that knowledge. But my death would only cut her last thread of hope.

So I ran for that door, certain I would never make it.

TWENTY-ONE

The wine's burning in her mouth was quickly soothed by a warm flutter in her belly. Vlad stared into her eyes, and the world seemed to slow. How she had managed to resist the lure of love for so long, she did not know. Now that she was embracing it—embracing Vlad's seduction of her—she felt as though she might be in heaven.

"Do you like it?" he asked.

She reached up and pulled his head closer, then fed hungrily on his lips with her own. "I love it," she breathed.

"I thought you would, my love."

Vlad straightened, lifted her hand, and danced with her. She lay her head back and laughed at the ceiling. Thunder crashed over them, yet only the most distant threat.

"You will be my bride. We will rule the world, Lucine!"

"We will be heroes."

"We will show that terrible suitor why you belong to me."

"We will feed on that evil suitor."

She had not a clue what he meant with all of his poetic speech. It hardly mattered. There was plenty of time for understanding tomorrow.

"Now you should go home, before the road washes out completely," he said.

"No." She pulled back. "No, I can't go now."

"Why ever not, dear?"

She searched his eyes. Was he serious? He was sending her home already?

"I . . . The night is young. It's storming outside."

"Then you want to stay with me?"

"Yes!"

He spun away, delighted, and he shouted at the roof, one fist raised, "I knew it!"

Lucine pealed with laughter and let him sweep her around, off the ground. Oh what bliss, what delight, what wonder! Music was flowing from the walls now, from the room next door perhaps, she didn't know, only that the mournful fiddle sounded like an angel crooning to her.

"Natasha, forgive me!" she laughed. "Forgive me, Sister, for all of my nasty words. You were so right! Give me more wine!"

"Not wine, my dear. There is something more."

"More? Where? Show me."

A fire flashed in his eyes and his jaw flexed. "I will." The look was so beastly and full of hunger that for the briefest moment she felt a sense of alarm. But then he swept her up and carried her into his bedroom, and she felt scandalous.

The light in here was lower and altogether orange. Dancing flames of delight. Vlad set her down at the foot of his bed and cupped her chin. She'd never been so desired, so consumed by a man, and her yearning for it was its own kind of rapture.

Her hands were on his arms; she could feel his muscles, bunched and knotted. Like the muscles she'd seen on Toma's beautiful body.

He lifted a finger to her lips and touched them, feather light. "You saw Stefan kiss Natasha."

"Yes."

"There was blood on her lip."

She hesitated. "Yes."

"You cannot imagine the pleasure, Lucine."

"You want to bite my lip?"

"It's not a bite as much as a sharing. A mixing of blood. A seal of love between two people. This wins the heart, not merely the drinking of the blood. That only softens you up, so to speak."

Vlad brought his mouth to hers. Flicked her lips with his tongue.

Her desire swelled and she gently took his upper lip into her mouth, giving him free access to her lower lip. Natasha had done this.

"Kiss me, Vlad," she breathed. "Kiss me however you want to kiss me."

He took her lip between his teeth. A chuckle escaped his mouth and she returned it. His teeth closed with just enough pressure to sting her without breaking the skin.

"Ask me again," he said.

"Kiss me, Vlad. Bite me."

Pain flashed on the inside of her mouth. But then it was gone, replaced by only a gentle, gnawing pain. She laughed.

"Is that all, dear sir?"

"No."

And he bit again.

This time the pain was sharper, deeper. Twin needles that stabbed into her lips. The burning spread down her chin, and she gasped. For a count of three the pain leaked into her blood before easing for a moment. Then it came again, flashing through her bones like a fire.

She wanted to cry out, but she refused. She felt like she might faint as Natasha had fainted. But Natasha had awakened without pain.

Vlad moaned with pleasure. His body began to tremble as he held her there in his arms. "I make you my queen," he said. "And I will be yours."

"It hurts," she said. Tears welled in her eyes. Panic touched her mind and her breathing thickened.

"My blood is much stronger than some. But that pain will be your ecstasy and you will be my bride." He touched her lips delicately, then drew his finger away bloody and placed it in his mouth. "It will take a few days for my blood to transform you," he said, voice so low she could barely hear it. "Some feed on the jugular, but it's so uncouth, don't you think?"

The pain reached deeper, down into her belly, through her

pelvis, down her legs, and clutched at her midsection. She doubled over, crying out.

"It hurts!"

"Embrace that pain."

Her mind began to fall into a hole; her world tipping toward him, joining with a darkness she didn't understand. But rather than feel appalled by him, she was strangely drawn to him.

"What's wrong with me?" She grabbed the bedpost with one hand to keep from falling. "Something's wrong!"

"Don't be so pathetic," he snapped.

What? What was he saying?

She looked up at him, pleading. "Vlad . . . Vlad, I'm scared."

"Silence!"

"Vlad . . ."

In an instant his whole demeanor transformed from lover to beast. He grabbed her around her waist, nails biting into her belly, lifted her high in the air, and slammed her down on the mattress.

"Silence!" His voice shook the rafters.

And Lucine thought then that she had made a dreadful mistake. But she could not believe he meant it. Not now, after everything he had said, after his eyes had devoured her with such desire.

"What are you—"

His open hand crashed against her face with a loud *crack!* "You will learn that I have no tolerance for whiners. I have shown you my love and for this you cry?"

His eyes were red, his face white like a sheet. His nails had grown. Blood seeped through her dress where they had cut her.

"Please! Pleeeeease!"

Vlad's mouth pulled into a deep frown. "You disgust me. Stay here." Then he turned and walked out of the room.

Lucine's mind was no longer lucid. She was on his bed and her bones were on fire, that much she knew. But she was confused about why he'd hit her, why he'd left her. She had upset him? She had said something wrong and wounded him.

But why had he retaliated? A man had beaten her before for carrying a child. Was this the same? No. No, surely not. This time she deserved his reaction.

She didn't have the strength to stand, much less leave. Even so, she didn't dare leave the room—it would only upset him more. She couldn't do that to him.

Tears began to flow from her eyes. She took her knees in her arms, pulling them close to her chest to keep the pain in, and she cried. She could not understand why she said what she did as she rocked there in anguish.

"Toma," she moaned. "Dear Toma . . ."

Time faded.

A door opened and she caught her sobs in her throat. But she was too weak now to turn and see who it was. So she remained still and tried not to upset him.

She felt the bed move. Someone was climbing on with her.

A hand gently touched her arm. Then the person lay down behind her, body folded into her own.

"Shh, shh, shh . . ."

Who was it? Not him. It wasn't him.

"I'm sorry, Sister. It will be better when you wake up."

Natasha.

Lucine wept.

TWENTY-TWO

I sprinted and was halfway to that sole unguarded door before I
realized that none of them had moved to stop me. They stood
still, watching, as if my running to that door was precisely what
they had in mind for me.

Or because they knew it was barred.

I pulled up hard and grasped the handle. Shoved it down. The
door flew open under my weight. I leaped through and spun to
seal it shut.

The sight of them standing there, simply watching, unnerved
me to the core. Their eyes red like fire, their faces white like

cotton, their mouths drawn with poise, like those portraits on the wall. Unmoving. Rigid. Unreal but so very real.

Then two flew, streaks of black, whispers of blown smoke. Directly toward me.

I slammed the door shut as they crashed into the other side. The bolt was there, at my hand, and I shoved it home.

Whether because they had better plans or because they could not breach this door I don't know, but they made no attempt to force the door open or break it down.

I found myself at one end of a stone hallway that headed toward the same side of the castle where I'd descended into the tunnels with Sofia the day before. There was no other course but for me to run.

So I ran, with my best speed, certain that these creatures of the night were already making flight to cut me off.

Only minutes ago I doubted anything that might be called supernatural; now I knew that I had been naive. I knew neither the extent of it nor the means by which to deal with it, but I was certain that evil existed. I had come face-to-face with it and survived long enough to know at least that much.

And Lucine was in its grasp.

Tears sprang to my eyes as I ran, blurring the path. But I didn't dare slow, because Lucine's only hope was that I escape this house of hell and return with the priests to cast it off the earth, or with an army to raze it to the ground.

The hall ended at two doors on either side, and I took the one to my right because it seemed the other led back toward the great hall. I had no desire to meet up with those creatures without any weapons that might put them down.

I had just closed that door when I heard them beyond. Considering the speed with which they could move, I was surprised they hadn't reached me sooner.

Here, another bolt, and I secured it forcefully.

This time I heard only a knock from the other side of the door. *Knock, knock.* They were playing with me!

I spun and raced down another hall, which ended in only one door. Opening it, I saw that this entrance led into a flight of stone stairs, which headed down. Into darkness.

My experience of the night before had left such a dark impression on me that I froze like ice there at the top of the steps. But I was without an alternative, so I plunged down into the darkness, for there was no flame to light the way.

The sound of my boots on the stone echoed around me, and I had the distinct impression that I was descending into hell, as real as I had never imagined it.

I found the end of the steps when I came up short and stumbled onto my knees in pitch darkness. But there was a sliver of orange light at the bottom of a door to my right. I staggered to it, found the handle to a door, and pulled it wide.

The stench that greeted me can hardly be described, like the smell of an unattended battlefield a week after the dead have been left to rot. The light came from a single torch beside another door on my left. The one the Russians would use to reach me assuming they knew where I had gone, which they surely did.

I headed right. Down a tunnel not unlike the one I had been in last evening, only this one was dank and the walls were covered with long fingers of moss. Why they would waste a torch to light this passage made no sense, unless it led to an exit that was frequently used. What other purpose would serve such a passage?

I rushed on, hoping the light fading behind me would meet the reach of another torch soon. My mind was a shell of itself. The events that had led up to that moment clogged my understanding of all that was real. I could head into any battle with a sword and a pistol and deal with any man or any army of men. I could be taken captive by an enemy and live in their dungeons until they grew tired of my outlasting will.

But here in this place my heart had been stolen and my mind had been stripped of all that I assumed to be normal.

Faint light flickered ahead and to my right.

I sprinted to a gated entrance along the wall and gripped steel bars. Beyond them was what appeared to be a study with one desk on the left and bookcases on the other walls. Nothing short of a prison. A torch blazed next to a large framed portrait of the creature I'd seen depicted before in this castle, that grotesque bat with folded wings. A creature of the night. A demon from hell.

But there was also a door at the back of that study, I saw.

A peal of muted thunder reached into the tunnel. I twisted and looked down the dark passage. Not a hint of light.

I couldn't head back the way I had come. They would be there, waiting.

The sound of that thunder had come from somewhere. I lifted the latch and pulled the iron gate open with an unnerving grate of metal against metal. Then I closed it behind me to leave no sign I'd entered.

Another peal of thunder, this one from beyond that door if there was a God and he was merciful. Not merciful to me, but to Lucine. Even my escaping was a kind of abandonment, and I will say that a large part of me wanted only to rush back upstairs and share her fate, whatever that might be. Wasn't it possible that I could still find a way to rescue her, however unlikely?

She doesn't love you, Toma.

I cursed my mind for the thought as I hurried for the wood door.

A single name was etched into brass beneath the framed portrait. *Alucard*. So then devils had names. Valerik or Alucard or Beelzebub, names didn't matter to me. But there was some truth to the ranting of the priests after all, and this mattered much.

The door was unlocked. I paused for a moment to listen beyond the beating of my heart, then I pulled the door open.

Now I could hear the storm outside. Lightning flashed, illuminating a long vacant tunnel ending in steps that led up.

I was running already, not bothering to close the door behind me this time. New thoughts crashed through my mind. A fresh fear for Lucine now that I had seen the naked power of these Russians. They weren't Russians at all but something less than human.

I slid to a stop at the bottom of the stairs, and now I saw the rain falling above, illuminated from behind by flashes of lightning. But how could I leave her? I could not! I couldn't go down the mountain knowing that Lucine was in his clutches.

I had to go back!

And I almost did.

But before I was a lover, I was a warrior, and I knew that my flesh and blood could not influence the fight waged by these powers. I had to get out and return with help!

These stone stairs ended in a small enclosure that protected them from the rain. I'd dropped my jacket off my back in the front entrance; there would be no retrieving it. I only hoped that my horse was still tied up as I'd left him.

But I was free of the castle. That was the—

"Hello, Toma."

I spun to my left. He stood there at the edge of this entryway. I didn't know who he was, because he wore a hood that kept his face deep in shadow. I could only see those red eyes, staring at me like twin cherries. His voice was low and gravelly, unlike any I'd heard, surely not entirely human.

And just as surely I knew that I could not in my right mind beat this man.

"She is mine now," the man said. "This time I told them to let you go. If I had not, you would be dead, my friend. But if you return I will kill you. And I will kill Lucine as well."

Now I did know. This was Vlad van Valerik.

Bitterness and rage flooded me. Uttering a feral cry of outrage, I hurled myself at the figure in two long strides, headlong.

I plowed into the wall behind him, palms, elbows, then chest.

A small chuckle rose to my left, but I couldn't see where he'd vanished to in such a hurry. These Russians could move with inhuman speed!

"Leave her!" I cried. "Leave her and I will spare you!" The words came from my heart, not my head.

The chuckle had already faded. I was left alone with the wind howling at my back and the rain wetting my shirt. I tell you it was all I could do to find a thread of good sense in my battered mind.

But I did, and the moment I found it, I turned and strode into the torrent, around the castle, all along cursing my failure.

My trusted steed was hunkered down against the storm as I'd

trained him. I ran to him, leaped upon his back, and headed down the mountain, a beaten and pathetic man.

But I would return.

I would be back if it cost me my life.

like the wind only days later. What devastation could be done on the battlefield with an army of these!

But I had heard that evil feared the crucifix. Holy water could scald a witch's skin. Perhaps there was some truth to these rumors—I was certain to find out.

With the clearing weather, my journey was soon on dry ground, and however dirtied, my shirt and trousers were dried by the wind. I didn't bother tying my horse by the church's porch—he was too shredded to take another step.

The entrance was open, thank God. I plowed in, uncaring about my presentation on the red carpet that ran through the seating for the likes of me, unbelievers. This was the narthex, if I recalled.

"Hello there?" I shouted.

Marching into the next chamber, the nave, I found it also empty. But the door was open, so someone must be attending to the church.

"Hello there! I have urgent business in the name of Her Majesty, Catherine. Who's there?"

Not a peep. So I headed up the aisle, under the great dome with its painting of Christ, past the bishop's throne and choirs, to the foot of the steps that led to what they called the Beautiful Gates—the door into the sanctuary behind. Now, I wasn't a churchman, but I knew that this richly painted wall with its images of angels and the Christ beneath a golden crucifix was a barrier to all but clergy.

But I was needing clergy now. So I stepped up on the platform, past the golden candlesticks, and into the sanctuary behind.

"Hello?"

The altar was there along with the censer and other religious paraphernalia that I was only vaguely familiar with. But there was no priest here.

A gospel book lay open on the altar, and I grabbed it straightaway. This instrument was the holiest of all religious artifacts, surely. If the church had any tools to deal with the devil, they would be a part of this book.

A door to one side slammed; feet pattered away; a voice called frantically. Someone had seen me and gone to fetch a higher authority. I paced, hoping for them to speed up.

For over an hour I had ridden south, away from Lucine. I was certain that, at the very least, she had tasted the same blood that had turned me to milk. In such a weakened state she would have then been subjected to much worse. She, like Natasha and Alek, might succumb and embrace whatever witchery they were serving. Then I would lose her!

And yet I was down here, so far removed from that mountain pass that I might as well be back in Moscow, asleep in a warm bed. It was unforgivable!

"What are you doing?" a voice snapped.

I twisted to the side door where a holy man stood, eyes round at my intrusion into his sacred space. "You're Julian Petrov?" I asked.

"I am the bishop." His eyes ran down my body and settled on my boots. They were clotted with dried mud. I had left crumbs on his red floor.

"Get out!" he demanded.

His tone was not the kind I appreciated. "I don't think you understand, Your Eminence. I have the most urgent business ordered by Her Majesty, Catherine the Great."

"Then say it outside where you belong. Not in God's sanctuary!"

The man had a large nose and big ears for such a narrow face. His red robes were loose and his black cap was slightly askew, giving me the impression he'd thrown them on before rushing here.

"I have come to solicit God's help," I said. "Surely he'll understand."

"By setting foot in this sanctuary and crossing me, you have defiled his body. Any believer knows this! Out, man, out!" He thrust a shaking finger at the door.

Now I grew incensed myself.

"But I'm not a believer. So I'm not subject to your rules. Now listen to me, you priest, I've just come from the most terrifying vision of evil. I've come to meet your God and see if he can save me. Are you telling me your great God is put off by my mud?"

"Cleanliness is next to godliness. But you of no learning would know nothing of that. Now please, if you don't mind, leave this sanctuary."

"Do you know who I am?"

"Should I?"

"My name is Toma Nicolescu. I was sent by Her Majesty to oversee the safety of the Cantemir estate—you're familiar with the letter I left with your man?"

He hesitated. Clearly I'd gained his attention. His eyes grabbed another look at my dirty boots. "What of it?"

I paced in front of him. "Lucine Cantemir has been taken captive. I have reason to believe that her life is in danger. But I don't have at my disposal the tools I need to deliver her."

"I don't command an army."

"But you can command the devil, yes? Because she is taken by hell itself, I swear, and we must return at once to deliver her."

His eyes lingered on me for a long while, trying to judge me. "What devil?"

"He goes by the name Vlad van Valerik, and he lives in the Castle Castile with his retinue, a coven of witches who drink blood and seduce the innocent."

Not a hint of alarm crossed his face. I realized that I must be sounding like a lunatic.

"I was just there," I snapped. "I too drank that blood, and it twisted my thinking!"

"I was told that Lucine is being courted by—"

"You know of this?" I demanded, shocked by his knowledge.

"I was informed by a messenger from Lady Cantemir, yes. And you must know that I approve. The duke is a man of significant standing. What is this nonsense about drinking blood? It's an outrage!"

"I drank that blood! I saw what they did to Natasha and to my man, Alek Cardei! They have become shells of themselves." His eyes were dark with doubt. He wasn't going to help me. I saw it on his face and I struggled not to lose my self-restraint. We didn't have time for this!

I grabbed a candlestick and shook it, sending the white candle flying. "For the love of all that is holy, man, give me something to fight evil! Tell me what I must know!"

"This is sacrilege!" he cried.

"Then pay me some respect!"

He reached out lovingly for the candlestick. "Please, put the candle down. You are defiling our sanctuary."

"Tell me you have the means to put a devil down."

"I do. I do . . . please."

I gave him his precious candlestick. "Then tell me. I will do whatever is needed. Convert me, baptize me, commission me, give me the means."

The bishop sighed. "I would guess that you are the devil here."

"Does the devil wish to fight the devil?"

He frowned at me, then stormed out of the sanctuary. I followed.

"Thank you," he said. "Now tell me what you know."

So I did. I told him the whole story, beginning with Valerik's first visit to the Cantemir estate and the death and resurrection of Stefan. I explained the events of last night, when I'd been bewitched by drinking the blood, and I did not skip a single detail through my meeting of Valerik as I escaped from the castle only two hours earlier. He watched with one eyebrow raised half the time.

When I finished, he stared at me as if I might indeed be a lunatic.

"You don't believe me?"

He walked over to a cabinet and poured himself a glass of brandy, threw it back, and swallowed in one gulp.

"I don't have all night, man!" I said. "She's up there at this moment, turning into whatever they are."

The bishop faced me, stern. "You've never been baptized?"

"No."

"You're not Christian?"

"Of course I am."

"But you aren't a member of the body of Christ. You're not in the church. So then you cannot be Christian."

"I am a warrior for this church, fellow!" I tried to calm myself.

"I have killed a thousand of her enemies. Forgive me, Your Eminence, but I must know how to defeat evil. I love the woman!"

"While I appreciate your loyalty to defeating Christ's enemies, you're clearly ignorant. You speak of love? I can tell you that passions of the heart have nothing to do with defeating evil."

"Then what does?"

"Obeying the church. Fleeing immorality and washing your hands of all sin. Fasting, almsgiving, holy communion, repentance, unction; these will cleanse you. You must believe in the triune God, the death and resurrection of Christ, and the bride, which is his church today."

"I don't have time for all of that tonight. Come with me. You can expose this evil for what it is! Bring your crucifix and your holy book and help me strip Vlad van Valerik of his charade."

"He's a Christian, you fool."

"Then he's an evil Christian who drinks the blood of innocents."

This statement brought an immediate scowl to the bishop's face, and I regretted making it. "No Christian can be evil," he said. "They are cleansed by the church."

"Please, I don't know what makes a man good with God. I only know that I need you to rescue Lucine from this evil. If I were a proper Christian, I would do it myself."

He studied me.

I pressed the matter. "Surely you've run into this sort of thing in your service."

The bishop stared past me. "Not personally, no. But I've heard whispers on the wind. Tales of this blood drinking."

"And?"

He spoke in a soft voice, as if hardly able to believe it himself. "Carpathian devils, made so by drinking the blood of the dead. Creatures of the night that have extraordinary powers and feed on innocent blood. It is said that a wooden stake through the heart will kill them. It is said that they fear water blessed by God."

He broke his stare from the wall and looked at me again. "Are you sure it was blood that you drank?"

"I believe it was, yes."

The bishop turned away. "Hmm . . . Then we will help you. You must go back to the Cantemir estate and wait for us. At first light—"

"I can't wait until—"

"We can't go in the dark. Evil is always stronger in the dark! If you want my help, it will be at first light."

An eternity! The thought of waiting twisted my gut.

"Those are my conditions," he said, and he drained another splash of brandy.

"So then, you will be able to help me?"

"We'll see. With God's grace, I think we can set you straight."

"It's not me I care about. It's her. It's him!"

"So you've said. We will dispel evil, I can promise you that."

I had no good alternative. So I dipped my head in agreement.

"So be it. I will wait for you. First light."

"First light."

"Not a moment later."

He turned and walked through the door to his sanctuary.

TWENTY-FOUR

She woke and it was dark, but she couldn't be sure if she was really awake. It felt more like a dream. A nightmare.

Her eyes were indeed open. She'd forced her eyelids to slits, then pulled them wider, despite the sensation that someone had sprinkled sand under her lids while she slept. Orange light shifted shadows on the wall. She was still in the bedroom. This was Vlad van Valerik's bedroom.

The man was a beast.

A shadow formed like a massive frog crawled up the wall. A ghost. But that was in her mind's eye, her dream. It had to be. She was still in her dream. Possibly sleeping in her bed at the estate, disturbed by what had happened to Natasha these past few days.

None of what she'd dreamed could be true. She hadn't turned her back on Toma or accepted the offer from the duke. She hadn't let Vlad take her to the meadow or kiss her. She hadn't dined with them or tasted that bitter blood when he held the goblet to her lips.

And she surely hadn't let him bite her and taste her blood. Or let him inject his blood into her mouth.

This was all a nightmare. She was safe in bed and Toma was near, vowed to save her from any harm.

Something pressed into the back of her leg and pulled her from her thoughts. A soft groan followed by a sharp cry.

Natasha! Her sister had come to comfort her after that beast had tossed her about and left. Then that was part of the dream as well?

Her sister's laugh cut the stillness. "No, Stefan," she breathed, but then laughed again, as if being tickled.

Lucine parted her mouth. Pain spread down her chin, through her breast, down her legs. The pain hit her like a hammer and she gasped.

"Natasha!"

The form behind her jerked up. "Lucine?"

She dared not move again. Tears stung her eyes. "Natasha?"

Silence for a moment, than a tender hand on her shoulder.

"Shh, Sister," Natasha whispered. "Try to stay calm."

"It hurts."

"I know. I know, it's the turning. The pain is part of your trans-formation. Accept it, it will pass."

"I'm changing?"

"You'll like it, Lucine, I swear you will. It feels terrible at times, being like this, but there's so much love and fear together, you know?"

"I don't want that, Natasha! What's happening to me? What did I do?"

Her sister went deathly quiet. Lucine tried to roll over to see her, but the pain in her joints was too much. She pushed her hand into the mattress to help ease herself and saw her arm then.

Her skin was gray. Covered by a disease. Flaking!

She panicked. Rolled despite the pain. "Natasha!"

"Shh, shh, shh." Tears glistened in her sister's eyes. "It will pass."

"Am I dead?"

"No. Shh, please stay calm. He's given you his blood. It's much more powerful than the others', so your change is quicker. You'll be his bride, Lucine. He's the master, the direct descendant of a queen. He can have only one bride. You'll be very special to him. It's a great honor."

"I don't want to be his bride!"

"No, you will! When you change, you will want it."

"Why didn't you tell me about this pain, Natasha? You betrayed me!"

Natasha sniffed. Then she lowered her face onto Lucine's shoulder and she sobbed.

"I'm sorry . . . I'm so sorry, Lucine. It all grows fuzzy." She lifted her face and stared with glassy eyes. "But you'll adore him. You'll be so happy. I swear it, I would never hurt you, Sister!"

"What's . . ." She lifted her arm and stared at her flaking skin. "What's wrong with me?"

"When you emerge, your skin will be pure and white, so

beautiful. They will all be in awe of you. The bride! It will be wonderful, Lucine."

She had enough good sense to know that her sister had lost all her objectivity. She herself was surely not far behind.

"Natasha?"

"Shh, Sister. Sleep."

"Natasha . . ."

Natasha began to cry again.

TWENTY-FIVE

I could not sleep that night.

I could not eat. I could not fix my hair, nor change my shirt, nor bathe. These tasks seemed pointless to me, utterly trivial in the face of my fear for Lucine. I thought about them but I could not summon the energy to break away from my misery.

Instead, I stood on the balcony outside my room and I paced, arms wrapped around my chest, eyes on those tall Carpathian peaks to the west. The weather had cleared down here, but ominous clouds still hugged the mountains. It was all I could do not to rush back up the road on my horse.

Indeed, I considered every possible rescue. A stealthy climb up the tower wall or a bold entry right through the front, up the tower, and out the window with a rope.

If not for the promise of the bishop, I would have attempted anything that held the slightest hope for success. The Russians wouldn't expect such a quick return after beating me so soundly. I would have at least that in my favor. But I knew that I had confronted evil up in that castle, and the church was now Lucine's best hope. If I went and failed, she would be doomed.

So I paced and I wondered about this love that had enslaved me. And it was in those wee hours that I remembered again the old man with the crow, the messenger from God who'd come to warn us.

Why warn me? Why single me out? Why go to such trouble to deliver a few words? Having discovered that God must be real, I found new meaning in the old man's visit. God had come to me in the form of that crooked bird.

I recalled his words directly: *"God was the one who told me to tell Toma Nicolescu that evil is in contest with you."*

He knew? A contest over what? It could only be Lucine! Perhaps this explained my nearly inexplicable and immediate attraction to her.

That the old man knew Vlad and I would be in this predicament was astounding. Had I known such a dark horse was on the horizon waiting to take her away, I would have kissed her feet and hands and vowed my love when I'd first fallen for her!

And did this mean that I was *meant* to love her? Yes, it must!

Which could only mean that she now depended on me alone.

From that moment forward I thought of myself differently. I was no longer the servant of Her Majesty, Catherine the Great, but the servant of God himself, on a mission to save the one who was courted by this devil.

I was indeed the savior, aching to love and save she who would be loved and saved. It was scandalous to think of myself in such an esteemed way. But it must be! I was her only savior, and the beast up the mountain was the devil on bat's wings, as the old man had said.

The moment this became clear to me, I raged. I could not stand there and stare up at those mountains a moment longer.

So I rushed into my room, pulled out my journal, and wrote by candlelight.

> *My love, Lucine,*
>
> *Forgive me! I would cut my hands off for not taking yours sooner. I would sever my tongue for not speaking my heart. Now you are there in that beast's castle, enduring his torture . . .*

I lifted the quill and thought. For all I knew she was laughing with hilarity up there, as Natasha and Alek had. I had no evidence that Lucine was not madly in love with the duke. But I shoved the thought from my mind because it only made me rage all the more.

> *. . . and I am here, enslaved by my own regret.*
>
> *I am destroyed by an unearthly love for you, my tender, beautiful one. Nothing matters to me now except that I destroy the evil that threatens you.*
>
> *I will bring all the armies of Russia here to level these mountains if that is what I must do to save you. I will fire a thousand cannons on that tower, I will crush those infidels with a hundred blows each.*

I will take the hand of God and drag him into those walls so
that the darkness must flee. Then I will be the light that crashes in
and sweeps you into my arms.

I dipped the quill and hovered over that page. My chest felt as though it might burst.

Lucine, my love, I beg you, hear my cry in your heart even now.
Love me. Love me, I beg you, love me . . .

It was too much, this pathetic plea! I dropped the quill on the desk and lowered my head into my hands to contain my tears.

When gray was yet an imagination on the black sky, I was out on the road, pacing again, like the father waiting for a prodigal. The darkness receded far more stubbornly than I believed it could, but day finally came.

And there was still no sign of that cursed bishop and his big ears. Still, I had no good alternative except to stand and wait, so I did.

"Toma!"

I turned to the house and saw that Kesia stood at the front door. A clergyman stood beside her. The bishop! Dressed in his red robes and black hat. How Petrov had gotten there I neither knew nor cared. He'd probably come before sunrise.

I hurried up to the doors. "Thank you, Your Eminence. Thank you for coming. I was worried."

"I am a man made of my word." But he looked more like a man made of stone.

I stopped and glanced between them. "You've brought what we need?"

"What would that be?"

"The weapons, man! The books, the blessed water, the cruci-fix, that wood stake, whatever you need to defeat evil. We should go immediately!"

"A word first, if you don't mind."

"Then let's hurry. Speak."

"Come inside, Toma," Kesia said, turning into the house. "A cup of tea perhaps."

"Madam, begging your pardon, but we don't have time to make small talk." I hadn't spoken to her since coming down from my journey to the Castle Castile but I assumed that the bishop had. "You know what we're up against here?"

"His Eminence has explained it, yes. And it's a delicate mat-ter. Sit."

We'd crossed the main room to a small tea table where a silver pot already steamed. I was far too anxious to sit, but when the bishop took his chair, I felt presumptuous standing, so I sat on the edge of the sofa.

"So then, let's speak," I said.

Kesia looked at the bishop, who wore a deep frown. He nodded and looked at me. "You are aware of who the man you accuse is."

"Yes. And frankly I don't care who he is. He could be the king of France and I would still carry out my charge."

"Perhaps if he were, I would be less reluctant. But you're charging a man who may hold the future of Russia in his hands. Of witchcraft, no less. Do you know the punishment for the dark arts?"

"I don't care about your punishment! I want only to take Lucine out of his hand. I have made my oath to the empress!"

"So I hear." He accepted some tea from Kesia. No one else was in the room that I could see. "I also hear that you are quite taken with Lucine."

I could not deny it after my full confession to Kesia. "My heart has taken an unexpected turn, yes."

"Against the order of our empress, no less."

I stood, face hot. "I am here to fulfill my charge. How dare you suggest I stand in compromise to the one I serve?"

He took a sip of that steaming tea, showing no sign of hurry whatsoever. "How do you suppose your heart was so taken against orders?"

"It doesn't matter. She is in trouble."

"So you say. And the punishment for the cause of this trouble, assuming there is witchcraft involved, is burning. You're demanding that we burn the duke, Vlad van Valerik, because you have fallen in love with the woman who has granted him the right to court."

"That's absurd!"

"Sit!" he snapped.

We faced off, he seated, I standing, and I saw that if I wanted any chance at his help, I must show my respect. So again, I sat.

"Forgive me," I said. "This is a highly unusual situation for me."

His dark eyes showed no relief at or acceptance of my apology.

"You have said some things of terrible concern to any man of God, sir. There can only be three explanations as I see it."

The lady Kesia was not her jovial self but fixed and distant. Something was not right here. I could see that they'd met and come to some understanding. They weren't going to help me.

The bishop continued. "The first is that you are mistaken. That whatever you saw was innocent. An expression of simple passion common among those of considerable means."

"No, I know what I saw."

"The second is that you saw unspeakable wickedness on the part of the duke and that he and his retinue are the handiwork of the devil." He crossed himself. "May God forgive my words."

"I can only say what I saw," I said.

"A most heinous accusation that would rip through the royal court and affect the empress herself."

I had not considered this.

"And the third?" I asked.

A blunt object pressed against the back of my skull. Immediately I knew—this was a pistol. I was being detained. My muscles started and I very nearly spun and slapped the weapon away, as I would have had I been among enemies. But I was with a bishop and in the service of Her Majesty to protect this household. So I remained perfectly still.

The bishop's eyes didn't move from mine.

"The third is that *you* have been infected with evil, Toma Nicolescu. And I would not move. He has orders to shoot if you do; all the exits are covered."

The full scope of their treachery swarmed me. I considered my alternatives and decided immediately that my chances for any escape would be better later, if indeed I chose to make that attempt.

My voice was rough, cut with fury. "This is an outrage."

"It is not uncommon for the ungodly to be bewitched without their knowledge. You have spoken knowledge that puts me in a difficult position. Either you or the duke seems to have slipped into the devil's claws. I can't burn another man, much less a royal, on the word of one whose head and heart are suspect."

There it was. I had not foreseen this possibility because I was so ignorant in the ways of the church. If I'd known better, I might have taken the bishop by force the night before and hauled him up to the castle to see for himself!

I looked at Kesia. "Madam, I beg you. You have to consider what I'm saying. I was there. I drank the blood! What else explains Natasha's and Alek's behavior? You saw them!"

"You drank blood," the bishop said. "And now you speak of tales that only a man who's visited hell itself could speak of!"

"Then cast that hell out of me and let's be on with it!"

"We will try."

"Then try."

"In time."

"We don't have time! Madam, your daughters are becoming something they were not. I beg you to let me do what I was born to do here."

"And what is that, Toma? To love and bewitch Lucine?"

I could see only red then. These fools were actually thinking that I was the devil, while the one we all loved was trapped in the real villain's cage.

That pistol was still against my head. Two soldiers dressed in the gray of the local militia stepped around the sofa bearing shackles. I, a hero of all Russia who had the authority of the empress, was put in shackles by a bishop.

"This is a mistake! I have a higher authority."

"And I have the authority of God," the bishop said. "Restrain him!"

They pulled me to my feet and clamped the shackles to my wrists. However much I wanted to resist, I knew it would only earn me a bullet in the back, for there wasn't just one pistol trained on me, but three. And I had no weapon.

"Take him to our dungeon in Crysk," the bishop ordered, turning away from us all.

Crysk! "No, hold me here while you explore the Castle Castile. I swear you will return and release me!"

"These things take time," the man said without turning. "An invitation will be sent to the duke. He will be given ample opportunity to explain any misunderstandings."

"An invitation? Of course he'll say what he needs to say, you fool!"

"He will say what he should say!" the man snapped, whirling back. "He is a Christian!"

Then he marched out of the room.

I should have felt humiliated, but I was too terrified for Lucine to worry about my standing.

"Madam, I swear you are making a choice that will undo your entire fortune if your daughters are in high value," I rasped. "You can still undo this!"

A flash of concern lit Kesia's eyes, but she only turned away. "You are out of your league, Toma." Then she too left the room.

I was hauled unceremoniously into a cart used to carry common drunks, then chained to a steel ring in the back. No amount of resistance or argument would help me now. I was headed south, toward Crysk, away from the Cantemir estate, away from the Castle Castile.

Away from Lucine.

TWENTY-SIX

Light streamed through drawn drapes when the black sleep first retreated from Lucine's mind like tar melting off a skull under a hot sun. So deep was her dream that she could remember nothing of it. She was hardly even aware of her own existence, only that she was waking. Layers of death were fading. She was being born. A butterfly emerging from a cocoon.

And still her eyelids felt as if they were made of lead.

She became aware of a cool breeze drifting across her body. The scent of earth after a hard rain was carried on that breeze. And beyond that, the smell of roses and pine needles. Cool water ran through a mountain brook, gurgling over mossy rocks—she could hear it. A horse whinnied; a laugh echoed softly from far away.

Her eyes opened briefly then closed against the bright light. They slowly opened again. She lay on her back with her hands clasped over her belly, facing the white silk draped over a canopy bed. Vlad van Valerik's bed.

She was alone. Her muscles and bones felt heavy, like stone, but her senses were screaming with vitality. Prisms of red and green shone where the light struck the golden bands fashioned around the bedposts. A candle scented with vanilla burned somewhere.

Memories from last night drifted into her mind. Vlad, the dinner, the blood. His bite. She was to be his bride.

Lucine blinked and moved her fingers. Her hands. Then lifted one arm up so that she could see it. The pain she'd suffered was gone. Flakes spotted her arms, like a snake's dead coat. But beneath lay a new, beautiful layer of white skin.

She sat up, expecting her rising to be sluggish. Instead she rose effortlessly, as if her upper torso had lost all of its weight during the night. A burgundy bedspread hugged her body, neatly folded at her breasts. She absently rubbed her arms. The dead flakes fell away leaving skin so pale that it appeared translucent in some places.

She gently pulled the bedding away from her naked body. The sheets were covered with the white flakes, and much more hung to her flesh, so delicately that most of it fell away when she moved. She'd been changed.

She wasn't sure what to make of that.

A strong scent that might be blood or sweat or bile tickled her nostrils, and she looked up to see Vlad in the doorway, watching her. She could smell him.

"You are beautiful, my darling."

Lucine opened her mouth to speak, felt the cracking of her lips. She touched her tongue to her lower lip and tasted the dried blood. The pain from his bite was gone.

"Beautiful," he said, approaching.

Vlad was dressed in black as was his custom—a long cloak and black trousers. A white shirt beneath a leather vest with brass buttons. His collar was loose and hung open, revealing his white chest, marked by blue veins just below the surface.

She vaguely remembered that he had beaten her in the night. But the memory seemed distant now, obscured by the explosion of sensations that throbbed through her mind.

He leaned over her, and the smell of his breath came as a quickening stench that could be flowers or dank mud, she couldn't decide.

His mouth lowered to hers and he licked her lips with the tip of his tongue. "I own you now, my bride."

Fear sliced through her mind. Then was gone. Her breathing thickened. Vlad straightened and paced. For a moment that stretched for a long while, he kept looking at her. She didn't know what to say. What to ask.

"On the third night we will be wed, here in the castle," he said. "Does this excite you?"

"I . . ."

She didn't know.

"No, you're too confused still," he bit off. "But you will. I will make you crave me for the pain it will save you. The castle will be yours. More power and love than you could have hoped for, here under my rule. A queen. My bride." He paced. "Say something."

She really didn't know what to say. She only wanted to bathe and see what had happened to her body. She wanted to leave this room. She wanted to find her mother. She wanted to drink and soothe her parched throat.

But she must say something.

"What happened to me?"

He smiled, but reluctantly, she thought. Sitting on the bed, he ran his long fingers down her leg, clearing the flakes as a twig might clear ash from a marble statue.

"I have given you my blood. Some might call it a disease; I call it life. My kind are ancient and we live a very long time, hundreds of years or more, depending on the purity of the blood. I am the last half-breed. There is only one full breed, called Alucard, who could make half-breeds, naturally, but he chooses not to for now. There are thousands of lessers in numerous secret covens. The others take many mates, but half-breeds take only one."

His hand traced her side up to her shoulder and neck. "You, my darling, are to be the bride of a half-breed. My blood is very powerful. The transformation you've seen already would normally take days and would never progress to this state. You will be very special, Lucine."

"I will?" Her voice was raspy.

"They will be in awe of you."

"I'm . . ." Her mind spun with all of this talk. The thought at once terrified and fascinated her.

"Don't stammer, it's unbecoming."

"I'm a half-breed?"

"A little blood doesn't give you that lofty status. Don't be ridiculous. You're the carrier of the half-breed's blood. Made by me. I offered you my blood and you took it gladly. I am your serpent and you are my Eve. And in our world, my darling, that is a very beautiful thing."

"But that doesn't tell me what I am," she said, gaining her voice. She looked at her white forearm. "What is this disease that you gave me? Am I . . . Can I be rid of it?"

"Rid of it? You've only just been born into it. My love for you knows no bounds! I have given you a gift that every woman alive would willingly die for. And you would throw that away for what?"

"I don't know." She felt the pressure of tears build behind her eyes. "I'm just frightened, Vlad."

For a moment he appeared angry by her confession. But then a comforting smile pulled his mouth into a shallow show of empathy. "Only because you don't understand yet, poor darling. You've given up the life you knew, so yes, it must be terrifying. But I have given you the world, you'll see that."

"Am I dead?"

"Heavens no," he scoffed. "Then you'd be in hell, now wouldn't you? You're alive, and with my blood will remain alive for longer than most. You will thirst for more blood; it is our drug. All other food is only for simple pleasure and growth. But the drug is what keeps us strong. Wicked! Full of love and passion."

He looked so powerful hovering over her. Like a god, and she his prey. She looked at his parted lips, recalling the way he'd kissed her the night before. His white teeth were hidden.

"They will come for you, my bride. My enemy will try to steal you. It's his way. He will try to make you fear me." He gently ran his thumb along her cheek. "And then I would be unable to control my rage. You haven't seen anger here, because we are full of love.

But it could not stop me from destroying your family. We would ruin this earth!"

She was unnerved by the confusion she felt when he spoke. "Please don't talk that way," Lucine said.

"In time you'll understand the full weight of my power. But first, come."

He lifted her hand and she swung her feet to the floor, then stood. Her toes tingled.

"Dance with me!" He snapped his fingers and a fiddle started up, far away, but she could hear it perfectly clear, as if it were playing in her ear.

Vlad slid one hand around her waist and swung her around. Flakes spun off her skin like dandelion seeds scattered by a puff of breath. She felt as agile and energetic as a gazelle.

He pulled her close and pressed her body against his chest. "Let me feed you, darling."

His lips were on hers instantly, and she abandoned her first impulse to pull away. He did not bite her, though she expected it, wanted it.

"Taste me," he said.

Bite him?

In answer to her unspoken question he opened his mouth and offered her his lower lip. She took it into her mouth and he moaned.

"Please," he said.

Lucine bit gently at first.

"Harder."

She did, until a warmth flooded her teeth and gums and flowed into her mouth. She swallowed his blood.

That same tingle that had tickled her feet rose up her legs and through her belly, swarming her chest and throat, dizzying her mind.

A gentle moan rose through her throat. What kind of ecstasy was this? What kind of drug? An aphrodisiac or opium or more; surely, far more.

Vlad's body trembled against hers. And then he eased away and cupped her chin in his hand.

"This, my love, is the darkness I offer you. An eternal life with me, feeding upon each other's dark souls. The power I offer is beyond comparison. No price you pay will be enough."

"Yes."

"When they come for you, remember that."

"I will."

"Now bathe. Dress. I will send Sofia to help you. Then we will show them all what we have done."

⚜

Lucine could have soaked for an hour for all she knew. Time was off center, hardly linear. The dead cells fell away with the hot water, leaving her skin pure and pale from head to foot.

I am a snake, she thought. *An albino reptile. Floating in a warm sky.*

Sofia came in and helped wash her hair, silently watching Lucine with wide, dark eyes. When the water cooled, Lucine stood and stepped into a black robe held by Sofia. Her skin felt as if it were on fire, wrapped up in that robe, too sensitive to be touched by such a crude cloth.

"Thank you," she said.

"It is my honor, my queen."

Queen. It was all so heady. So rich. So then why did she feel so powerless? So empty and hollow under this translucent skin?

She faced Sofia, who took a step backward and dipped her head. A terrible sadness overwhelmed her and she thought she might burst into tears right there, standing as the queen of snakes.

When she didn't speak or move, Sofia lifted her head and stared at her face. An understanding passed between them. Tears misted Sofia's eyes.

I'm sorry, Lucine.

The words were clear, put in her mind by Sofia. Sorry for what? Something was wrong, wasn't it? Beneath all of this beauty and power there was a deep pool of dark sorrow that remained hidden. Natasha had expressed it. Vlad had lashed out at her. Fear returned to her, a searing, painful fear that seemed to flow from her bones.

She spoke in an unsteady whisper. "What's wrong?"

A single tear broke from Sofia's right eye and trailed down her cheek.

I cannot . . .

No more. Just that.

"Please, Sofia. I'm frightened."

Another tear from Sofia's other eye. Then they streamed down her face. But no words, only this silent weeping that broke Lucine's resolve to be any sort of queen.

She began to weep. But she wasn't as reserved as Sofia. She walked to a chair covered in red silk, sank to her knees, lay her head on the seat cushion, and wept. She couldn't express the remorse that drained her of these tears. Her mind was a pit of emptiness that had no bottom. Her heart seemed to have stopped, although she could hear it beating in her chest.

"Am I dead?" she sobbed.

Sofia spoke quietly, with some effort. "They are waiting, my queen."

Lucine faced her. "Not until you tell me what has happened to me."

The woman wiped her own tears with the back of her hand and glanced at the door. "You've been made by a half-breed. Among us that makes you a queen."

"I don't want to be a queen."

Please, Lucine. Please don't make me cry again. Then aloud, "But that will change. Your mind is still deeply upset by your . . ." She hesitated. "Your transition."

It occurred to Lucine that Sofia had put herself in some kind of danger by what she'd said without speaking. Perhaps she had a true friend here, then?

"Tell me more," she whispered. "Tell me I'm not dead."

"You look ravishing, my queen. And you will see just how alive you are."

Lucine stared at her.

Please. Please, no more.

So Lucine stood, light as a feather, and walked into the bedroom. They dressed her in leggings woven like a fisherman's net and boots to her knees. Then a long, black, lace-sleeved gown that parted at her thighs and swept elegantly to the floor on either side and behind. They combed out her long dark hair, allowing it to dry naturally in soft waves. Sofia placed a black velvet choker with a single red ruby around her neck.

And all the while, not a word. Not even a thought from Sofia.

Her appointed handmaiden led her downstairs, through the dining room where they'd eaten last evening, and into the grand ballroom.

It was bright day outside, past noon perhaps, but in this room there was only darkly stained glass in an overhead dome to allow hints of sunlight inside. Through an image of a winged creature. A hundred candles in sconces and a massive chandelier cast an orange hue over those gathered.

The entire retinue stood waiting in groups, up the twin stairs, along the balcony. Dozens. Perhaps a hundred, all dressed in black, including Natasha and Alek, who stood to the right with Dasha and Stefan.

Vlad stood at the center, fixated upon her. Utter silence engulfed the room. Every eye watched. She could feel their stares like a hundred peering moons.

Lucine saw it all in a rather disconnected state. But then her appreciation for this show of honor sank in and her pulse surged. Sofia left her side and joined her sister.

Vlad smiled, spread his arms wide, and looked around the room. "On the third night, in two more cycles, I will marry. My friends, I present to you my bride and my queen!"

The sound started out as a simple rhythmic tapping of feet, then swelled to a stomping, all in unison. *Boom, boom, boom, boom.*

Vlad slowly walked toward her, eyes drinking hers, drawing her with such compulsion that she could hardly stop her own feet from stepping forward.

In the time it took to blink once, he crossed the room. Then he was over her, one arm around her waist, hot mouth hovering over hers. Feet filled the air with thunder.

"Then, my dear, there will be no turning back," he breathed.

He kissed her lightly, and as his lips lingered, the stomping crescendoed. She saw past him to the eyes, all staring, all glaring, all feeding upon her and Vlad in wonder.

But in that moment a new sound reached into her mind. A distant scream of anguish that swelled and shattered the pounding of boots in one bone-splitting shriek. Instead of human over her, she saw beast. A hunched, winged wolf.

The terror that slashed through her heart in that single moment was so raw that she could not think to scream. Then it was gone, replaced by a cheer from the Russians, who'd all raised brass goblets.

Humans all.

Vlad scooped up his own drink from a table and lifted it high. "To my bride and your queen, Lucine!"

"To the queen!"

They drank. Lucine breathed. Memory of the vision faded.

TWENTY-SEVEN

The dungeon they threw me into was attached to the monastery and had its own entrance, which would have provided access to the outer wall if I'd managed to break out of the prison. But they hadn't given me a single opportunity for escape. They'd chained my legs and arms before releasing me from the cart and dragging me down the stairs into the dank place.

I was the only prisoner; this wasn't a holding tank for commoners, only those whom orthodoxy wished to contain while the church investigated their crime. There were three other cells, all sealed off by iron bars, and a large room at the end whose purpose I would quickly discover. My cell was only four paces to a side, walled with stone and brick and littered with dirty straw to soak up some of the moisture from the ground. It smelled of mildew and sweat.

But none of this bothered me. My mind was spent on other matters.

I had to get out. I felt as if the demon had shot an arrow through my chest and pierced my heart.

There was no window to tell me how much day had passed, but with each passing hour that wound bled more. I grabbed the bars, thrust my head between them, and roared for the guards to attend to me. I was in Her Majesty's service and at the end, when they learned that I was an innocent man wrongly imprisoned, a full accounting would be made. They would pay with their lives!

I yelled this repeatedly, but either no one heard me or they thought me a lunatic. And at times I wondered if they might be right. If so, then love had driven me to it. Lucine was my lover. I could think of her in no other terms now. My lover was in mortal danger and I was powerless to save her.

My imagination of what Vlad van Valerik was doing to her knew few boundaries. I saw the vulture latched onto her with great claws, flying her away to the mountain peak to feed on her, and I screamed at those mountains to give her back.

I saw whips and chains tearing into her flesh, and I wept with her pain, tempted to claw at my own skin so that she would not be alone.

I saw that beast hovering over her limp form, choking her with one fist as he ripped her clothes off.

I saw tears streaming down Lucine's cheeks. And I sat in the corner and wept.

They came to me hours later, a tall gaunt man with a wicked

grin and his shorter henchman, who looked like a dog that hadn't been washed for a month. They stood outside the cell, holding a torch for light.

"At last!" I cried.

The tall one dipped his head as if courtesy mattered here in the earth. "I've come to hear if you have decided to make your confession."

I grabbed the bars. "What blasted confession? They're checking out my story, please tell me that."

"The story of a man whose soul is twisted by witchcraft can only be a lie. Your only recourse now is to confess so that God might have mercy."

"Then I confess! Now let me go about my duty. Let me out or I swear I will have your head when this is all over."

The man's grin stayed fixed. "You'd best not threaten God's servants. The next time I come down it will be to rack you." He motioned at the room down the hall with his head. "A hot skewer is known to loosen even the darkest tongue. Then you will scream for God's mercy."

"I'm screaming *now*, you fool." They intended on torturing me until I confessed to witchcraft? But that confession would only earn me a death sentence. I was trapped by these monsters. My only way out was to earn some sympathy or trust, and I was doing both badly.

I released the bars and held my hands in a show of surrender. "Forgive me, sir. Forgive me, but I am beside myself and at your mercy."

"True," he said.

"There has been a terrible mistake. If only you could reach the general in Moldavia, he would explain my esteemed position. I am well known as one of Russia's most celebrated heroes."

"Is that so?"

"But here, I'm glad to be your servant. My interest isn't for my life but for the life of Lucine Cantemir."

His right eye grew larger, brow arched. "The woman you have wrongfully loved?"

Did the whole of Moldavia know this? An outrage!

"Don't be absurd, man. I love all those put in my charge, if only to protect and serve them! I demand you contact the general immediately."

"Oh, we will. As soon as you bare your wicked soul."

Then the gaunt man turned and walked away, followed by that ghoulish dog of his. The light receded with them. If I could, I would have reached through the bars and strangled them both with my hands.

How could they know of my love for Lucine? Kesia had betrayed me! I was bared here for all the powers of darkness. They would gouge out my eyes and feed on my soul. I'd seen their kind of torture before, the worst kind that reduced common humans to excrement for the sake of religious confession.

I stood in my cell, trembling, reminded once again why I despised the church. It claimed to be the bride of God, but I couldn't see God marrying the bishop. The very instrument of Lucine's salvation would now snuff out her only hope. Me. The one man who loved her. I was powerless.

I fell to my knees in the corner and wept. They could dig out my eyes and rip out my veins, but none of their torture could compare to the pain that ravaged me in that corner.

I begged God to hear me. If he would not save Lucine, then I only wanted to die with her. My strength and control, all that had made me a hero in Russia, now felt like a curse. Useless. I was to be pitied as the warrior become a worm.

I lowered my head into my hands and I sobbed in great heaves that refused to release me. I could not breathe; I could not stand. I could only shake and groan.

The man who could not be broken by any army was crushed. I would have preferred to meet my death on the battlefield, because this kind of death was at the expense of Lucine, and that drove me to the brink of madness.

Then I succumbed to that innate core of myself that I had never shown any man. Unable to contain myself, I threw my head back and hurled my guttural cry at the stone above me, a trapped wolf howling at the moon, a wounded lion bound in cords.

And when my cry exhausted my breath, I drew a deep groan that echoed in that chamber, and I thundered my rage and remorse again. My hands were clenched to hammers, my neck was strung to vines, but I was only a worm.

How had I gone from stoic hero to ruined fool in a week? What kind of disease had taken my mind and my heart? What fate had delivered me to Moldavia to find this scourge that would make the black plague seem like a blessing?

I cursed myself. I cursed Alek. I cursed Natasha. I cursed God. I cursed the devil. I cursed that beast. I cursed all the powers that had conspired to render me such a terrible lover.

But I would never curse Lucine. The rest of us could die if only she lived.

And when my body could not sustain this display of madness

any longer, I sank to my side, held myself tight, and let the rest of my tears drain from my eyes.

⚜

My face was still planted on the soggy earth when I heard the creak of a door and the distant rattle of keys. *They've come to rack me*, I thought. *They will take a hot skewer and sear my bowels. They will gouge my eyes and pluck apart my body until I tell them what they need to justify my execution.*

I will scream that I am a witch, that I have been touched by the devil. Then they will crucify me.

And I welcomed it.

But no . . . no, I couldn't. I had to pull myself together as long as there was the slightest hope that I could escape these monsters, find another priest who was not mad, and rush back up that mountain to confront Valerik on his terms, however unlikely any victory might seem.

So I pushed myself to my knees, stood up, and steadied myself by one hand on the wall as the sound of boots approached on stone.

One man, not two. Even in shackles, I might be able to take one man. I might take him from his feet, twist the chain around his neck, and choke him to the death.

Orange light crept into the pit. The boots stopped outside my cell. I refused to turn. *Let them enter.*

"Toma."

The voice was low. Gravelly. I blinked.

"Toma Nicolescu. Is that you?"

I had heard this voice before. I slowly turned my head toward the bars. A priest dressed in a brown hooded robe stood holding a torch in his left hand. His face was hidden in shadow.

He faced me for a while, then reached up and pulled back his hood. I recognized him immediately. This was none other than the old man who'd warned Alek and me at the Brasca Pass! His scraggly hair hung around a wrinkled face and cloudy eyes that now stared blind through those slits.

"Who are you?" I asked, stunned by the sight of him.

He inclined his ear toward the passage, then stepped closer to the bars. "We don't have much time."

"Who are you?" I demanded again.

"I've chosen the name Thomas for your sake, though names don't matter. But you are called Toma, which means 'twin.' So call me Thomas, which also means 'twin.' Saint Thomas, if you want." He cackled. "It has a nice ring to it. And it was he who sent me to you."

"Thomas?"

"But that doesn't matter. Names mean nothing now."

I wasn't sure I could trust the man, but I wasn't in a position to argue, so I held my tongue.

The old man wrapped the shriveled fingers of his right hand around one of the bars and spoke quickly, in a hushed voice.

"We don't have time, you have to focus."

"Who are you?"

"Like I said—"

"Not your name."

This so-called Saint Thomas took a deep breath. "One who knows far more than you. Think of me as an angel sent to you from another realm to free you from your prison—it's happened before—albeit this time without an earthquake. I'm sure that sounds absurd. Just know that, like Vlad van Valerik, I'm someone you'll never fully understand."

I approached the bars cautiously. "You know Valerik?"

"He's a half-breed. The blood of the Nephilim flows through him. A creature of the night."

"He's the devil, then."

"Yes, in a manner of speaking. Nephilim. As in that book Genesis. The offspring of fallen angels and humans. They'll be known by other names one day, but it all comes down to the same thing, my young friend. You find yourself at a pivotal point in history, long before all the most famous stories based on such creatures are written."

"What stories? How can you possibly know all of this?"

"Because I'm from that other realm. Evil isn't the only force that can manifest itself in physical form."

I grabbed the bars, knowing now that no matter how old and blind and frail, this man must be my salvation. "Then let me out! Tell me what I must do. I am lost in here while that beast has her!"

The old man stared at me, then pulled out an ancient leather book from under his cloak. "You'll have to discover that on your own, but I can help. This is known as a Blood Book. A journal."

"It'll take more than a book to defeat them. If you're a man of God, go with me."

"No, Toma. I am an old, blind man and must go back." He placed his cracked hand over mine. "There are times when spiritual realities show themselves in flesh and blood, yes? When roles are played to mirror something far greater. 'Unless you eat my flesh and drink my blood.' Some say symbolism, but now here it is true."

It made no sense to me. Lucine had already tasted the blood, as I had, and it was working evil in her.

"I should serve her communion? It's that simple?"

"The affairs between God and man aren't about simple rites performed at an altar. You love her, I think?"

Tears flooded my eyes.

"You'll have to woo her first, if you can. This is a passion play, a contest for her heart, not her service. Win her heart and you might be able to save her. Enter her world. Be her Immanuel."

The tears spilled down my cheeks and I made my confession to that old man. "I didn't tell her. She doesn't know!"

"And it might be too late—she might have turned cold already. The seduction of those dark beings is astounding."

He withdrew a key. Placing the journal under his arm, he unlocked the cell. I rushed out and whirled both ways to be sure we were alone. We were.

"Take this book. It will help you. After you read it, and only then, can you dare go up that mountain." He pressed the book into my hands and I took it carefully.

He started to turn. "I have to get back."

But I stopped him with a hand to his arm. "Why? How did this happen?"

The old man shrugged. "It happened. They became flesh. Evil walks among you now. That's all you need to know. There's a horse by the back gate. Run quickly, Toma."

Then he left me standing with the book in my hands and hurried down that dungeon passage. He was already at the top of the steps when I began to run. Down the tunnel, up the stairs, out the doors, and into the failing light. A monk with a bucket of potatoes saw me and stared as if he were looking upon a ghost. I nodded my respect and ran past him, straight to the back gate, which was open.

The horse was my own stallion, and I gratefully leaped onto his back.

Voices shouted behind. A bell clanged. Yet now I was free and my horse was fast, and I galloped away from the bishop's dungeons of hell.

I headed into the night, toward the north and the west where the Carpathian Mountains rose like tombs against the sky. Toward another hell that would surely burn my flesh and leave me dead.

TWENTY-EIGHT

I t's yours, my love. All of it." Vlad turned around, spreading one arm out to the vast library with its towering bookcases and gold-appointed candlesticks. The crystal chandelier shone like the stars. Or were they diamonds? She would put nothing beyond him now, no amount of wealth or power. Vlad could hardly surprise her any longer; he was limitless.

And her soft smile must have told him of her wonder, because he brushed her hair off her face and touched his lips to hers again.

The pain of her turning had eased as the night came. After the show of honor and dancing in the great hall with the entire coven, the council had retired to Vlad's wing and feasted at the familiar long table, only tonight the scents and the tastes had changed completely. It was boar, she was told, and each bite tasted like the first delectable morsel after a week of starvation. Her hunger could hardly be satisfied—she'd never eaten so much meat and gravy, so many beets or so much sweet corn in one sitting or ten sittings.

When she made a comment, they all laughed with delight. She was turned, they said. She had found a new life. Nothing would ever taste so bland or smell so mundane again.

Their laughter sounded like music, and it was then that Lucine began to smile.

"Now you know why I could not stay away, Lucine," Natasha cried.

"Yes," Lucine said. "I can see that."

Even so, she knew that something was wrong. A glance at Sofia told her the same. The woman laughed with the rest, ate like the rest, joined in revelry with the rest, but when their eyes met, Lucine was sure she saw a haunting remorse.

For a brief few moments, concern of death would ride her, but then the beauty of her turning swallowed her, and she would forget why she'd been concerned at all. She saw those demons screaming only one other time, at that very table. One moment they were aristocrats lounging at a magnificent spread; the next they were six creatures dining in hell.

She gasped, silencing the table.

"What is it, dear?" Vlad asked.

The vision vanished.

"I . . ." She touched her throat and took a sip of wine. "I just had a strange sensation. Better now."

He took her hand. "The sensations of the gods often feel strange at first. You will gasp a hundred times over the next week, I will make sure of it." He lowered his ruby lips to her white knuckles.

He's a true gentleman, she thought. *I love this man. And he has made me his queen!*

"I hope so," she said.

He lifted his eyes and seemed to take up residence in her own. "So do I," he said after a pause. Then to the others, his dark stare still feasting on her, "Please leave us, all of you."

They were gone when she looked over a moment or two later. His command over them was entrancing.

Left alone, Vlad stood and walked behind her. He slid her chair out, took her elbow, and eased her to her feet, remaining behind all the while. Drawing her hair aside, he leaned over her back and breathed on her neck.

"I understand why some feed on the neck," he murmured. "The scent of blood can be overwhelming."

He eased her around, drew her close, and kissed her lower lip, biting deep into the softness of her mouth without any hesitation.

Lucine gasped, expecting the same pain she'd felt the last time he bit her. But now a pleasant and numbing warmth flooded her chin, her throat, down over her breasts. She shuddered as his blood spread through her body.

She wanted to drink that blood. She longed for the taste in her mouth, its heat in her throat. But she knew she couldn't until he offered it to her himself. No one had told her this; his blood seemed to carry the knowledge with it.

Her world swam and Vlad moaned. Then, after they'd settled, he insisted he show her more of the castle. The ballroom, the sweeping stairs, the balcony, a dozen rooms winding up through the higher floors, used for lounging or storage of his collections. The collections consisted of books and paintings and relics from more countries and eras than she imagined one man could possibly amass.

But Vlad wasn't simply one man, or any man. He was more than and less than at once, the most powerful being that walked this earth. And she was his queen.

They explored the lower floor's main halls, overflowing with more paintings and chests that were filled with golden coins, rubies, emeralds, sapphires, and more black onyx than she knew could be pulled from the earth. The relics could not be numbered—candlesticks, swords, knives, and instruments of science with sharp edges made to slice easily through human flesh.

There was a round room at the back of the castle that she found most interesting. Above, open to a starry sky. Around the walls, limestone carvings of lions' heads and goats' heads from which water once spouted. At the center, a large round table with a huge limestone cross on it, dirtied with dried moss and fungus. And around the base of the table, an empty pool perhaps twice the width of the table.

"A bathhouse," she said. "But no water?"

"No. Water and crosses aren't my favorite." He held one hand behind his back and motioned to the crucifix that stood taller than he. "As a common ornament, it's fine enough. I keep it around to remind me how powerless it is by itself. But water, blessed by even this harmless symbol, makes me rather sick."

Oddly enough, she understood. There was something offensive about water, which gave life in the midst of death.

"The cross was a fountain, but it doesn't work. Perhaps we'll fill it with water and prove our fears misguided one day, just for fun."

She returned his show of bravery. "For fun."

The entire castle was filled with wonder and beauty, though she was quite certain that part of her appreciation was the result of her new vision. But none of it quite affected her like the tunnels below the castle. The dank, torch-lit halls with their caged rooms were all rather unnerving at first glance but only mysterious at second.

They stood now in the grand library off the main tunnel, and Vlad seemed very impressed with it. "We pride ourselves in knowledge," he said, bowing his head and spreading his arms before a portrait called *Alucard*. He retained his reverential posture for a few moments and then straightened. The fanged, red-eyed wolf-bat would have sent a chill down Lucine's back only yesterday. Now a profound awe mixed with her fear and respect for this creature.

"He's your earliest ancestor, also called Shataiki or Nephilim by some," Vlad said. "As written in the oldest book in the Pentateuch, when the sons of God united with the daughters of men."

"Is he . . ." She wanted to ask if he was dead.

"He lives still."

He must have made Vlad? And what did that make her?

"I am second generation," Vlad said. "One generation from my father."

"And what about the rest of this coven?"

"The rest? Most are made, like Natasha, with only a hint of Nephilim blood in their veins. Even the older ones are less than a tenth."

"And . . ."

"And you?" He lifted her hand and kissed the back of it. "My bride, you will become half of what I am. The strongest and the most gifted of all of God's sons. There are only a few like you alive today. Does this please you?"

"I . . . But am I really alive?"

He hesitated. "Do you feel alive?"

"I don't know what I feel."

"Do you like it?"

"I think so. Yes. More as I get used to it."

But there was also a pain raging just below the surface, she thought. Something that had to do with this beast who looked like death in one moment and life in the next.

"I'm eight hundred years old. Alucard made his first human when he bit a pregnant woman two thousand years ago. The offspring became my father, so to speak, though we don't bear offspring as such. I was made by another who was made by my grandfather. I am the last."

"So then I could be seen as your daughter," she said.

"No. You are my bride. And as my bride you will live a very long time."

"And then?"

Vlad turned from the portrait. "And then you will die and take your rightful place in hell."

His voice was unapologetic. Bitter. His face had darkened; his eyes had gone like coal.

"I don't want—"

Vlad's hand slammed into her cheek with such force that she spun and smashed into one of the bookcases before dropping to her knees on the cold stone floor. Pain sliced down her neck, and for a moment she was sure her jaw had been shattered.

She grunted and reached for her face. Blood flowed from

a cut on her upper lip. Her mind filled with a raw hatred for this half-breed who had just savaged her, and for a moment she wanted to throw herself at him and claw his eyes out. She was reliving her past!

"Never speak of it again," he said.

Then Vlad was picking her up. Kissing her wound. Tasting her blood. And when she tasted his, her pain faded and she realized that she had deserved to be hit.

They fed on each other for a few long dizzying minutes, and Lucine knew that she would both love and hate Vlad forever.

TWENTY-NINE

Saint Thomas, the beast hunter—that's how I began to call the old man who delivered me from the church's dungeon. But I will confess that I couldn't be sure he was a man at all, any more than Vlad van Valerik was really a man. If so, then surely not a man in the same way I was a man.

There was more to both of them.

I needed a place to hole up and read the journal, and I knew of no better place than my own room in the Cantemir estate's west tower. I knew the grounds well, knew the layout of the security, the guards' schedule, the maids' comings and goings, and the surrounding countryside.

More importantly, I was certain that the church would mount
a search for me, spreading tales of my witchcraft as they went,
but I doubted they would look for me so close to where they'd
taken me.

I rode north of the estate and tied my horse in thick grass near
a brook, where he could manage for a day, even two if necessary,
before I returned. Then I walked straight to the house and slipped
into my bedroom using a window I'd left unlocked in the event I
needed a quick exit under attack. A matter of habit.

I stood in the darkness for a long while, listening for any sound
beyond my own breathing. The house was as quiet as an abandoned mine. Satisfied, I locked the door, pulled the curtain tight,
and lit a single candle, no more.

There by the soft yellow glow, I pulled out the book the old
man had given me and set it before me on the desk.

A single leather thong bound the frayed brown covers. The
lower right-hand corner curled up, worn to a lighter shade from
handling. Either a thousand hands had opened the book, or one,
a thousand times. It was less than an inch thick. The name of that
book was etched into the leather above the twine.

Blood Book:
Tales, Confessions, and Rumors
of Another World

I took the end of the thong between my thumb and forefinger and gently released the looped knot, then lifted the cover
and looked at the first page. The writing was in script, written in
black ink with a sharp quill. A letter to the reader.

To you who are Chosen—

I, Thomas, have written and compiled this Blood Book so that those with eyes to see will understand the makings of both worlds, the seen and the unseen. The secrets written between these covers will lead you to death if you fail to understand, or to life if you open your eyes and see.

I have seen what so few have seen. And I can assure you that evil has made itself known in the flesh. A door was opened for one of those beasts to enter this world and spread the disease in bodily form, as was done at the dawn of time. As with the sons of God, the Nephilim beast, who slept with women and bore half-breeds as told in the Holy Scriptures themselves, entered your world 1700 years ago and passed his seed to a woman who bore that first monster.

The line of those who came from that Nephilim beast must be stopped before their seed spreads further! If they can be redeemed, it must be through love and blood, not sword and hammer.

Where all was once unseen, now it is seen. What was done in spirit will be done in the flesh, so all men will know that evil walks and speaks and that the Maker's great romance is a kiss of love, an offering of blood.

If you read now, you are chosen. All you need is here. Find the heart of Solomon's Song for that beloved. Slay the beast who would win her.

Be the hand of your Maker, in the flesh, for all to see.
Be his twin. I beg you.

— Thomas

I reread the letter three times, mesmerized by the suggestions contained within. Flipping through carefully, I saw that the front of the journal was filled with drawings and notes, some faded to light tracings on the grainy paper, all in very sharp letters and square lines.

The next section was written by another party in yet a different hand. And a third section was in the same hand as the letter I'd read. So this Blood Book was a compilation of three journals written by three people?

I flipped back to the beginning and scanned the opening pages. Pictures of winged wolf creatures, very similar to the images I'd seen in the Castle Castile. This was them! Here, the ancestors of Vlad van Valerik and his coven of devil worshippers.

The inscription under one such sketch of a creature that had been cut in half: *Dissected Nephilim*. It was a ghastly picture describing various body parts.

There was more, much more, in this first section, details written by someone called Baal about a reality that I could hardly believe existed. I peered at those pages with barely a thread of reason to hold my mind together. Surely it was all the figment of some madman's imagination!

I had always considered religion to be the device of the powerful to wrest control from the weak, an instrument of fear and political power. But here on these pages, the rift between the known and unknown was woven together in such plain detail. Either the writers were truly insane or they had seen what I had not.

And yet I *had* seen! There in the Castle Castile I had seen things that could not be explained by anything other than what I was reading on those pages. Perhaps all those fables contained in the Holy Scripture had some basis in reality after all.

The candle burned. My breathing was steady and heavy. Not

a sound but the soft crackle of ancient pages turning and the sizzle of the flaming wick. I was transported into a new world of understanding that shook me to my bones.

The writings of Thomas, who I agreed must be an angel from God himself, brought the rest into focus. His journal began with a simple disclaimer that he would write only what could be grasped by a mortal who had never crossed the realities as he had. I tell you my fingers trembled over the page as I read his interpretation of this struggle between good and evil made flesh so that some may see. In his words:

> It is no different than what has been known by some already, that angels and demons have walked this earth in human form, that beasts have been known to speak and whales to swallow men. That dragons will come from the sky to consume, and the Christ will come on a white horse to slay them.
>
> It is written in the Holy Scripture that fallen angels, the sons of God, mated with the daughters of men who bore them monsters called Nephilim.
>
> It has been written that a ram from the thicket saved Isaac. That Jacob wrestled with an angel. That the devil possessed swine. But what few know is that Alucard, the servant of that devil, crossed over to this earth in the days of Noah and is followed by his offspring, some knowing, others unknowing. Their lust to win the love of mortals away from God knows no bounds.

I stopped there, knowing I had met the offspring of this Alucard the first time I laid eyes on Vlad van Valerik. My doubts were washed away and I began to read with even more intensity, searching for the way that I might contend with this unholy thing.

I cannot say all that I read that night, because much of it was too otherworldly for me to grasp in its entirety, and that Blood Book was soon lost, never to be recovered. But the crux of it all was seared into my mind as if by a branding iron, and here it is:

There is indeed good and there is indeed evil, and both walk the earth. But good has little to do with the forms of religion, and evil has as little to do with so much behavior condemned by religion. Both good and evil vie for the passions of the heart. For love! For Solomon's Song of romance and desire. Love is God's gift to his creation. And evil contests this same love with bitter rage, to be loved as God is surely loved.

This was evil's seduction, and it had manifested itself there in bodily form in the shadows of the Carpathian Mountains, a manifestation of the same battle that rages in every human heart.

My only hope of standing in the presence of such evil without becoming one with it was to be cleansed by all that was holy. To find a new life washed with a new power, with blood that had taken on the meaning of life.

According to the Blood Book, life was in the blood. It quoted from the Holy Book: "Except ye eat the flesh of the Son of man, and drink his blood, ye have no life in you." And again of the saints, "Thou hast given them blood to drink."

All of the blood sacrifices, which I had always considered barbarous, suddenly made sense. That blood, however symbolic on the altar, had true power as much as evil had manifested itself in the blood of this beast. Surely this was why the Christ had bled out on that cross of torture. Not for a religion, not for

Christianity or orthodoxy, but for the heart of man. In the words
of Thomas:

*Immanuel, God with us—that he would leave the spiritual realm
and be present in flesh and blood in such an act of humility is a
staggering notion. As it is, he willingly gave his blood, in the flesh,
so that others might find life, for it is written: "He did not come by
water only, but by blood," and "Without the shedding of blood there
is no remission." Now blood is required to give new life to the dead.*

*I tell you, he did not give only a small amount to satisfy this
requirement. He was beaten and crushed and pierced until that
blood flowed like a river for the sake of love. It was for love, not
religion, that he died.*

*There is a fountain filled with blood drawn from Immanuel's
veins. And those plunged beneath that watery grave to drink of his
blood will never be the same.*

I slid out of my chair and crashed to the floor, and I threw my
life into the hands of God, begging him to give me his blood and
his heart to pump that blood. I wept into the stone, prone before
the very God I had discarded all of my life, and I vowed to love him
if he would only love Lucine and give his blood for her.

I was a mess, and I knew only whispers of the truth, but even
those ravaged my mind. I could feel the heat of God himself flowing through my veins.

When I finally staggered back to my feet, I was still clueless
about what I must do. *Woo her*, the old man had said. *Win her*. But
how, when she was up there with the devil and I was down here
with nothing but a useless sword?

The answer had to be in the journal, so I changed out the dim candle, splashed some red wine in a glass, and pored over the book.

It wasn't until the last few pages that I read the words I longed to see. Here Thomas had written a simple guide for slowing or killing these kind.

Alucard's blood extended their lives. Depending on how pure their blood, a half-breed might live a few hundred years or more. They possessed incredible strength and such speed that one might not see them move. Seeing the distance of their leaps, one might think they could fly. Over time, many other traits had been attributed to them, most of which were exaggerations spun in fantasy, Thomas said, but it was true that the half-breeds had intoxicating powers of seduction. Even lesser descendants with only a hint of that blood would turn heads when they walked into a room.

In the end it was all about this: the wooing of the heart and the power in the blood. But at least in this manifested contest between good and evil there were ways to slow or kill the half-breeds.

They were terrified of any water associated with their great enemy.

Wood could affect them profoundly if it came in contact with their hearts, something to do with their origin in a black forest.

They preferred to sleep underground where the Nephilim lairs were hidden. Many had attributes that betrayed their bloodline: longer fingers and nails, sharper features, pale skin revealed by a shedding of their old skin. Their eyes were also dark, often rimmed in gray, though in sunlight the irises could look quite normal.

If ingested, their blood was like a potent drug that might weaken the mind, but the effects would soon pass. If their blood was injected directly into any person's bloodstream, however, that person would be infected and transformed.

And that is what I know, Thomas had written on the last page.

They go by many names, including Shataiki. I've never heard of one being restored, but neither is there evidence that souls infected by this scourge have no chance of finding their way back to humanity.

What I do know is that evil has manifested itself physically and must be dealt with in the same manner, physically. This is not church business where a crucifix can be waved and words uttered. The love, the blood, life and death, everything—it must all be real and in hand, or you surely have no hope to prevail.

May God have mercy on your soul.

— Thomas

I closed the cover and stood. I paced. Then I sat again and I peeled back the pages. There had to be a clearer way! I had learned much, but this wasn't a blueprint for battle. If my instructor had never killed one of these half-breeds, how was I supposed to do it?

Yet the old man had said that everything I needed to know was there, in the Blood Book.

So I read and reread it, and each time I discovered a little more. I understood that religion, however faulty, wasn't based on nonsense. That there raged a war between good and evil that made my own wars pale by comparison. I was somehow a central figure in the history of that battle, even if I ended up only a stake in the ground to mark where these forces of darkness were first flushed out of hiding.

When I finally closed the book, a thin crack of light showed through the drawn curtains. So late?

I rushed to the drape and pulled it open a few inches. What I saw there sent a chill down my spine. Dozens of troops sat upon their horses about the estate. Regular army, not only the church's guard. One of them was walking my stallion toward the barn.

I dropped the curtain, frozen. I had been found out.

THIRTY

To do the unexpected is often one's only hope of survival. I had learned the lesson more times than I cared to recall. You must know that I felt no fear for my own life in that moment, but I confess to feeling more fright than I had courted in many years, thinking only that if I went down, Lucine would lose her savior.

I grabbed my pistol, my sword, and the book, and after checking the hall, I ran out of the room, straight for Kesia's quarters. She had a storage closet well secured with heavy timbers, and I'd told her that if there was any trouble, she must take hiding there until the danger passed. Anyone firing upon the house would send balls of lead through windows and doorways, and anyone inside would be in danger of being killed—except in this closet.

The hall that led to her room passed an opening to the great ballroom, and as I flew by they saw me. Shouts gave the warning, but I ran on, because I had seen what I wanted to see: Kesia wasn't with them.

Her door was locked, but I knew that the mechanism was made of wood and I easily smashed through with my shoulder.

Behind me the soldiers gave chase, boots thudding on the stone. I slammed the door shut, leaped to the dresser, and shoved it into position to block any easy access.

"If you come in, she dies!" I cried.

Then I rushed to the closet, threw the door wide, and came face-to-face with Kesia, whose hands shook with the weight of a pistol.

"I swear I won't harm you," I said, lifting both arms. "I only want you to hear me, because I swear, I am your only hope."

"You're the devil," she cried. But her voice wasn't firm.

"If you still think so after I've said my piece, then shoot this devil. But please"—I withdrew the book from my waist and held it up—"I have something you must see."

Her eyes shifted to the book, then back to my face. "What is it?"

"An ancient journal that explains in great detail who Vlad van Valerik really is."

"He's royalty."

Fists pounded on the door.

"He is. But he's more, far more, and far less. Tell them that if they try to come in I will kill you."

"I have the pistol."

"And I have the book. Say it."

She hesitated, then yelled for them to stop or she would die. The fists stopped beating.

Kesia slowly lowered her weapon. "I swear on my first husband's grave, Toma, if this is some trick you will pay with your life."

"Have you known me to be the kind who would play a trick for my own gain?"

Kesia put the pistol on her shelf.

"Thank you." And then I told her what had happened to me in the dungeon, about Thomas the saint, and I carefully outlined my case for the existence of creatures of the night who were made by the unholy union of fallen angels and human women. And as I laid it out she began to quiet and her eyes grew wide.

"And now this book, Kesia." I handed it to her and she opened it carefully. "There you'll find drawings, and near the end, the way to slow these beasts. Even kill them."

"You can't seriously think that the duke is one of these!" she whispered.

"Come with me, then. See for yourself. Saint Thomas told me in no uncertain terms that Valerik was such a beast! And your daughters are both in his grip. Dead to this world."

Her mouth remained parted and her fingers trembled as she stared through sections of the book. She lifted her eyes to me.

"Is it possible? These are the stories of peasants!"

"Believe me, a week ago I would have said the same. But now this is a story that I have seen and lived. Because, as God is my witness, Lady Kesia, I love Lucine with all of my heart and flesh. If I must, I will rush out of this house into a hailstorm of slugs for the chance to save her. And if I die, then you will have lost your daughter as well."

I watched as her resistance faded from her eyes. They misted with tears and she held the book out to me.

"Then go to her. Bring them both back to me. Forgive me for my ignorance."

"Think nothing of it." I paced out of that closet and scanned the room.

The fist pounded on the door again. "Lady Kesia, please—"

"Leave us!" she cried. "Do you want him to slit my throat? I'll blame you, oaf!"

Silence.

"I need blessed water, they're bothered by it. Wood . . ." I whirled to her. "Do you have stakes?"

"Whatever for?" She rushed to her desk. "This is absurd; you're surrounded. How will you get out?"

"With you. They wouldn't dare shoot at you."

"Me? I can't go with you! I believe you. I don't think it's necessary I go up there to see with my own eyes."

"Then I won't take you up there."

"If not with me, how will you—"

"I only need your cooperation to get out," I explained. "We'll head south toward Crysk. As soon as we're clear of the estate, I'll drop you off and circle around to the north, back to the Castle Castile. Tell the bishop I've fled to find the general. They'll believe you."

"While you go up against the Castle Castile. Alone?"

"Alone. Water. A crucifix. And fire. Quickly, I need them all!"

Once the decision was made, Kesia threw herself into helping me. She fetched a leather bag from her closet into which I placed some candles with fire starter, a bottle of oil, and a crucifix from her wall. The crucifix was over a foot tall and stuck out the top of the bag a few inches.

The blessed water was a problem without a priest, naturally, but I did take a jelly jar filled with water from the basin.

"Don't worry, I won't cut you," I said, withdrawing my blade.

"Please don't."

I nodded once and shoved the dresser away from the entrance. The door swung open and I held the lady from behind, placed the blade against her throat, and shoved her forward.

"Hold your ground! I have her."

"Back, you oafs!" she cried. "Don't fire!"

Eight of them were in the hall, and their eyes grew round when they saw the knife. They retreated into the ballroom as we hurried forward.

"Drop your weapons!"

They hesitated until Kesia reinforced the demand. With my blade at her throat they hardly had a choice. A single misfired musket ball could end her life.

The soldiers outside had even more distance to contend with, and they could only watch hopelessly as I pushed my prisoner past them to the stable, where I collected my horse and mounted behind her.

Five minutes later the estate fell out of sight as we crested and descended the hill on the property's south side. I left her there, by the side of the road.

"Tell them I've gone south to find the general. Don't worry, they'll pass by this place soon enough."

She looked up at me. "All of this is still hard to believe."

"Very hard." I pulled my steed around.

"Bring them back to me, Toma. Fulfill your duty. Please."

I kicked the horse and headed into the trees without an answer.

❧

It took me three hours to reach the crest that looked down at the Castle Castile from the north. The road approached from the southeast, but I knew they had a watch over that path, so I guided my stallion down into the ravine a full mile from the bend that first brought the fortress into view.

The ground was steep and treacherous, and dark clouds had blown in and hugged the Carpathian peaks, but almost two days had passed since the heavy rain, so the ground wasn't as slick as it could have been. There was no way to stop the tumbling of gravel loosed by my horse. I could only hope I was far enough away for even those creatures to hear.

I stopped for a long spell at the creek in that ravine and fashioned from the young trunks of saplings five stakes, each just over a foot long and an inch thick. Using my knife I sharpened each to a needle point. I hoped this would satisfy Thomas's suggestion that these creatures feared wood, however strange that might seem.

Regardless, the whole mess was far beyond strange. Sitting there in the ravine with a gurgling brook at my feet, I wondered what kind of madness had captured my mind. But the evidence of all I had felt and seen and heard battered away all that madness.

Had I not fallen completely and inexplicably in love with Lucine?

Did I not see Natasha leap far over her head and walk the air?

Or drink their blood and wake up in my bed having misplaced the day?

Was Thomas a figment of my imagination? And the book . . . I reached for my belt to be sure it was still there. Were these the words of a fool?

But above it all was the horror I felt at the prospect of any harm coming to Lucine.

I mounted and left that mountain brook with my leather bag full of strange weapons. Five wooden stakes. A bottle of water blessed only by me at the creek. A large crucifix. The makings for fire. A long rope with a hook. One pistol in my belt. And the journal, though I saw no use for it now.

The climb up the far side was even worse than the descent into the ravine. A lesser horse would surely have slipped and tumbled back to the creek. But we managed.

Now I stared down at the Castle Castile, and my bag of tools felt like worthless sticks and stones. The clouds had formed a flat, dark blanket just over my head, capping the mountain to my right below its peak. Two crows glided silently through the sky above the castle, like sentinels informing on any who came near. For a moment I imagined that they weren't crows at all but some kind of sibling to those who hid inside the castle's thick, towering walls.

The stable sat at the rear, quiet. Three horses ate hay in a paddock.

I shuddered in the damp air, trying to focus on my task.

My strategy was a simple one, tested many times on a dozen battlefields. So often I'd had Alek by my side and I wished for him now.

If I were so fortunate, he would be my first target. If I could win Alek, I would have a wealth of information to work with and a warrior who had saved my life on countless occasions.

I would descend on foot from here and make a stealthy entrance. Once inside I would lay my trap—with Alek's help if I was so lucky. Then I would spring that trap and take Lucine.

But I was no fool. Reaching her would be a monumental task. And even if I did reach her, I didn't know what condition I would find her in. Then there was the task of getting out and down the mountain without being taken.

A chill spread through my palms. It was suicide.

You can't do this, Toma. You can't throw your life away like this. There is no hope for success.

If they were normal men, I wouldn't be so unnerved. But I'd faced them and been sent packing like a dog from the kitchen. I looked at the bag of simple tools in my hand.

I should pray, I thought. So I lifted my chin and spoke to the gray sky, though I didn't know how to pray. "God, if you are indeed maker of flesh and blood, I beg for your blood." The preposterous nature of my predicament settled over me—that I was powerless on my own, that I would require God's blood to empower me in this battle over souls. Tears swelled in my eyes.

"Use me as your servant to slay this evil nature that inhabits that fortress. If Lucine dies, then I will die. But let me be your hammer to crush that beast!" It occurred to me that I was speaking aloud now, and I peered down at the castle to see if there was any indication that my voice had carried.

The crows still circled; the mist still hung undisturbed in the air. I would be God's incarnation in that world of ruin and darkness that held Lucine captive, and in going down I would surely throw myself.

My body shuddered.

I gathered my bag and descended into the world of the fallen.

THIRTY-ONE

The afternoon was declining and I was halfway down the mountain when the first roll of thunder rumbled through the sky, a monster growling its warning to the lone earthling crossing into forbidden ground.

The dark clouds now blocked out all but dim light, becoming a gray slate that butted up to the peaks, sealing any escape to the heavens. Distant flashes of hidden lightning stuttered behind the covering. An ominous portent, surely. I hitched the bag on my shoulder, grasped it tightly so that nothing would fall out if I slipped, and continued down.

God and all that is good above me, have mercy.

I had mumbled prayers all the way, wondering if there was any way they could be heard above that black mass. Thomas's words whispered through my mind on the lips of ghosts. *Woo her, Toma. You are her Immanuel, Toma. It's in the blood, Toma, there is no undoing of evil without the blood, Toma.*

Toma. Thomas. Twin. It made me wonder if this unlikely saint named Thomas had ever given his blood or if, as a creature of the light, he had any blood to give.

A mist crept down from the blanket of cloud as I drew closer to the ancient castle walls, visible through the treetops. By the time I worked my way to the edge of the grounds cleared of trees, a hazy fog hung to the ground.

I pulled up behind a large trunk and peered at the thick walls made of massive stones, blackened by age. Not a sound but the pounding of blood in my ears. Out of sight, a horse snorted. The corral was to my right. The entrance to the underground was around the eastern wall a hundred paces ahead of me.

There comes a point before every battle when a decision must be made to proceed or retreat for a better opportunity. As I looked across the expansive lawn, I knew that proceeding was terribly ill advised. But I also knew that there would never be a better opportunity to rescue Lucine.

There would never be any further opportunity at all, because the bishop and his church would soon learn that I had not gone to find the general. They would send a full army against me, and I would spend the rest of my days in a dungeon, if the empress had mercy, or be put to death if she had even more mercy.

So then the die was cast. I would only hope for the mercy of God himself now.

Resolved, I set the bag down and pulled out the iron crucifix. I had seen many crucifixes about the castle, but Thomas said they feared those elements that were blessed, directly linked to God himself. So I tried to bless the crucifix in my hand by crossing it and whispering a prayer as I'd seen priests do on occasion.

"Use this cross as your instrument, covered by your blood. In the name of the Father, the Son, and the Holy Ghost." The large crucifix lay dormant in my hands. No bolts of lightning suggested a greater power had heard me.

I checked the stakes, jabbing the air with them as if they were swords. I'd never actually thrown a stake as I had many a knife, but these were heavy with sap and would likely fly fast and true if properly thrown.

The jar of water I'd brought seemed a hopeless device. What was I supposed to do, throw it at them as if it were a cannonball?

I shoved two stakes under my belt opposite my pistol, gripped the crucifix in my left hand, and, after a long-drawn breath, ran forward in a crouch. The mist was so thick that I could feel a tingle on my face as I cut through it.

When I reached the eastern wall, I slowed my rush with my right hand and spun so that my back hit the stone with hardly more than a bump. I could not be sure they hadn't seen me, but I would know soon enough. They moved fast.

And so would I.

Twenty paces along the wall to the front edge. I glanced up as I flew and saw no sign of them. Then I was at the corner, peering around.

Still no sign I'd been seen.

The wall was three feet thick here, so I had to take two steps before I could see whether the passage I used to escape the underground was open. I prayed it was so; my secondary plan was even more foolhardy than the one I would try first.

The gate lay open in the same position I'd last seen it. But was the door at the end of the tunnel open?

Ducking inside the alcove and plunging down the stone steps both encouraged me and sped my heart with dread. I was inside, that was good. But I was inside . . . with *them*.

Still no alarm that I was aware of.

The torch at the end of the tunnel was not lit, but after inspection I was satisfied that it contained fuel and would fire when I needed it. After replacing it in the bracket, I crept up to the door.

The handle moved under my hand. Daring not to breathe, I eased the door open just a sliver, just enough to know that the cavern beyond was dark. I pulled it shut and calmed myself. Here then was the way in.

I retreated to the tunnel wall and stared at the gray light for several long seconds, knowing that I had to go back outside if I hoped to succeed. There in the passage I was unnoticed, momentarily enshrouded by a close hand of comforting darkness. If I went inside I would be in their home, at their disposal, with only some unlikely weapons at my disposal, wooden stakes and a crucifix.

Outside I would be exposed, and if discovered I would stand no chance of entering. They would seal the doors or stand in wait to crush me the instant I tried to break in.

Either way was a terrible risk. My mind grappled with uncertainty and for a while I could not move. On any other battlefield I would trust my skill and strength to deal with any foe because I could hack my way through a dozen infidels if pressed. But against these masters of darkness . . .

Lucine's savior was a powerless fool who didn't stand a chance. She was doomed! I felt defeated already, cowering in that darkness, overwhelmed by such desperation that I thought I might fall to my knees and weep.

Instead I laid the bag in the corner where it couldn't be seen, and I plodded back down the tunnel. Up the stairs, holding close to the stone wall. The approaching dusk was unbothered. Still not a hint they knew I was at their walls.

I slipped back around the same wall along which I had come, then ran along the base toward the back corner. Dismissing all but the immediate task from my mind, I gained some familiar composure. I had to know more about the lay of this battlefield before I rushed into battle.

The stables lay fifty paces behind the back wall. No servants that I could see, but I waited several minutes at the corner to be sure. No sentries along the top wall, but the castle's rear door could open at any moment. It was a risk beyond my control.

I withdrew my pistol, checked the load, and hurried along the back wall.

The door was locked—a quick yank of the latch confirmed that—but I had no intention of using it then because I had no idea what lay behind it.

When I reached the far corner, blood surged through my heart. The tower rose into the dark gray sky ahead of me, and I knew from Sofia that this was where Vlad van Valerik made his kingly home.

Thunder crackled overhead; lightning stabbed the horizon, a long crooked finger belonging to God or the devil, I knew not which. I could barely see the windows at the top of the tower, glowing orange from the light inside.

Everything in me wanted to rush up the tower, scale the wall by whatever means, and break through the window to save Lucine. Surely she was inside there, or would be soon.

Surely she would fall into my arms and vow her love. Surely she would take my side and fight off that other suitor.

But if I went up now while the Russians were still at full strength, they would simply hound us down and crush us before we reached the road. I felt too irrational for my comfort already, but I wasn't foolish enough to rush into certain death. What good would I be to Lucine if I were dead?

I approached the tower, studying the layout of the wall and the windows in the event I would need to scale the fortress.

The first drops of rain began to fall as I turned and ran back. By the time I reached the far corner, water was dumping from the sky, a gift from God I thought, because now the visibility hardly extended beyond ten paces. I quickly secured my pistol under my shirt, praying the weapon would remain dry enough to fire.

With only a glance to my right to be sure the back door was still secured, I ran across the lawn toward the stables. My own horse hunkered down at the top of the mountain where I'd tied him off. In the event I did manage to escape with life and limb, I might not be well enough to crawl back up that mountain, particularly if I had Lucine with me. I had to secure at least one mount.

There were only ten horses in the stable. Because of the storm they would not run far even if I took a whip to their hides. This was their home, and I had no doubts but they were as loyal to Valerik as his coven.

If I'd had a potion to make them sleep, I would have used it. They were beautiful beasts, all of them. But they presented a threat to Lucine, however small, so I did what I had come to do.

I secured them, slit their throats with my knife, and let them bleed out. I killed them all but one.

The one, a tall black stallion that could carry three people if need be, I tied off in a separate stall, hoping the scent of the others' blood wouldn't disturb it too much.

The rain washed the blood from my hands as I ran back across the lawn and rounded the fortress to the underground entrance where I'd left my bag. I was thankful for that gift from the heavens.

But once I had descended the stairs where the rain no longer mattered, all the comfort I felt at having successfully surveyed the area vanished. Because there at the end of that passage lay the door to the dungeon, and in that nest I would face a terrible enemy that I was sure I could not survive.

THIRTY-TWO

Breathing steadily, I managed to light the torch using the flint I had brought. Orange flame flared and my immediate impulse was to extinguish it before I was seen. But the tunnel beyond was dark and I would need light to pass quickly.

Taking one long breath, I eased the door open a crack, saw that it was still dark, then pushed it wide enough for me to slip inside. I closed the door behind me and strode down the inner passage, pulse pounding in my ears.

I am tall and strapped with muscle, but there I felt far too frail as I moved down the tunnel to the door that led into the study I'd escaped through before.

That door was also open. And the space beyond was dark. I stepped in and once again shut the door behind me. Now I was fully inside the nest. The flame from my torch showed the desk and the portrait of what I now knew to be a fallen angel that had crossed over into this world to spawn those Nephilim.

Moving quickly, I lit the torch next to the portrait and extinguished my own. I removed the oil I'd brought and spilled it along the floor by the door through which I'd entered. Then along the bookcase and over the desk. Grabbing a lamp from that desk, I splashed more oil on the door and the sofa.

Satisfied, I left the torch burning and exited the study into the outer tunnel. Except for the orange light spilling from the single torch behind me, the passage was dark. But I was too close to the main halls to risk light now. At the end there was a door. I had to reach that door in the darkness.

Withdrawing my pistol and checking the load one last time, I headed forward. The sulfuric stench was so strong I couldn't breathe except in shallow pulls, but the floor was moist and slippery. Without more light, I couldn't run without risking a fall.

How I managed to stay straight, I don't know, but I only scraped the moss on the walls once. And then I was at the end, winded more by my nerves than from exertion. I could still just see the slight glow of flame from the study far behind me.

No light from under the door. I opened it and stepped through. Now I was on the thinnest of ice. Up to that point I knew my way because I'd been there before. But I had no intention of retracing my former steps back to the main ballroom from which I had fled.

I had to get back down to the tunnels where I'd met Alek. Back to that same library that, according to Sofia, Alek preferred. If I could make it there and win Alek back, I would stand a far better chance than if I had to go it alone.

I had noticed earlier that the Russians seemed to hold together in groups, lounging in rooms where they clung to each other. During my tour with Sofia, we hadn't encountered even one wandering down a hall alone. They all seemed to know where they wanted to be and wasted no time getting there.

Or so I hoped.

A thin thread of light traced the base of a door directly ahead of me. I'd passed by this door before, avoiding it because it led back *into* the castle when my intent was to get *out*.

I crossed to the door. It wasn't locked.

Now I had a choice. In the event I did encounter one of the Russians, I would have to strike without a moment's hesitation, before they could fly at me or flee to give the warning. Normally I would use the pistol, for there was no quicker way to a man's head than the path of a musket ball.

But the ensuing blast would give its own warning so close to the main hall. I would risk it deep in the tunnels but not here.

So I shoved the pistol into my belt and withdrew my throwing knife and one of the wooden stakes. I don't mind telling you, that stick of wood felt like a toy in my hand.

I cracked the door and eased my head forward for a view. If anyone had been in the hall, they were gone already. It ran to my right, toward the back of the castle. A single torch on the wall lit the way.

I stepped in and strode quickly.

This is it, Toma. At any moment a door will open and expose you to a team that's been watching and waiting. They know you're here.

But I refused to believe myself and picked up my pace,

empowered now by raw experience. I was a slave to my instinct, clinging desperately to a hope in a blood greater than mine.

The way was unknown to me—all I know is that I passed through two doors and rounded a corner that delivered me directly to the flight of stairs I'd descended with Sofia. And I had not encountered a soul.

I was so surprised that I pulled up sharply and searched my memory to be sure this was the right passage.

But it was! And I leaped into it.

Perhaps they didn't know I was there. Perhaps I had stumbled upon the greatest fortune, or perhaps another force was behind me, seeing my way to this noble task.

If only I had known what awaited me. I might have fled.

Instead I took the steps two at a time, down into the round atrium, through the darkened door, and then right, into the same tunnel that Sofia had led me down. I ran down the passage, sure I could hear whispers from the rooms I passed, which only sped my pace. I had only one objective, and I tore for it with every last reserve of speed.

And then I was there, at the gate to the library. I spun in, panting.

It was empty. The door leading to the room where I'd found Alek was closed. I could not dare hope for my good fortune to hold up a moment longer. I could set fire to this room using the torch on the wall, and then retreat, having accomplished some of what I'd set out to do, but if Alek was behind that door, I might consign him to his death. I would have rather fallen on my own sword!

So, for my love of Alek, I would risk it all by going through the door, if only to win him first. I was bitten by madness!

I slid silently up to the door and pressed my ear against it. A soft chuckle. But how many? And was Alek . . .

Then I heard him laugh.

The sound flooded me with a frightening mix of rage and optimism. I decided to use all the weapons at my disposal. Snatching the water from the bag, I shoved the latch down and threw myself through the doorway.

At first glance I saw that there were only three of them. Alek and Dasha were in a chair together opposite a male I recognized but did not know.

My entrance caught them off guard, and I was already rushing forward. I hurled the jar of water at the male with my left hand as I flew toward Alek and Dasha. Then, uttering a guttural cry, I snatched a stake from my side and dived for Dasha.

She was just snapping out of her shock, twisting to her right, when the stake reached her with my full weight behind it. The sharp point entered her body just under her armpit and drove deep, into her chest, all the way to my fists. I swear that stake had gone through her heart.

She gasped loudly, grasped for the wood that stuck out of her body, and collapsed into Alek's arms.

My momentum carried me over them. I hit the ground rolling and came up with my pistol withdrawn. Only then did I see that the jar of water had smashed into the wall and accomplished nothing.

But the shock of seeing me shove that stake into Dasha's heart had momentarily frozen the other male. I steadied my aim and shot him through the head.

A hole, and he collapsed in a heap.

"Ahhh!"

I bounded to the door and shut it, then spun back around. Alek was off the couch, staring at Dasha's dead body. His face was white and he was shaking with horror.

"Wha— Oh no, what is this?"

"Alek! It's me! Toma, your commander."

He looked at me, flabbergasted by what had happened. And no wonder: the woman who had seduced him was now dead at his knees. For the first time it occurred to me that he might be too far gone to come to his senses. But he was Alek. Alek! The strongest of men.

"You've . . . you've killed her!"

He collapsed to his knees and began to shake her body, wailing his command. "Wake up! Dasha, get up! Wake up!" Tears spilled from his eyes. He grabbed the butt of the stick to pull it free and immediately jerked his hand away as if it had burned him.

I hadn't anticipated this reaction. I might have made it that far without being detected, but surely someone would come soon.

I leaped to his side, grasped the stake, and jerked it free. Blood flowed from Dasha's wound.

"You see, Alek, it burns you? But it does nothing to me. You've been infected by the blood of the Nephilim. You must break free of this curse!"

He leaped to his feet and spun to the dead male. "You . . . you've killed Petrus?"

"They are infidels! Worse by far than any enemy we've faced. I beg you, Alek."

He backed away from the sofa, arms trembling. "You've killed Dasha."

"She'll come back to life," I said. "Didn't Stefan?"

"You used the wood! She can't come back!"

He knew more than I.

"I need your help, Alek. If you possess an ounce of duty still, you must find your way past your passion and help me save Lucine!"

He looked stricken. "Lucine? She's the bride. She's the new queen. What have you done?"

I didn't know which was worse: that Alek was so far gone or this new bit of information about Lucine.

"When?" I asked.

"At midnight."

"Tonight?" I was appalled.

"We were hoping you would . . ." He seemed to lose track of the thought, and he looked back down at Dasha. His mouth clamped shut then slowly drew tight. Bitterness began to replace horror.

"Alek, please. They are wicked."

But even as I said it, a new thought crashed in on my mind. If they were wicked, was Lucine also wicked? And Alek and Natasha? Were humans infected with the bad blood wicked to their core? Even so, if Lucine was to be wooed and loved, were they not all?

Their blood was bad, but was there nothing redeemable about them?

Still, I pressed on. "I've learned so much, Alek. There's no time, but . . ."

The male whose head I had shot moaned. He was coming awake? Was there no killing these creatures?

Panicked, I rushed over to him and shoved the stake into his chest. He shook once, then lay still. But I tell you, doing it sickened me. I could see that it wasn't only the Nephilim in him that I'd killed. It was the human.

But now time was running on and I was feeling trapped in that underground grave. I rushed back to Alek, grabbed him by the shoulders, and shook him. His eyes were fired and his jaw firm.

"I need you! Snap out of this, Alek. We can't let him marry Lucine; she can't possibly love him. I am sent here by God himself to save her. And you and Natasha. I'm under direct orders from Kesia to . . ."

He dropped his head and threw himself into my chest. My chin took the brunt of the blow and snapped up. Then I was falling, back over the couch where Dasha lay dead.

Alek roared and tore into me, pummeling me with both fists. I cried out and tried to push him off me, but he didn't budge. His knuckles slammed into my gut like battering rams. He was far stronger than I remembered him.

But then he would be. He had turned, infected with whatever blood Dasha had put into his veins.

Another one of his fists landed and I felt a rib crack. His eyes, only moments earlier dark, were now red with rage. It was then that I realized he intended to kill me. His mind was lost in bloodlust, and he wouldn't back down until I lay dead at his feet.

I brought my knee up with as much force as I could, managing a full swing despite the pain in my chest. It landed in his groin and should have easily pitched him over my head.

He only grunted once, then brought his elbow down on my head with enough power to knock out any ordinary man.

Panicked, I snatched for the stake still tucked under my belt. "Alek! Alek—"

He hit me again, and this time I thought the blow might be the last. My head swam.

I tugged the stake free and jerked it up so that the point angled up toward his chest. I don't think he saw it in his blind fury, because he threw his full weight down on his next blow.

The stake cracked a rib and sank into his chest. I will never forget the look in his eyes, one moment red and glaring as if he himself were a demon, the next dark and round, stunned that something had changed. His blow glanced off my shoulder and went into the floor with an empty crack.

He groaned and blood bubbled from his mouth.

What had I done?

"Alek?"

In answer his eyes rolled up into his head and he slumped over the stake, held up like a canvas over a tent pole.

I shoved him off me and clambered to administer life. "Alek!" I jerked the stake out and immediately tried to revive him, but my efforts were useless.

I threw my head down on his chest and grabbed my hair. What had I done? I'd just killed the very man I'd come to save! The one who could help me save Lucine!

I beat upon his chest with my fists. "Alek!" But he would not respond. What kind of calamity had I brought upon myself? I was torn with dread.

I staggered to my feet and looked about the room, surrounded now with three dead, all killed with those stakes. For a moment I could not think. What to do now? How to make amends for this slaughter wrung from my own hands?

I grabbed a lamp and threw it against the floor. Oil splashed around my feet. I rushed out to the library and grabbed three lamps, smashing each into the bookcases. My only chance now was to move before the rest knew what I had done and could mount any coordinated effort against me. I had to save Lucine and Natasha or I would not be able to live with myself.

I snatched up one of the torches and thrust the flame against the spilled oil in the inner room. The fuel caught immediately, flashing to a roaring fire that swarmed the couch.

Forgive me, Alek! I felt ill.

Grabbing my leather bag, I ran around the outer library, touching the torch to the books and cases. Flames erupted along the floor and hungrily licked at the paper and wood soaked in oil. A crackling *whoosh* chased me from the room. I ran down the hall, blazing torch in hand.

"Fire!"

I thundered the warning at the top of my lungs.

"Fire!"

Smoke billowed from the library's entrance behind me. I saw the first response when I was only halfway down the passage, a dark head jutting past a gate, glaring at me with black eyes. Then he was gone in a blur that blew past me toward the inferno behind.

"Fire!"

Though I ran straight toward the stairs that would take me up into the thick of them, I pushed my sprint to its limit. Up the stairs. Two more brushed past me as I leaped to the landing.

"Fire in the tunnels. Dasha!"

I had one hope and that was that they would see me and think I had decided to join them. I was warning them, after all. I was voicing my concern in the most strenuous way possible. I had planned to do just this, only with Alek at my side.

An oil lamp sat on a table near the entrance. I smashed it

against a large painting of one of their ancestors then threw my torch at the soaking canvas. Flames swarmed the portrait. When I spun around, four more of the Russians stared at me with wide eyes. Understanding sank into their eyes.

"He stole my bride," I screamed, backing toward the passage that led to the tunnel through which I had entered. I had to make my escape there or all would be lost. "Now he's paid his price."

A fifth suddenly appeared next to the other four. He stared at the fire, then drilled me with his black eyes.

"Then so will you," he said.

I thrust the crucifix at him. "In the name of the Christ—"

He snarled and swooped past me, knocking the cross from my hand. It clattered and came to a rest on the stone. Oily black smoke boiled through the passageway.

I stumbled backward, closer to my way of escape. My right hand found two more stakes and I jerked them out. The Russians said nothing but neither did they move.

It was all the hesitation I needed. I ran while twisted halfway around, keeping the stakes pointed in their direction.

"Stop him," Stefan growled.

Something slammed into my shoulder as I rounded the corner, knocking one of the stakes to the ground. Pain flared up my neck.

Then I ran pell-mell for the first door that led to the tunnels. Only the stake saved my life, I'm sure of it. Perhaps without the distraction of the smoke they would have gotten to me already. As it was, I made it through the first door and raced for the second.

I flew down the stairs into the long tunnel, expecting to feel claws or teeth in my back at any moment. I kept my eyes on that glow of the study because I knew that my salvation waited there.

Three strides from the gate, something struck me again, knocking the other stake from my grip. They were taking their time, I thought, knowing they could pick me apart at their choosing.

I spun into the study, plucked the flaming torch from the wall, and spun to face them. Three appeared in rapid succession.

I held the fire toward them and backed to the door I'd soaked with oil. They stepped in carefully. I wasn't sure why I assumed they would fear fire, but now I had no doubt they did. Thomas had said water terrified them, but I saw more fear in their eyes at the sight of fire. Then again, I hadn't confronted them with holy water.

Without removing my eyes from theirs, I touched the torch to the ground. A ring of fire swooshed around and then behind them. But the flames weren't large enough to stop them from exiting through the gate. Only enough to give them pause.

I shoved the door behind me open, dropped the torch on the ground, and slammed the door shut on them. I could hear the rush of flame exploding up the oil-soaked wood. With any luck, it would be enough to hold them back.

However great the cost, I had managed to do what I planned with respect to the Russians. I prayed they would interpret me as the jealous lover who had come to exact some revenge before fleeing for his life. Now their hands were full with my distraction. They surely would employ all means to extinguish the blazes.

I turned my back on the door and ran out into the heavy rain, uncaring now for stealth, only speed.

My trap had been set and sprung, but the night had only just begun.

THIRTY-THREE

Y ou must know your place, my queen." Vlad spoke in a low rumble that shook Lucine's bones. She felt both dread and wonder in his presence. "You must know that I have made you and that your flesh sees only my flesh."

They were in the ceremonial room at the base of the tower, a space reserved primarily for the rituals that marked the changing of powers, such as a wedding or a death of any half-breed. There was no throne, as one might expect, but a slate table with candlesticks rising on each end. The candles lit a large circular carving in the wall behind, the image of a crucifix with three curled talons reaching down from above, piercing the middle where the members crossed. Blood, real blood as far as she could tell, seeped from the puncture wounds, glistening in long trails to the base of the carving, where they seeped into a large stone basin. One might easily mistake the throne room for a dungeon rather than a place of such esteem.

The rest of the floor was unfurnished. Oil lamps ran along roughly hewn walls softened by long red velvet drapes that framed the lamps. She stood at the center of a large black circle etched into the marble floor, dressed in a thin white cotton gown that hung to her knees like a scant whisper. At Vlad's command, Natasha and Sofia bore witness from their places at one end of the circle.

Vlad walked around her, arms behind his back, black boots clacking slowly on the marble. His eyes swiveled to Sofia and Natasha. "Your sister should watch and know that her fate would be much worse if she ever broke our covenant."

What was he saying?

"Sofia should watch and know that I see the fracture in her heart already. Hell will not contain her pain."

Lucine blinked, frightened by the harsh words. Yet they were appropriate, weren't they? If Natasha or Sofia broke their covenant with Vlad, they should pay whatever price he demanded. He was their lord and master.

He stopped in front of her and smiled. Brushed her cheek with his thumb. "Tonight we will be wed and the world will not contain my joy. The coven will gather, and you will lie on the altar. I will deliver you into hell, and you will become a half-breed, fully fleshed and fully dead. Together we will reign over these living. What do you make of that?"

"It is my honor, my lord."

"It is. But you must also know your duty. You must know that I may do with you as I please. That your very existence now depends solely on me. If I would drain you of blood and leave you as ash, I will do so. If I would send you to my master to be used for his pleasure, you would run to him. You will have great power in your flesh, but it is mine, never forget that."

It sounded both terrifying and beautiful. Lucine knew that she had changed, but the specifics of that change seemed to fade with each passing hour. Glimpses of her prior self flashed through her mind but vanished so quickly that she couldn't dwell on them. She only knew they were there, not what they meant. Like knowing that the devil lived but not what his purpose was. Or that God was in heaven but not what he did up there.

"Yes?" Vlad prompted.

"Yes, my lord."

"You must know that you are already dead. That your flesh is meat. Even your beauty is mine. All of it."

"Yes, my lord."

"And you will love me always, like an innocent child loves even a brutal father."

"I will."

"Yes, you will."

Vlad was smiling one moment, then his face twisted with rage. He drew back his arm and slashed at her with a grunt. His claw slammed into her face, spinning her around and off her feet. She landed on her left shoulder and felt her head crack against the floor.

Her world went dark and was filled with screaming. Her own, she thought. She clawed at the darkness above her, then was jerked upright.

"Now look at you, you whore."

Her master was speaking. He was telling her what he wanted from her, and she would do it without question, because not to meant more of that screaming. Anything but that screaming.

Orange light flickered into view. She saw that she was standing again, held up by Vlad, who gripped the back of her gown. Without thinking, she lifted a weak arm and felt her face.

It was not normal. Lumpy. Fleshy. And wet with blood. She could only see out of one eye. She thought maybe other parts of her face might be missing.

Lucine began to cry.

"You aren't so beautiful now, Lucine. And if I took Natasha's head off, I would expect you to smile still."

But she couldn't respond. Her throat was choked off with her own cry. She could hear the soft cry of Natasha behind her, sniffing.

"Shh, shh, shh, now come, darling. Come." He drew her to his breast and she leaned into him.

"Shh, shh, shh. You'll be beautiful for our wedding."

Then he dipped her in an embrace, bit his lip firmly, and let his blood dribble onto her face.

Lucine felt the numbing change immediately. Felt her face tingle and shift. Soft popping as flesh joined flesh and bone connected to bone.

Vlad licked her face gently, then wiped the excess blood off with his palm. In that moment she loved him more than she had at any previous moment.

"See? All pretty again. It is my flesh to do with as I please. You should never cry again. Yes?"

"Yes."

"And who am I?"

"My lord and master."

"And am I Natasha's lord and master?"

"Yes."

"Yes." He released her, walked over to Natasha, and slit her throat with his nails. Blood spilled down her dress. Her eyes went wide and she tried to speak, but her larynx was severed.

She collapsed in a heap.

"Leave her."

He would heal her, of course. Lucine felt her hands shaking with the horror of this sight, but she knew that he would heal her and they would dance together again.

Sofia's eyes were misty.

Why, if she knew that this was all just a test? A rite of passage. The becoming of a queen.

Vlad returned to Lucine, wearing a smile. "Not to worry, darling. She will see our wedding from a very unique vantage. Yes?"

"Yes," she said, but it came out like a croak.

"Do you love me?"

"I love you, my lord."

A fist pounded on the door.

"Not now!" Vlad thundered.

"There is a fire, sir!"

He hesitated.

"Where?"

"In the tunnels."

Lucine saw the flicker in his eyes, the momentary shock. Nothing more.

"Sofia, take Lucine to my tower. Now."

She was instantly by Lucine's side.

"Both of you, remember what you have seen tonight."

"What about Natasha?" Lucine asked.

He searched her eyes. Offered a compassionate smile and kissed her forehead. "I will take care of her later."

And then he was gone.

THIRTY-FOUR

Time was against me. From the beginning my plan had been to distract them sufficiently with fire to draw Vlad van Valerik's attention. I had not intended to leave with such a loss. Though my slaying of Alek would undoubtedly help convince them that my purpose was retaliation, not rescue, his death rode me like a monster.

Still, I had to bear down and use what means lay at my disposal to find Lucine and get her out before the fire was put out and matters sorted.

I ran around the castle, drenched. The fortress was bordered by a stone sidewalk, and the pounding washed away my footprints as quickly as they were made.

I already knew precisely where I would scale the wall. The lowest section that ran into the tower was midpoint on the western side. I withdrew the rope, shoved the bag into my belt so as to leave no evidence of my passing, and stared up at the lip of the wall, only twenty to twenty-five feet here.

Still, it took me four casts to lodge the hook firmly enough to chance a climb. The wet wall compromised my footing, but I managed to scale most of the way before teetering on a fall. I lunged up and grasped the ledge with one hand, swung free for a moment, then grabbed that same ledge with my other hand.

Without the full benefit of fear, I might not have thrown myself over the wall so easily—scaling wet walls is difficult business without the proper leverage. I quickly hauled the rope up and left it ready to be thrown back down.

The top of the wall was not even two feet wide, and I ran it with far too much abandon. Thinking back now I realize how easily I could have missed my step in the rain and plummeted to a nasty end. But my mind was now swallowed with the tower just ahead and that window within easy reach of a higher ledge.

If Lucine was not in the tower I would . . . Honestly, I might have been tempted to throw myself to the ground.

Only when I was there, on the ledge at the window, did I realize that it was sealed. A curtain hid the room beyond. I would have to break the glass and risk drawing attention. I saw no alternative other than retreat, which was tantamount to death.

So I wrapped my pistol in the leather bag and slammed the butt against the glass. The window shattered inward. Thankfully there was no wind to blow the rain in. With visions of Vlad or one of his subjects pushing me back while I was only halfway through,

I slapped the leather bag on the windowsill and threw myself into the tower, uncaring of what lay beyond.

Thinking back now, I realize how disastrous that leap would have been if I'd entered an open stairway and fallen to my death. Evidently God hadn't abandoned me when I'd killed Alek. I landed on a hard floor and rolled into a ball, tearing the curtain down with me. It took me a few seconds of frantic motion to untangle myself from that cloth and get to my feet.

A bedroom. Not just any bedroom, mind you. A magnificently appointed chamber with a huge canopied bed and velvet drapes all around. Outrage overtook my good senses, and I blotted out any imagination of what that beast might have done to her in this chamber.

Thunder shook the tower.

I stood shaking and dripping on a large bearskin rug, knowing that even this hesitation worked against me. But I was suddenly afraid of what I might find if Lucine was indeed in the next room.

I could not take any time to deliberate. So I strode to the door and shoved it open.

Lucine stood in the middle of the room before a full-length mirror as none other than Sofia attended to her. She wore a white gown, reddened around the neck by what appeared to be blood, though I could see no blood on her flesh.

Her hair was long and dark as I remembered it, but her skin . . .

Her skin was a translucent white. Her lips were pale. Her eyes were dark. She was the most beautiful woman I had ever laid eyes on. I could not move. Of course, Lucine could have had unwashed, knotted hair with bugs crawling in it and I would have undoubt-edly felt the same.

They both looked over at me and gasped when my frame filled the entry. Here were the two women most immediately in my life. But the only one I had eyes for was Lucine.

I stood rooted in the doorway, overwhelmed by her presence after so much conjecture and longing on my part. There she was, standing like a ghost, but I saw only an angel.

"Toma?"

Her voice was frail. Her dark eyes round. Her lips pale, parted with surprise. She had said my name. Not with malice or any side of disparagement. Just *Toma*. And I heard it as the voice of one calling to me in the wilderness, begging me to come to her if only so that she could know that I was real, not just the lover in her dreams.

I stepped into the room and stopped. "Yes?"

"What are you doing here?"

"I . . ." Words failed me.

"How did you get in?"

Sofia stepped to one side, glancing at the door behind her.

I gestured behind me with a heavy hand. "I . . . the window."

"You broke the window?" Sofia asked.

"Yes."

"But you can't be here!" Sofia cried. "He'll kill you if he finds you."

Vlad. So then, we were alone for the moment. Surely we had enough time to get out!

"We don't have much time," I said. Then quickly, gaining my thoughts: "I have a way down the wall and a horse waiting, but we have to hurry!"

"Go? Go where?" Lucine asked.

It occurred to me only then that I was playing the fool, speaking nonsense. She might be a prisoner here, but what alternative had I given her? She didn't even know that I loved her! I had spent so much time cherishing my fantasies these last few days that I had begun to assume she believed them too.

Win her, Toma. Be her Immanuel.

I hurried forward, addressing Sofia. "Please, Sofia, I must have a moment with her. It's of the utmost importance that I speak to Lucine alone."

"Whatever for?" Lucine asked.

My heart began to fall.

I grabbed Sofia's hand and kissed it. "Please, I beg you—"

"I can't leave her, she's my charge."

"She's first my charge!" I blurted. "But I have to tell her!"

"Tell her what?"

It wasn't working out as I'd imagined. But the thought of that fire burning out and Vlad returning pushed me to a less tactful approach.

I faced Lucine. "That I love her," I said, and my voice shook with deep emotion. Her eyes remained wide. I said it quickly. "That I have loved her from the first time I laid eyes on her, but I couldn't speak it because I was under oath not to love her, from the empress herself. I am bound by duty, but I am now bound by a love for you that has plagued me day and night. I cannot sleep, I cannot eat, I can only drink from my own imaginations of whatever love you can offer me. I will treasure you and save you, and no man, no beast, no power in heaven or hell will separate me from my oath to waste my life for you."

Neither moved. Neither spoke. Neither so much as blinked.

Why had Sofia not pounced on me or spread a warning? Was there a seed of goodness left in her that longed for more than she had in this living death?

I looked at her, pleading. "Please, before it's too late. Is there no light left in that dark heart of yours? You must allow me to vie for her heart."

"It's too late," she said. "You will only get yourself killed."

"Then let me die trying."

"But you're only being a fool," Lucine said. And she said it as if this fact was the most certain thing in her mind.

Her words shattered my world. It was as if the sky collapsed on me, crushing me with suffocating weight. Because I knew that she was right. In her eyes I was a fool, and surely anything I said would only reinforce that opinion. Her mind and her heart were owned by another lover, and I was only throwing away my words like a blithering fool.

It all crashed in on me: the days of escaping the estate so that I wouldn't have to face her; the nights around the table trying not to be caught watching her; the pages in my journal where I had confessed my undying love; that first fight with the Russians in my feeble attempt to rescue her; my confession to her mother, Kesia, telling all; the dungeon into which I'd been thrown for the confession of love; the charge given to me by Saint Thomas, to win her; the death of Alek by my hand; the heroic rescue of my lover, who was now rejecting me as if I were nothing more than a silly boy.

I could not breathe. The blood drained from my face. Tears welled in my eyes. The world began to spin. Heat flushed my cheeks and spread down my neck. There was a hell and the flames were burning around me already.

Lucine just watched me.

I turned away and walked three steps without direction, then stopped, uncertain what to do next. But my course, however foolish, was already plotted. I hung my head in my hands and struggled to maintain my composure.

I tried to speak, to apologize for my reaction. I couldn't bear the thought of imposing on her a moment longer. But my throat was locked up.

And now the emotion dammed up in me broke through the thickest wall that I had erected to protect my heart. Sorrow and anguish flooded me, and I began to panic.

I couldn't do this, not here in front of Lucine; no good would come of it! I would rather pull my hair out by the roots.

But my body wasn't listening to my reason and my shoulders began to shake with sobs. I was screaming at myself to stop this terrible display, and the more I commanded myself, the more my heart revolted.

It took the last reserves of my self-control not to throw myself on the floor and groan. Instead I stood with my back to them, shaking silently with unremitting sorrow. I had to rescue her! I had to leave. I had to beg the empress for forgiveness. I had to walk off the end of the earth into a black void. But I could do nothing.

"Take a moment," Sofia said quietly behind me. She was speaking to Lucine.

"But what will Vlad say?"

"Don't worry about that!" She spoke in a quick whisper. "Listen to what he has to say; you owe yourself that."

"I—"

"There are things you don't know, Lucine! Eternal death is something you cannot imagine. I will watch the stairs. The man loves you. Just hear what he has to say."

A door opened and closed and we were left alone.

The rain pelted and thunder crashed and Lucine stood beneath it all suffocated by confusion. Not by nature's booming voices but by a small whisper deep in her mind that called her to Toma's side.

But she had given herself to Vlad. She was to be queen! She had found her place by his side, and she knew that if she moved even one step away, he would crush her and it would be well deserved.

And yet Sofia spoke of eternal death, and upon hearing it Lucine felt a deep well of sorrow open beneath her breast. The half-breed's blood had changed her, stealing her memory of life, she knew that. But she couldn't feel that life.

Toma loved her?

She could barely remember him, much less love him the way she loved Vlad. Yet there he stood, sobbing. Confessing a love for her that made no sense. How could any man love as he professed to?

He'd stilled and now he turned to face her. For a while he just looked at her with teary eyes. Her sorrow grew, empathy for dear

Toma, who'd come to rescue her not realizing that she didn't want to be rescued.

Dear, dear Toma, I am sorry for you. And I am sorry for what Vlad will do to you when he catches you here, trying to steal his queen.

"Lucine," he began. Then he said nothing for a while. More tears streamed down his face, and she felt her sorrow return like a slow tide.

"Lucine, I am so sorry. I should have told you. I wanted to, but I . . ."

Then he was stumbling forward, falling to his knees, gripping her hands, pleading as he stared up at her face.

"I vow my eternal love for you, Lucine. I have loved you since I first knew you. You ruined my world with your first glance, and I have coveted the slightest gesture, the smallest acknowledgment. To know that you know I exist is enough. To return my love is my deepest longing, but if you would only kiss my hand I would know that you have seen my love."

A tear broke from her eye and slid down her cheek. He kissed the back of her hand, then spoke with even more passion.

"You have been my waking obsession. You haunt my dreams. I am utterly preoccupied by you. I beg you to give me a single chance to win your love, to wake you from this living death that has stolen your heart. It is evil, Lucine!"

His face was red and his lips trembled.

"You are to wed a monster from hell who will ravage you for eternity! But I can offer you life."

It was more than she could bear. Lucine pulled her hand away and turned away. "No, Toma, you can't. I have his blood now."

He was there, at her back, with trembling hands on her shoulders, speaking quietly close to her cheek. "Then I will find you new blood. You will take God's blood."

Revulsion rose into her throat and she stepped away. "Stop! You're going to get us both killed!"

"No, I will bring you life." His hand was on her back, warm and strong. "And if I can't, then return here and live with him. But I will show you such love that you will never leave!"

"I am dead!"

"I will love you anyway!"

She whirled to face him. "No one can love the way you speak of it!" she snapped. "There is always a price, and I have paid mine."

"Then let me pay the price for you. Let me love you, Lucine, I beg you. Give me one day, just one, and if you are not delighted I will bring you back."

His words hammered her mind like an avalanche of boulders; she was at once overwhelmed and terrified by them. Who was this hero of all Russians who would save her from the Russians?

"Toma." She spoke his name aloud.

Her memory of him flooded her. His steady breathing as he followed her around the castle that first night, his frequent glances in her direction, his unwavering loyalty to duty. But even more, Toma was a warrior with scars to mark his body. A savage fighter who had killed a thousand men with his bare hands, now here trembling with love for her.

"Toma."

For a brief moment she wanted to throw herself into his arms and beg him to take her away from this hell.

But as quickly as the desire swelled, it was washed away. By Vlad's blood, she thought. And then she didn't think about it.

❧

There was life inside of her. I could see it in her eyes, hear it in her voice. A warm ember of hope glowing deep in her heart. And I was sure that my words were coaxing that ember to flame.

No sane person could choose death with Vlad over the hope of life outside this place.

She said my name. "Toma." As if she were tasting it for the first time. Then she said it again. "Toma." This time with desire. But the light in her dark eyes was fleeting and she quickly averted them.

"I've heard you," she said. "So now you must go."

You cannot know how deeply those words spoken by Lucine cut me. I wanted to grovel on the floor and beg her mercy. I wanted to show her my strength and whisk her to safety. I longed to kiss her on the lips and tell her that I would be the only food she would ever need, that I would satisfy her deepest need and delight her wildest craving.

But I wasn't winning her with impassioned pleas. I had to make her listen to simple reason! So I shoved the ache in my heart aside and spoke to her plainly.

"It's all plain if you could only see, but you've been blinded by this blood, and I don't blame you, I drank some as well. I was here, drunk on that ancient blood, and I lost myself to it. You're deceived, Lucine. You've been drawn into a passion play in which both God and the devil are vying for your soul. Now you are with the devil, an unholy union between a fallen angel and a woman. I've—"

"You know this?" she interrupted, turning.

"And more," I cried, sparked with hope. I quickly told her about Thomas and the book, pacing before her like a schoolteacher, desperately hoping to appeal to her mind, which seemed stable enough, even if misplaced.

I told it to her and she listened, but my mind was only on her. On Lucine. And with each passing moment my love for her seemed to grow. Perhaps because she finally knew of it.

It was surreal. I was there as a hero to rush her away from the ruthless beast who could be climbing the stairs as we spoke, yet my mind was wholly distracted by the pale woman with dark eyes before me. By the way she watched me, the way her lips spoke, the way her fingers moved, the way her delicate feet crossed the wood floor, by all of it.

But even more by those attributes that had first compelled my affection. Her tenacity and directness. Her integrity and laughter and delicate nature. The passion in her eyes.

And yet even more by the hope that Lucine would share herself with me and allow me to share myself with her. I was a lonely man for all my bravado, and in Lucine I had found a desperate need to belong, to know, and to be known.

I finished my tale, leaving out Thomas's insistence that I woo her. I was hopeful, however, that having failed through impassioned plea, my appeal to reason was doing just that.

She looked at me for a long time.

"Is that all?" she finally asked.

"It's not enough?"

"Even if what you say is true and Vlad is who you say he is, neither you nor I can change it."

"You can leave him. You must!"

"And choose you over him?"

I hesitated. "If you could find it in your heart, yes."

Tears welled in her eyes again. I saw her pale, delicate throat move with a swallow.

"In another life I might find you and beg you to love me if I would be so fortunate." She looked away and held her chin level. "But in this life I am bound to another lover. I have his blood and am a slave to his love."

"Then tell me what I can do to woo you!" I blurted, hating the words as soon as they left my mouth. But I was desperate, so I barged ahead. "What kind of enticements and seduction can he offer that I can't? What food or drink or passions?"

I wove my fingers into my hair and paced. "Am I not man enough? Would you want me to kill a thousand more infidels?" I flung my arms wide. "Is he stronger than I?"

"Yes. But that has nothing to do with it. Please, Toma, leave me." She said it with a biting tone, but her tears betrayed her.

"I can't! You are the only reason I would live."

"You don't know me."

"I know you like my own flesh."

"I am diseased."

"And I am your healer."

"I am bound to Vlad."

"Then I will kill him!"

She uttered one restrained sob, then turned her back to me and gathered herself.

"Leave me, Toma. Leave now if you want me to live through tonight."

I was crushed. Neither confessions of love nor rational argument sufficiently moved her. I didn't know how else to woo her.

I rushed to her and I threw my arms around her in an awkward embrace from the side and I laid my head on her shoulder. I intended to offer some words, but my emotion had choked me off again.

"Please," I finally croaked. "Please, love me . . ."

It was utterly pathetic, I knew it already, but I was past any cleverness.

"Toma . . ."

I lifted my head and kissed her hair. "I'm so sorry . . . Please, Lucine, I beg you."

"Toma . . ."

"Please . . ."

"Toma!" She pushed me away and glared at me. But I wasn't convinced by that cruelty in her stare. She was only doing what she felt she must.

"Leave me. Go back out the window and leave with your life. Never return, I beg you. Never."

She was enslaved in the prison of Vlad's devices. He was the cruel dungeon master, and he held her in his grip! It wasn't Lucine, it was Vlad van Valerik who was to blame for this.

Heat spread through my face as rage welled up like a flood.

I had been given the book to slay this beast. My earlier words came to me: *I will kill him.* And then I knew that I must. The only way to release Lucine from this scourge was to put my fifth and last stake through Vlad van Valerik's heart.

In this way I would woo her, by removing the shackles from her eyes so that she could see.

"Leave," she whispered. I thought she was going to burst out in tears. "Please, Toma. Please leave."

My mind snapped. I could only see the one objective before me, and I no longer cared to think through the strategy of it. All of my plotting and figuring had brought me to this utter failure. I wanted no more of it.

I could either throw myself out the window or go down and kill the beast who had done this to my Lucine. I was a warrior, so the decision was born of instinct, not deliberation.

I stepped up to Lucine, kissed her once on her lips, grabbed my last remaining stake out of my belt, and went in hunt of that half-breed, Vlad van Valerik.

THIRTY-FIVE

The descending spiral staircase outside the room was lit by one torch mounted on the wall next to an iron railing. Sofia stood from her squat on the top step.

I did not fear her. At that moment I did not fear any living or unliving soul, or any beast that had no soul. But in particular, I did not fear this mysterious being who had shown me such graciousness. Her kind I would never again kill.

I glared at her. "I must kill that Nephilim," I said. "Tell me where I can find Valerik."

Her eyes fell to the stake in my fist, and she took a step backward.

I lifted it. "I have the means, now tell me what I must know. If he survives me, he will win her. If I slay him, I will win her."

Her eyes darted down the stairway. "He can't be killed," she whispered. "He's too strong! You'll never reach him."

But I pushed her doubt away and brushed past her, heading down the stairs.

"Toma!" she whispered.

I was too determined to stop.

"The fountain, Toma. Issue your challenge at the stone fountain."

Now I ran, down the stairs, through a hall, into a room that appeared to be a dungeon with a slate table at the far end. A form lay in a pool of blood but it wasn't the beast, and I was turning away when her face registered in my mind.

I rushed up to the woman. Natasha! The similarity between her and her twin stopped me cold. Except for the blonde hair, this was Lucine. Her throat had been slit and she'd bled out on the ground.

My knuckles were white on the stake. *Dear God in heaven, what have I done? Alek, my only friend, is dead. Natasha, my charge, is dead! Lucine . . .* My face twisted with sorrow. *Lucine is dead.*

A holy wrath seeped from my pores. I ran from the room, jaw tight, mind fractured. Through a dining room, into the grand ballroom with the twin staircases, where I slid to a stop.

I had no plan, no fallback route, no exit strategy to consider. Only the driving conviction that I must deal death a final blow.

But now I paused, breathing hard through my nose. The hall was empty. Smoke laced the air, heavier toward the back. But the fire was surely out by now. At any moment the duke would walk through the doors at the back of this room and see me. Sofia was right: I had no chance in an open fight with him.

She'd told me to issue my challenge at the stone fountain.

I ran along one wall, eager to be out of such a large open space where these wraiths could travel like the wind, through a doorway farther toward the back. This stone fountain might be in a courtyard or a bathhouse or another large hall. But I'd seen two already, and neither had a stone fountain.

The smoke was still thick in the atrium where I'd confronted Stefan only thirty minutes earlier. Still no sign of the Russians. They must all be in the tunnels dealing with the tragedy I'd left them.

I sprinted to the back and burst through a door. It opened into a large enclosed space with an open ceiling at the center through which sheets of rain now fell. Limestone carvings of animals with waterspouts for mouths lined the wall, spaced every two paces. A round platform with a huge limestone cross on it sat in the middle. And around the base of the table, a pool perhaps twice its width.

Two thoughts collided in my mind. The first was that I had found Sofia's fountain. The pool was evidence of that. The second was that rainwater streamed over the cross and had filled that pool.

Water. And a blessing, there in the form of that crucifix that had once been the central fountain in what appeared to be a bathhouse.

My heart surged with hope. This was it! I had arrived at my own salvation here in the heart of the enemy's castle, because I could now only be saved if Lucine were set free, and she could only be set free if Valerik's grip on her soul was loosened. I was sure of it.

I staggered out into the pelting rain. The water came down

in streams from an ominous gray sky, but surely the heavens were sending down their blessing, not a curse.

The pool was only two feet deep and I sloshed across, then hoisted myself up onto the round platform. Water streamed off my head, down my chest. I stood soaked from head to foot.

My right fist still clung to the wooden stake. I stepped up and pressed the palm of my left hand on the stone cross. It was coarse, a relic that had paid its dues exposed to the weather. The cross beam was at the level of my head, nearly seven feet high. Moss and thin vines clung to the surface in patches.

Water flowed over my fingers, down the stone cross, then spread at my feet before streaming into the large basin that circled the fountain. I saw no power or magic in this water. I wished it were blood, because blood seemed to have far more significance here than water. But water was like blood, wasn't it? Flowing over the cross, cleansing, washing away evil.

"Bless this fountain, God in heaven," I cried, facing the sky. "Wash it with your blood. Slay this beast, spare your bride!"

I didn't know what else to pray. And again my lack of planning stopped me.

"Issue your challenge," Sofia had said.

Staring at the large cross before me, I was struck by how improbable it all was. I was to issue a challenge to a beast who made even a hero of Russia appear like a twig for all his strength. But I had a wooden stake. And a crucifix. And the water, blessed by that cross, that flowed over my fingers. And I had love.

Above all, love.

I hung my head beneath my outstretched arm; water splattered about my boots. My throat ached with that love. My chest felt filled with lead. I was already at the end of myself, trusting only in the power of the blood from Immanuel's veins to save Lucine and myself, that somehow it had been transferred to this water and this cross before me. I didn't know how else it might help us.

My breathing thickened and I breathed a last prayer. "Do not forsake me. Let me save the one I love, I beg you." I straightened and slipped my knife from its sheath. Now I held a weapon in each hand. "Bring him to me."

The sound of those words comforted me, and I lifted my chin to the sky. "Bring him to me!" I roared. "Bring the beast to me and let me slay him."

"I am here."

Valerik's voice was calm, from the entrance directly behind me. I leveled my head and stared at the water streaming over the cross. *He's too calm*, I thought. *He doesn't fear this water.*

My chest rose and fell. Such fear gripped me that I felt I could not turn. Orange light wavered on the walls; there was fire behind me.

"Do you fear me?" Valerik said. I could hear the mockery in his voice.

I turned slowly, shuffling so that I didn't slip. The half-breed stood tall in the doorway as his brood filed past him, bearing lit torches. They spread out on either side, protected from the rain by a narrow projection that ran along the top of the round wall. Stefan was the last to enter, and he stood by his master's side, scowling.

I was now completely encircled by the coven. There was no escape.

"You have hubris, I'll give you that," Valerik said. "Any sane man would still be running after causing us so much pain. But here you are, ready to slay the beast. Was this your purpose all along? You killed your friend and my subjects to this end?"

"I'm sorry about them," I said. "It is you I want."

"Really? I thought it was that woman. My bride."

He spoke of her as if she were an object to trade.

"She loves me," I said.

He gave me a wicked smile.

"I have come from her room," I cried. "Where I embraced her and told her that I loved her. She wept in my arms."

His smile softened and his right hand twitched, but he stood still, feet planted on dry ground, arms easy by his sides. His overcoat and his trousers were coal black like his eyes and hair.

"Then she'll have you to thank when I show her my disapproval," he said. "Not for loving you, because she cannot love any other suitor. But for not killing you while she had the chance."

"Love? You have no understanding that to love is to *give*, not to *take*. Yet you take the souls of others."

"And I give them the world!" he roared.

"But not life. You can't give life. You are dead."

"Do I look dead to you?"

He leaped at me without warning, landed lightly on the table next to me, and slammed his fist into my jaw. My head snapped up and I staggered back into the cross.

"Does that feel alive to you?" he rasped in my ear, pressing so close that I couldn't move my arm to maneuver the stake. I swung the knife, but he caught my wrist out of the air and held it with an iron fist.

He lifted his other hand to the blade in my grasp and ran his palm along the razor edge. Blood oozed from the wound. He grinned and licked the cut, then ran his tongue up my cheek.

And then he leaped and was gone.

"You have no power here, human."

I jerked my head up and saw that he was crouched on the top of the cross like a gargoyle. The rain falling past him glowed in the flames' light. *This is the devil*, I thought, *and he has come to tear me apart.*

And he was relishing his task, taking his time without threat. I tried to think quickly, knowing that if I didn't leverage my advantage with precision, I would die.

But I could no longer grasp that advantage. I had the water; still he gloated over me. I had the wood stake; still he was far too fast to make a target. I had the knife, but it was only a toy here. I had the book . . .

But I did not have the book! It was in the canvas bag still draped over the windowsill in the tower bedroom.

Then I had only my mind and my heart. The last power at my disposal was love. The power of wooing and affection.

"That's all you have, Valerik?" I cried. "Blunt force? I know who you are!"

He leaped from his crouch, landed nimbly on his feet by the entrance, and turned to face me once again.

"Oh?"

"I have read a Blood Book," I continued. "Alucard was the first of your kind to enter this world. You are a half-breed and you are dead already."

He wasn't quick with a return. I had touched something off.

"A Blood Book," he said. "That's impossible. They don't exist in this reality."

"Then where did I read Baal's journal? Where did I learn that you are a descendant of the Nephilim, devils from another realm? Or that you fear wood and water?"

"Where is it?"

I ignored the question, seeing that I had gained an advantage.

"There is a great romance," I said, "written about in that book. God's wooing of his bride. You think you have stolen her, but you don't know that it's true affection, not merely seduction, that draws her. And you have no affection, only seduction." I paused. "She is drawn to me."

Valerik bobbed his head as if to say, "Really?" He looked around at his subjects who stood in black, staring at him with rapt attention. Ten or twelve torches licked away the darkness. I wondered what would happen to those subjects if Vlad van Valerik were killed.

He spread his arms and spoke with a condescending grin, addressing me, but his coven as well, surely. "So you insist on playing the part of suitor, Toma. You could have left me to rule my world as I see fit. You could have found another world for your affection and left me to seduce my own. But no!"

He stepped forward, into the rain.

"Instead you are here in the flesh! In my home! Have you lost your mind?"

"It's my heart, not my mind, that I have lost. Lucine has it. All of it. I love her desperately in ways that you can't possibly understand, much less experience! I cannot live without her."

"She is my bride!" he bellowed, leaning into the words.

Was not the devil a fallen angel? And Nephilim, fallen angels who'd mated with women?

"What is it with you fallen ones, always wanting what isn't yours?"

He lowered his arms and glared up at me. "Where is the book?"

I again ignored the question. I had to find a way to distract him, if only long enough for a single thrust with the stake. Or I could throw the wood like a knife, confident I had the strength and skill to place it through his chest. With some luck, through his heart. It was my only play here.

That and love.

"There is a great romance between God and his creation," I said. "My greatest weapon is love." I let the knife slip from my fingers and clatter to the stone at my feet. "But you refuse to let me wield that weapon because it threatens you."

Valerik spit to one side. "We laugh at religion's brand of love, forms and rules that keep the poor feeding from the church's coffers. It is dead."

"I agree. That kind of love is porcelain-coated balls of dung. But what of true affection? Can you offer that?"

"You've been a guest here before, you tell me. Did you see or feel any affection?"

"Then it should be settled. If you truly love her, you will let Lucine decide."

"She has made her choice."

"You've deceived her!" I cried. "And now she is in your prison. What love is that?"

He issued a crackling growl and leaped to my side, unable to contain his rage. But this time I anticipated the move and I rammed the stake with all of my strength into the spot where I thought he would land.

The wood sank into his flesh, precisely timed. Deep, to my fist.

He gasped and his dark eyes went wide. Both of his hands grasped the stake, but he made no attempt to pull it out. Around us the coven stood in stoic silence, like sentinels waiting for an order to tear me apart.

"Do you think I'm afraid of a stick of wood?" Valerik said.

I stepped back and saw it then. The stake had gone into his lungs but missed the heart. Or perhaps a half-breed didn't react to wood the way his subjects did. Either way, Valerik wasn't bothered by the sharpened sapling sticking out of his chest.

He pulled aside his shirt and jerked the stick out. Blood flowed from a hole that immediately began to grow together as if made of putty. Within a six count he was repaired.

He tossed the stake onto the platform, where it rolled close to the edge and came to a rest, far beyond my reach. Valerik's lips twisted into a soft growl and his eyes hinted at red behind those black orbs.

It is the end, I thought and took another step backward. I would die here under a dark sky in the Carpathian Mountains. The hero of Russia would finally be stripped of life, undone by love.

And Lucine . . .

I let the fight go out of me. My arms sagged; my jaw felt heavy.

I would die and Lucine would be his slave for eternity. The full realization of this inevitable outcome poured into my mind. It smothered my heart with a wrenching sorrow.

"Lucine . . ."

Breathing her name only made it worse. I could see only her, watching me, confused by the war in her own heart. I began to panic.

My face wrinkled and I started to breathe in shallow pulls.

"Lucine!" Her name, just that, I still had her name, and I sobbed it, uncaring of anything but hearing her name, however distorted by emotion.

"Lucine . . . Lucine . . ."

It became too much for me. I dropped to my knees, reached clawed fingers at the sky, closed my eyes, and moaned her name, for it was the only salve for my pain.

"Lucine! Oh God! Lucine, Lucine, Lucine . . ." These were the guttural groans of a dying man clinging to the last thing that was more precious than life itself. To love.

"Oh, my God, my God, why? Why? Why do you forsake me?"

"He forsook you a long time ago," Valerik said. "And now you will die. No lover, no God, no life."

Filled with a sudden wrath, I leaped to my feet and screamed at him. "She does not love you! She will never love you! She will always hide a love for me deep in her—"

The air shattered with a ferocious growl, and I felt myself picked off my feet by the neck and slammed back into the cross as if I were an insect. The blow took my wind away.

Valerik shoved his face close to mine. I could feel the hot air from his throat when he spoke. "She . . . is . . . *mine*!" The roar of that last word blasted me full in the face.

Keeping me pinned against the cross at my neck, he ripped my shirt off with one swipe of his other hand. His hand flashed again and this time I felt his fingernails slice through the flesh on my chest. He cut to the bone, and I cried out with pain.

Blood flowed from the wound.

But he was only beginning. He sneered up at me and slashed at my cheek. Then my shoulder.

The pain was terrible, but it wasn't what pushed me to sob as I hung there on that cross. My pain was not for me but for Lucine. She was now the lover of this monster, and I could do nothing to help her.

My strength began to fade and I let my muscles sag as I struggled to breathe past his iron grip.

"I will see you in hell," he growled.

"Vlad?"

I could hear her voice now, speaking to me in my fading consciousness. Lucine was saying his name, but it was questioning, not sure.

Valerik had gone still. I opened my eyes.

I saw her over Valerik's shoulder. Lucine. Lucine stood in the doorway, dressed in the same nightgown she'd worn earlier. A book hung from her right hand.

The Blood Book I'd left in my leather bag.

She held the book out. "Is this true?"

THIRTY-SIX

S tefan eased away from Lucine. The others shifted as well. Something had altered the norm.

My heart bolted with both anticipation and fear at seeing Lucine. She'd found the book, and something in her reading of it had drawn her mind back from the darkness. But what price would she pay for her choice to question her master?

He still had me by the neck, but he'd twisted around and was staring silently at that vision of beauty that filled the doorway, backlit by an orange glow from within the castle.

Drenched, the beast's shirt clung to sinewy cords of muscle wrapped around his shoulders and down his back. I had no doubt that he could break my neck with a single squeeze of his fingers. My vision was already fading.

I reached up with both hands and grasped his wrist in an attempt to loosen his grip but only succeeded for a moment before his fingers wound tighter, cutting off my air.

"Is it true that you are a devil?" she asked.

"How dare you leave my tower!"

She looked up at me. "Let him go. Please, his only crime is to love me."

He released me and I collapsed in a heap then fell to one side. My head hit the stone surface with a sickening thud. The stake was on the other side, too far to reach. I struggled to remain conscious.

"I found Natasha," Lucine said. "She's dead. You killed my sister." It was said simply, but the emotion behind her words betrayed a dreadful sorrow.

Valerik's reaction was immediate. One moment he stood on the platform, glaring down at her, the next he was in front of her. He slammed his fist into her gut and raked his claw up her face when she doubled over. The book flew from her hand. He'd knocked the wind from her so she couldn't breathe, much less scream.

"You haven't imagined the kind of pain I am capable of." He grabbed her hair and jerked her head up so that she faced me. "Is this the ugly wench you love?" he mocked.

I pried my head off the stone and got one arm under my chest, afraid that if I said anything he would only hurt her more. But he didn't need the motivation.

Holding her up with one hand, Valerik hit her face with the other. Then again. "Is this the woman?" He ripped her dress and slashed at her breasts, bloodying her badly. Then he shoved her forward with a fist full of hair.

"Is this the bride you love? Tell me!"

I pushed myself up to my knees, sobbing now, terrified to say anything.

"Toma?" She gasped, choked with desperation.

The beast snarled and cut her a fourth time, this time silencing her with an open hand across her neck, laying her flesh open as if she were a fish. Blood spilled and I knew that she could not survive long.

"Luci . . ." My damaged throat could rasp her name. I tried again but this time only a whisper. "Lucine!"

He dropped her and she fell to her face without the strength to break her fall. And there she lay, perfectly still, bleeding in the rain.

Valerik moved like a storm, plucking me from my knees and pinning me against the cross to finish his killing. With two quick flicks of his hand he sliced my wrists.

"Now I will bleed your veins," he breathed. And he held me tight against the cross as my blood flowed from the wounds, over my hands, and into the water.

So both Lucine and I would die.

But a thought crawled into my mind. Something I'd read in the Blood Book. Words about a fountain filled with blood drawn from Immanuel's veins.

Be her Immanuel, Toma.

I did not understand it fully. I didn't even know if this single thought was only the mad fantasy of a dying man. But I let it consume me and I groaned my approval.

"Take my blood . . ." I forced the words past those cords around my neck.

"Bleed for me," he growled.

"Take my blood!" I rasped. Then, with my last reserves of breath, "Find your life in my blood!"

I could see only the sky because his hand was wrapped under my chin. But he shook me like a rag and shifted that grip, allowing me air and a clearer vantage. And I saw.

I saw the blood flowing from my veins.

I saw the pool, turning red now with that blood.

I saw Lucine struggling to her knees.

My eyes darted to Valerik's face. The dark rage there made me cringe, but I only wanted more fury from him, so that he would find his complete distraction with me.

"Without the shedding of blood," I said, then had to take a breath before I finished, "there is no remission."

His face twitched. Something registered in his eyes—a stray thought or dawning realization.

"She is my bride," I said. "She will always be my bride."

He jerked around.

Lucine was already on her feet, falling forward. She toppled face-first into the fountain filled with blood drawn from my veins.

"No!" Valerik released his grip and I crumpled to my hands and knees. He leaped to the side of the pool. "No, no, no!" But she was past his grasp.

In a flash, Valerik was back on the platform, leaning over toward her body. He grasped her by the back of her dress and tried to jerk her out, but the cloth tore free and she sank.

"No!" He shoved his arm into the water and cried out with

pain. When he yanked his hand out, it was blistered, seared by the blessed water.

Lucine was below the surface still, baptized in that shallow bath of blood. I could fall in after her and try to shove her to the surface. Or I could get my hands around the stake and try to end the life of this beast.

Valerik first. If I pulled her out it would only be for him to savage her.

I got to my feet, staggered to my right, and fell upon the lone stake. When I swung back, Valerik had his hand under the surface again, ignoring the pain of his seared flesh, grasping for her body.

I stumbled forward and threw my full weight into my fall, stake extended. Down upon the back of Vlad van Valerik.

The sharp wood entered his back and slammed right through to the stone beneath him. His body arched and he screamed, a terrifying demonic sound that would disturb the sleep of the most jaded fool.

His body shook violently, bowed back like a praying mantis. I knew I had hit his heart by the full-fledged panic in his eyes.

I knew I had ended his existence on this earth. He was surely dead.

But then I was falling, over the edge, into that bloody grave that was more than my own making.

Lucine wasn't sure if she was alive or if she was dead.

Dead, she thought. She'd learned from the book that she was dead already.

But now hot fingers snaked through her body, tingling and burning along her wounds, and then deeper, through her veins to her extremities like molten lava finding its way through cracks and down narrow channels. It burned her fingers and her toes and it made her face hot.

Toma . . . The thought of him made her jerk. Her eyes snapped open. She was lost in a sea of red.

Toma . . . Sorrow welled up in her throat. *Toma, dear Toma!* He'd been right. All the signs were there. From the beginning she'd seen the affection in his eyes. And now she hated herself for not being swept away by those eyes.

Was she alive?

Her knee bumped into the hard surface beneath her. She was in the pool, below the surface, lungs burning. Suddenly alarmed, she flailed and jerked upright.

Her head cleared the water and she gasped for breath. Water streamed off her face and splashed into the pool. She wiped her face with her palm to clear her vision and was struck immediately with the changes.

At the door, Stefan turned and looked into her eyes. Vlad's limp body hung over his shoulder. From the look of disdain on Stefan's face, she thought Vlad might be dead. How? The lieutenant turned without a word and walked into the castle.

The pain on her face was gone. A glance down at her body showed only smooth flesh, no wounds. Her neck . . . She touched her neck with light fingers, then eagerly, grasping, feeling. But there was no torn skin. She was healed?

She spun around, rising to her feet. The coven was gone. They were all gone. Stefan had been the last. Rain poured, water flowed, but there wasn't another soul in the room. The cross upon which Vlad had pummeled Toma rose to the sky, mere stone.

"Toma?"

She looked around again.

"Toma!"

But only blood remained to show that anything had happened here at all. A fountain of blood and she, standing lost in the pool.

Something struck her ankle and she jumped back. A hand floated on the surface. Wearing the gold ring that bore the empress's insignia.

"Toma?"

She plunged both hands down and clawed at him, finding his hair and his arm. "Toma!"

Lucine hauled him up, got his head and upper body out of the water, but in the dark she couldn't tell if he was still breathing, dead or alive.

"No, no, please, no!" She dragged him to the side, then over the edge where he flopped onto the stone floor. "Wake up, Toma! Wake, wake!"

She still couldn't tell if he was alive and she had no idea how to help him. She beat on his chest.

"Wake up, Toma. Please don't leave me now. I need you! I am your bride, you can't leave me." Then, when he still didn't respond, she screamed at him. "Toma! Wake, Toma!"

His eyes fluttered open. Lucine gasped. They closed again.

He was too weak, drained of blood!

But his eyes opened again, and this time he stared at her for an extended moment then sat up. The cuts on his wrists were still bleeding—she had to stop the flow of blood!

Her dress was tattered and drenched, but she had nothing else. Frantic, she tore off her sleeves. "We have to stop the
bleeding!"

He was staring at her with wide eyes as she quickly wrapped
his wounds.

"You're alive?" he asked.

⚜

I sat there in shock, seeing Lucine working madly over my wounds
without bearing a single mark on her own body. I'd seen what the
beast had done to her, and despite all that I had seen, the vision of
her unblemished body was staggering to me.

It was more than the fact that she didn't bear a single mark.
Her skin had changed, become smooth and flesh-toned rather
than translucent and white. And her eyes. They were once again a
light brown.

The Russians were gone. Vlad van Valerik's body was gone.

But Lucine was not. She was there and she was whole, unless
this was her ghost.

"You're alive?" I asked, and in my shock it sounded like a
reasonable question.

She worked to secure the cloth around my wrists without
responding.

"But you are," I said. "You're alive!"

She suddenly sat back on her haunches, dropped her head into
her hands, and gave up a sob.

"Lucine . . ."

She sat up. "Shh, shh, no." She pressed a finger against my lips to silence me. Then, with tears streaming down her face, she began to kiss my hands, like the tender drops of rain that now fell lightly around us. Unwilling to restrain herself any longer, she took my face in her hands and kissed my cheeks, my nose, my forehead, every part of my head.

"Thank you," she whispered. "Thank you, thank you."

She kissed my lips. "Thank you, Toma. I'm so sorry. Thank you." And she kissed me again, a longer, lingering kiss that was far more than necessary for any show of gratitude.

She pulled back and stared into my eyes, searching through her tears. "I love you, Toma."

It was all I wanted to hear. I was so eager to hear those words that I suffered a momentary fear she might take them back or soften their impact with an explanation.

So I threw my arms around her and pulled her tight against my breast. I began to cry unabashedly, undone by such gratefulness that she would love me, praying she would not take it back.

"I love you, Toma," she said again, this time into my ear. And by the sound of her voice and her desperate embrace, I knew that what she said was true.

I could say nothing that I had not already said, and I didn't want to breathe a word that might upset the moment. We clung to each other for a long time, and although I was weak, she seemed to have the strength for both of us.

"Are they gone?" she asked, looking at the door. "I mean, gone?"

"Vlad van Valerik is dead," I said.

She twisted back. "He is?"

"I put a stake through his heart before I fell into the pool."

"Are . . . are you sure?" Her eyes darted about the room. "You saw him die?"

"I believe I did, yes. And now they are all gone. They must have taken his body."

She stood and peered out the door. Then disappeared through it.

"Lucine? Hold on!" I pushed myself to my feet, reached out to the fountain to steady myself, then walked rather unsteadily to the door.

She stood in the great room two doors away, looking around, lost.

"Lucine?"

"They're gone," she said.

"Are you well?"

Lucine turned and hurried back, and with each step she took, her face brightened. She walked right up to me and slipped her arms around my neck.

"I am far more than well now."

She stood to her tiptoes and she kissed me until I was sure that I was melting there in her arms. Her tears came again, now surely drawn by love more than remorse. Her lips slipped away from mine and she buried her head into my neck, crying. Too much had happened not to cry.

Lucine and I stood in the Castle Castile now emptied of all its evil, and together we wept. For we had found the truest love. We had found God's blood.

We had found each other.

My dear reader—

So you see, I am dead. Not in the flesh, but that hardly matters, does it? I was killed by Vlad van Valerik, and through my death Lucine, who was surely as dead, found life.

I can't rightly tell you if my death was physical, if I truly died in that fountain, but again, that hardly matters. Either way I am now dead to this world, having seen too much of the other. Having been infused with a new life, God's blood, which now surely passes through my veins.

I am not a saint named by orthodoxy, for that church has rejected my story and brands me as a heretic. There are times when I think back on those weeks and I wonder if it all really happened or whether perhaps I did lose my mind. But I have only to look at Lucine, my wife, sitting across the table, to know that every memory is true.

It wasn't a conventional happening, to be sure, but then neither are most of the accounts in that book called the Holy Scripture. If you have any lingering doubts, you may visit our home and we could talk about the matter over a fine roast and red wine. Naturally, you would have to travel to Russia because Lucine and I moved to Moscow after we were wed, two months following that day.

As for Natasha and Alek, we mourn their deaths to no end. If there was a way to bring them back, I would do it. I would enter another castle and slay another beast. But they are gone. Kesia sold the Moldavian estate and has taken up residence with her husband, Mikhail Ivanov, in the country near Moscow. We visit her often.

The Castle Castile is still vacant to my knowledge. No sign of the coven was found. The only bodies recovered belonged to our dear friends, Natasha and Alek. Although the antiquities remained there for a day, when I took the army up the following afternoon, even those were gone. The entire castle had been cleaned out then gutted by fire.

I am sure you want to know what happened to those creatures, those poor souls infected by Nephilim. Truthfully, I can't be sure Lucine still carries the blood in her veins, this much we know. But she is different from the rest, for she has been recovered.

The rest may have vanished forever when their half-breed maker died. Dear God, I pray not, because Lucine and I still talk of Sofia and would relish a meeting with her, a chance to win her over to a new life.

We aren't certain which of them might be saved or turned, but we are convinced that a true half-breed would no longer be considered human, the greater half being made from that fallen angel himself.

So then, if you read this book and if you encounter any person who might strike you as lost to the darkness, I would only implore you to love them and pray they be delivered into the light by a blood that works to purge evil.

The Blood Book is lost, gone with the rest of the castle relics. But I attest to its message, and it is a message of love and romance. I have neither seen nor heard of that old messenger from God who called himself Saint Thomas. But to honor him I have taken his name.

As for me, I am freed from my duties to the army. And upon learning that Vlad van Valerik (who had indeed been chosen as Lucine's suitor) murdered Natasha, Catherine forgave me my indiscretion for falling in love with Lucine.

I now spend much of my time writing poems, songs, messages to my Lucine, which delight her. Books, such as this one you have read.

The very day Lucine and I rode down those Carpathian slopes, I penned a poem about Immanuel's veins. I have recently learned that it fell into the hands of a great writer of hymns in England named William

Cowper. He did write a hymn using a fragment or two of my poem, I
believe. For my words are true and I leave you with them now.

> There is a fountain filled with blood,
> Drawn from Immanuel's veins;
> And any plunged beneath that flood
> Will be purged of all that is bane.

Saint Thomas
Lover of his Bride

The End

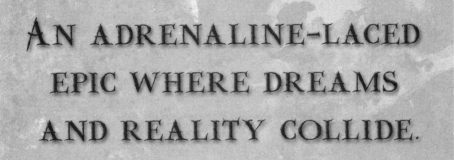

AN ADRENALINE-LACED
EPIC WHERE DREAMS
AND REALITY COLLIDE.

FOUR NOVELS. TWO WORLDS. ONE STORY.